ALL THINGS LOST

THE TERRITORY SERIES
BOOK 1

D.L. BUNCH

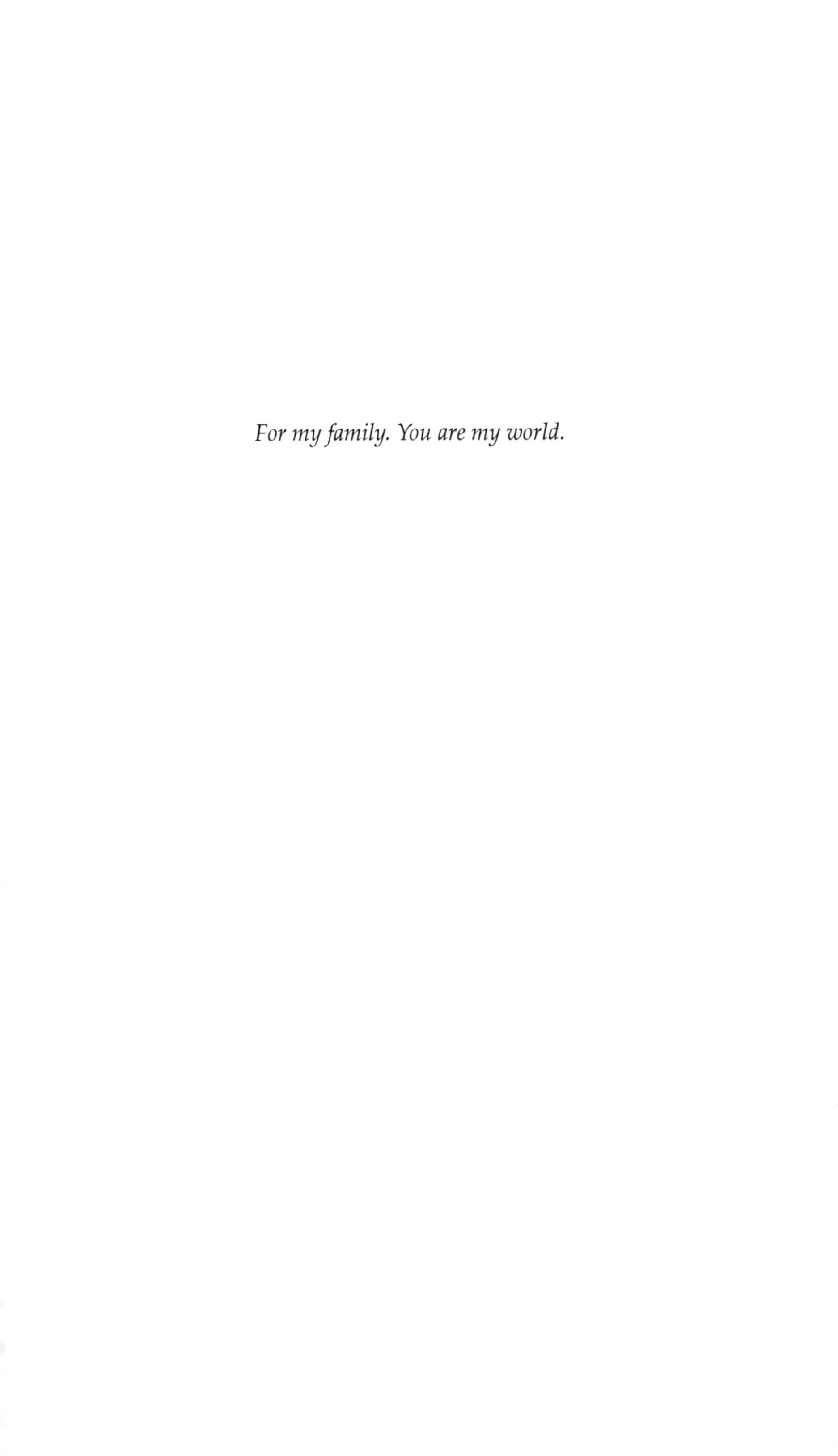

For my family. You are my world.

ACKNOWLEDGMENTS

First and foremost, I'd like to thank my family. They've been supportive, helpful, and most of all, patient with me through the process of writing this series. Next, I'd like to thank my editor, Ayden Rails, she's done a fabulous job of pointing me in the right direction on these final drafts. I appreciate everybody who's read some iteration of this along the way and have given their valuable feedback. And last, but definitely not least, thank you to my beta readers, Suzanne Toruk, Jay Logan, and the Taos Toolbox crew. You all are the best!

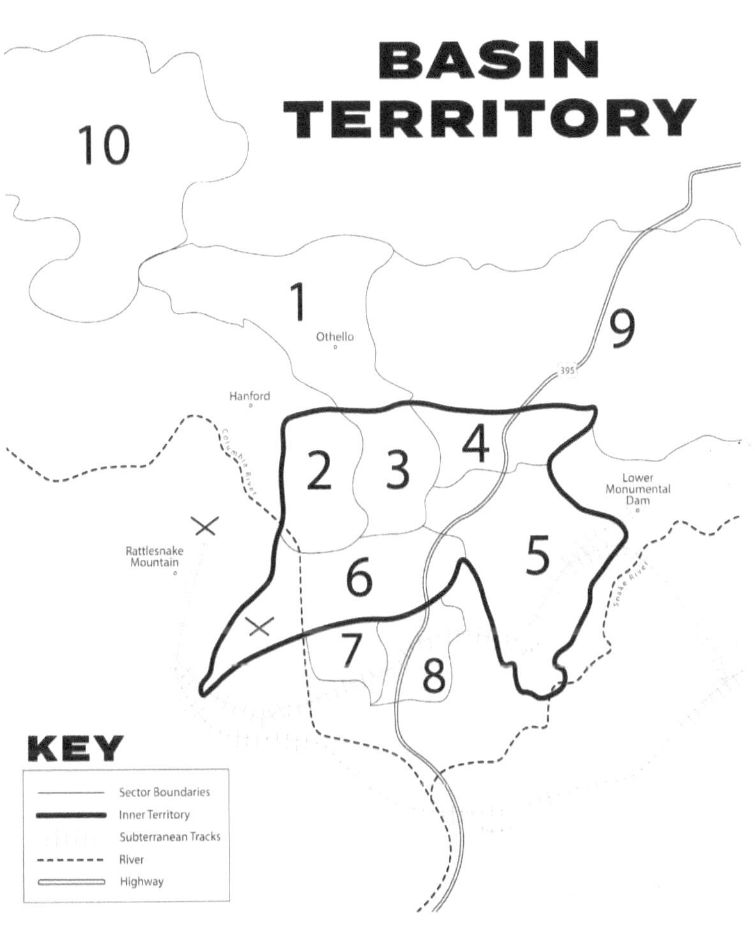

BASIN TERRITORY
10
1
Othello
9
395
Hanford
Columbia River
2
3
4
Lower Monumental Dam
Rattlesnake Mountain
5
6
Snake River
7
8
KEY
Sector Boundaries
Inner Territory
Subterranean Tracks
River
Highway

PRELUDE: JEROME

Thursday, September 8, 2072

When Jerome Warren thought back, he pictured air-conditioned suites and room service, turquoise pools and frothy piña coladas in distant resorts. Each represented a milestone on the ladder he'd scaled to the peak of success—the rewards of a grueling climb. He no longer pined for the sleek cars, fancy yachts, or dinners schmoozing with the nation's powerbrokers. No, he longed for the small comforts that evoked a simpler, kinder era. All of the things he took for granted.

He gazed through the grimy, cracked window of the dilapidated farmhouse, a faint breeze slinking in. Sweat trickled down his face and spine, pooling at his lower back. The air moved like a blast from an oven, offering no respite, only a mocking reminder of the world he'd lost.

Jerome's grandson, Jorge, sat forward, poured another glass of water from the pitcher, and handed it to him, brows drawn together in concern. The wide, pock-marked table sat like an island in the room, the office chairs around it creaky and old, one of the last vestiges of a more civilized time.

The brackish, warm water nipped his tongue and dribbled down his chin. He swiped it away in annoyance.

"You should have stayed home." His grandson thumped laced fingers against the hardwood of the table in front of him.

Jerome snorted. "Like you're ready to take any of these folks on yourself. Some day, but not yet."

Jorge's eyes flashed, though his dear Maria had raised the boy right, and he didn't talk back–boy, ha, he was nearly twenty-two. A battle-worn man these days.

"I've dealt with every group of traders and scavengers that has passed by Colville in the last two years, Grandpa. You keep talking like these people are going to be any different."

Jerome ran his hands over his damp pate, trying to pat down what few patches remained on his seventy-year-old head. Should he tell his grandson that the world's ills probably originated close to this very spot? "The Basin Territory is fair but secretive. If you don't focus on their secrets, you'll be fine. It's all a bunch of horse-pucky anyway. Get in, bargain high, and settle where you need the numbers to be. And for crying out loud, don't give in too soon."

He leaned back and tried to ease a sudden sharp tightening in his chest. It abated, and he finished the rest of the water from the pitcher.

"You still could've sent somebody else. If you keel over before we make it back home, Mom will never forgive you–or me."

Jerome waved the comment away. Kids these days. He still had a lot of good years left.

The clock on the wall ticked. The chairs rattled.

After thirty minutes in the stark, boiling room, irritation turned to anger. He figured it for a negotiation tactic. Jack Allen was supposed to be leading this trade, and the man was the wily sort. Before the Collapse–the utter destruction of society that left them all scrambling for survival—Jack had been a defense lawyer, then a military officer during the wars. He could argue for an ocean-front property in Idaho and make perfect sense. It made for interesting negotiations but also tricky ones. His grandson would learn why these folks were different–and why you had to be careful.

He stood and stretched his legs, suppressing a groan. What he wouldn't do for an aspirin right about now. His old bones ached from the seventy-five-mile journey by horse and cart through sagebrush hills and following clogged, unmaintained roads. Add in the heat, and it had been downright grueling. By the time the massive Basin Territory wall had come into view this morning, his knees were so stove-up that when he stood, he'd almost fallen from the cart. Not that he'd tell Jorge that. The kid would have him stowed away for good, then.

He had given up hope of the negotiation ever getting underway when a tall young woman strode in. A tight bun held her black hair in place at the base of her skull. Neat little sweat patches ringed the underarms of her t-shirt, the only sign the heat affected her. She wore dusty jeans with sturdy boots, the typical clothing for everyone in the Basin.

Resources like water and electricity abounded in the Territory, though Daniel tried to hide it. The bitterness sat in Jerome's throat, hard and unyielding. He swallowed it down and resisted the urge to smooth down one of the loose patches on his thin denim overalls.

Two men followed her in and flanked the door, their hands resting on their gun belts. In the past, only one guard ever accompanied the negotiator, and never in such defensive positions.

Jerome frowned at the new negotiator, finally recognizing her. Mia Burgess.

I'll be damned.

Jorge must have sensed his unease because he sat forward, eagle eyes on Mia.

She perched on the seat at the end of the table beside Jerome, the ledger in her hand thumping against the wood as she set it down. She frowned at the empty pitcher, and Jerome resisted a satisfied grin.

"Mr. Warren, it's good to see you." Her lips compressed into a strained smile, worry lines fanning out beside her serious, gray eyes. She opened the mottled green book to a tab marked with *Colville* and folded her hands on top. Mia looked him dead in the eye. A good sign. Most people were unable to lie when they did that.

"Good to see you too. I was starting to think today wouldn't happen." Jerome let the jab slip, testing her.

She didn't waver, didn't crack a smile, didn't even blink. Her fingers tightened briefly on the book, a fleeting twitch, before settling back into place.

His eyes cataloged the gesture with interest. So, maybe not an ice queen like his people said she was.

"Sorry about that. We had a situation come up. Now, you're here for the annual allotment, I understand?" She said.

"Yes. This is Jorge Salva. He'll be taking over for me next year. Jorge, this is Mia Burgess. Daniel's daughter. I met her last year."

Jorge raised an eyebrow at the name of the Basin Territory's notorious leader and offered the woman one of his most charming smiles. "Nice to meet you, ma'am."

She blinked. "And you, Mr. Salva. Let's get down to business, shall we? Your reports?"

Jerome slid a paper off the pile in front of him and handed it to Mia. "Our population report for the year. We took in eight refugees from over the mountain, and twenty-three babies were born. Only five deaths. Two from an accident and three from natural causes."

A sour taste crawled into his mouth and settled in the vicinity of his gut. The dissection of his settlement felt more invasive every year—yet another reason to pass the reins to the younger generation.

At the mention of the report, the expression on Jorge's face turned from charming to grim in a blink. Yeah. Jerome had left this part out on purpose.

"Nobody moved on?" She ran her finger down the columns.

"Not this year."

She nodded. "Produce report? How are the greenhouses?"

He handed her the next page. They maintained greenhouses for supplemental produce grown in small amounts year-round. Ten years ago, both structures had cost them a year's salt production. The food grown was well worth the price, but it still gnawed at him that it counted against a bigger yield from the annual negotiation.

She scanned the document, and Jorge clenched his hands together on the table. Jerome remained detached and kept handing Mia reports: water production from their wells, mining operations, and resources traded with other settlements. The Basin considered everything before discussing basic food requirements for the year.

Mia perused the last page and met his gaze. Her frown lines deepened. "The increase in your population concerns me, Mr. Warren. There has been too much growth. We're only able to provide you with your current tonnage at the same rate of trade."

His small settlement maintained a delicate balance between having enough people to work the mines and having enough food and clean water to keep them alive.

"What if I add twice the amount of salt and increase the tonnage of ore?" Jerome's foreman would have a fit, but they depended on the corn, potatoes, and grains they bought in bulk from these people each year. All were commodities that they couldn't grow with their limited water supply. "We're not asking for handouts."

"I understand, sir, but our yield depends on the weather, and as you know, it has been–" She paused for the briefest of moments, a look of consternation flickering across her serious face, "–more erratic lately. We are only able to provide the current tonnage at the current rate of trade. We have other settlements to consider."

"Isn't this supposed to be a negotiation?" He shot back.

Jorge tensed beside him.

"Not this year."

"But we have families on the brink of starvation." Jerome's voice cracked on the last word. He massaged his aching shoulder and tried to maintain control. "We weren't going to leave people to die. You know what is going on out there! I want to speak to your father."

Mia ignored his last statement, a bad habit she must have picked up from Daniel. "It's going to be a difficult year with the ongoing drought getting worse. I know people are getting desperate. Maybe you should consider encouraging your families to hold off on having more children until more food is being produced."

Jorge lurched to his feet, the wheeled swivel chair shooting out and hitting the wall behind him. "That's callous of you. I thought you people were fair-minded. The horror stories from the other side of the mountains are—please, we don't have your resources."

The two guards in the room stiffened, hands settling on their weapons.

Pain shot down Jerome's arm, radiating through his chest cavity. He rose to shaky limbs and his chair slammed to the floor, colliding with Jorge's.

Mia waved off the guards.

"How can you sit there and patronize me, young lady? I lived through a civil war, a plague, and the worst famine in recent history. What have you had to live through behind your wall?" He clutched his chest, panting. "What have you had to suffer?"

Jorge steadied him with one hand. "Grandpa? Are you all right?"

Jerome shoved him away with a weak push, eyes fixed on Mia.

"I'm sorry we're unable to be more accommodating. There will be open negotiations next year. Your first food shipment will be ready in two weeks at the North Train Yards." Concern flashed on her face. "Can I get you something, Mr. Warren? More water, maybe?"

Thoughts tumbled one right after another in a jumbled haze. Black dots spotted his vision. *We're all doomed.* "I'll take nothing from you except what…I'm…owed."

Outside. He needed fresh air. Now.

The guards came to prop him up, but he stumbled past them out the door, his breath coming in shorter and shorter gasps. Pressure built in his chest, threatening to explode with one wayward pinprick.

The young people these days skimmed the surface of true despair. The deaths they experienced were only drops in the bucket of what his generation had seen. What they had reaped in war after war, plague after plague. And now the drought had amped up again, risking another famine. The horrible stories of strange behavior spreading like a disease, where there were even reports of cannibalism. Where had they all gone so wrong? How could they all stop repeating past mistakes?

Scorched air hit Jerome's lungs, and he collapsed to his knees. His waiting cart stood by a lone poplar tree, the traveling companion he and his grandson had picked up a blur in the stark sunlight.

So close, yet so far away.

Things had gotten so much better in recent years. Colville would have to start severe rationing again. More hardship. Less of everything.

His heart augered down, a pain like a vice through his entire body.

Jerome closed his eyes, gray sweeping in from the peripheral.

"Grandpa, stay with us." Jorge's intense, panicked voice echoed down a tunnel of agony and disorientation.

Jerome crumpled the rest of the way to the dirt, multiple hands reaching, grasping him.

Dust choked his nostrils and coated his tongue. Shouts echoed around him, the wind howling through skeletal treetops. His chest tightened, each breath a faint, fading gasp. A chilling calm enveloped him as death gripped his heart.

"Arrr..." He tried to reassure his grandson, his beautiful daughter's only child, but it was too late.

He had failed. They all had.

Part 1

The Past: Eva

2044

"Life can only be understood backwards; but it must be lived forwards."

— *Søren Kierkegaard*

PROLOGUE

From the journal of Dr. Eva Zapada,

To some enterprising soul, a record of what was:

Where do I begin? Begin. Ha. Beginnings happen in many places, don't they? Look at births and deaths, a natural cycle, like the Ouroboros consuming its own tail for eternity. Both begin and end something anew. Do I start when I first met Daniel? Or when I took the job in Handford's Manhattan Underground Complex? Do I go back even earlier, before the First Wave of the Resource Wars, or ten years later, after the Collapse of society finished us off? All those years run together like trains at a switching station. Now all the major scenes of my life flash through my mind like reels on the old movies. Constantly moving forward, but never staying in one place for too long. So much death. So many new beginnings. Maybe in the future, some enterprising soul not yet born will take the bits and pieces of now and combine them into a fuzzy picture of what happened then. How it all fell apart like cracks in a glass, forking out in jagged lines before bursting into pieces. What will that person think of me and what I've done? Or of Daniel, for that matter? Will we be painted as villains or something else entirely? Our lives have straddled the grey areas for so long, like tightrope walkers balancing on a cable between two massive skyscrapers. It's taken everything to continue, to fix what we broke. All we have now are new beginnings—in whatever forms those take.

April 2044

D r. Eva Zapada needed Xanax and a stiff drink. Neither would stop the visions of suffocating under tons of earth, steel, and concrete, but maybe, just maybe, one or the other would allow her to fall asleep. Her *abuelita* would turn over in her grave, believing nature—or Vix Vaporub—provided for all ills. But her grandmother had been raised in a traditional Mexican household and didn't believe in easy fixes—unless, of course, *Vaparu* was involved.

Eva tapped her watch. 1:03 a.m.

Giving up any attempt at sweet oblivion, she kicked off the tangled blankets and scooted out of the coffin-like bottom bunk. The top bunk was worse, the space between the ceiling and bed even more minuscule. It made Eva glad she didn't have to share the room. She avoided overnight stays in the underground laboratory as much as possible, but on this particular occasion, her project manager gave her no choice.

Relieved by the empty, wide-open hallway, she drew in a deep breath. Pharmaceuticals and booze were out of the question, but the mess hall had to contain tea or something else that would help.

Fluorescent lights hung from the ceiling on steel bars, bright and impersonal. The colored lines painted on the concrete floor guided people along sterile passages, the government's utter lack of care for aesthetics glaringly obvious. Cameras on the ceiling watched her every move, something she'd learned to ignore.

At one time, the nuclear site on the surface, nestled in the desert of Southeastern Washington state, had been a part of World War II's Manhattan Project. The vast subterranean

Manhattan Complex was developed later during the years of the Cold War with Russia. As with most things associated with the government, there was the tip of the iceberg that everybody saw, and then everything else underneath.

The mess hall door hung open, a single dim bulb glowing above the long counter along the back wall. Over time, some upgrades had trickled in, but not all. A sleek stainless-steel fridge and stove, paired with a brand new microwave, clashed with weathered metal countertops and chipped plastic trays stacked by the industrial sink. The adage "If it ain't broke, don't fix it" thrived here, oddly out of place given the flood of money coursing through the facility.

Shadows lurked in the dark corners of the room; the outlines of tables were darker against the murky gray half-light. She put her finger on the switch, and one of the shadows moved. Eva swallowed a startled yelp.

"Please, don't."

The voice belonged to Dr. Daniel Burgess, one of two Special Projects Leaders in the MUC. In private, her assistant, Rani, jokingly called him the Overlord. She claimed SPL was too tame for the man. She should know, she'd worked with him forever. Dr. Burgess sat with elbows planted, forehead between his hands, and long fingers threaded through dark hair.

"I didn't mean to disturb you, sir. Just coming in for some tea, then I'll be gone." She skirted his table, her eyes finally adjusting to the dimness, and made a beeline for the fridge and microwave.

"Not a problem, Dr. Zapada. Trouble sleeping?" His eyes were dark pools in the grey half-light of the room. In the light of day, they were a unique color, not quite blue, but not quite hazel or brown. A fascinating mixture of colors.

Many of her colleagues called him intimidating and intense, his intellect making his demeanor borderline rude on the best days. Not that he noticed. Tonight, he seemed…subdued.

"The bunks are a little confining." The microwave beeped,

and she took out the cup. Eva dipped the herbal tea bag in the warm water and sighed. It was time to return to her coffin.

"You don't have to leave on my account. Come. Sit. I need to run something by you anyway."

Eva hesitated. Dr. Burgess's black tousled hair stuck out in odd angles; his dress shirt was rumpled with the top buttons undone. She had worked as the lead for her current project for over a year, and every time she'd discussed updates with him, he'd never had a strand or lapel out of place.

Eva shuffled in her slippers to the table and sat, wrapping her hands around the warm mug. He clutched a whiskey glass, the golden elixir gleaming amber in the faint light. If the half-full bottle beside it was any indicator, he'd been here for a while. Dr. Burgess raised the tumbler to his mouth and took a sip. This was the first time she'd seen him drink alcohol. She didn't even know any existed in the MUC.

"What can I do for you, sir?" Eva sipped her tea, the herbal sweetness warm on her tongue. Maybe she could ask him for a shot? That would certainly put her to sleep.

"Not call me sir?" He cocked his head to the side.

She blinked a couple of times. Was the man drunk? Had to be. He never strayed across that invisible line between professional and unprofessional. And that comment bordered on the latter.

"Then what can I do for you, Dr. Burgess?"

"Why don't we just go with Daniel tonight? It's been a while."

"Since you've been called by your first name?" The surreal informality of the conversation unnerved her. It was a highly classified facility with real-world implications—and HR. Calling him Daniel felt…intimate.

"In my line of work, people rarely call you by your first name, even off-duty."

"What about family?" Eva half-expected Daniel not to reply. Nobody knew much about him, other than his service record.

"All my family is gone. Dead in the First Wave." Sadness tinged his voice, and he took another sip of his drink.

A spark of sympathy shot through her. Many people died in that first volley of the Resource Wars now ravaging the world. She, too, had lost most of her family in that wild week ten years ago when China and Russia, in their Eastern Bloc alliance, had strategically detonated the first bombs. Thankfully, she still had her parents and sister.

"What can I do for you, Daniel?" Eva let the name roll off her tongue, the vowels taking on Spanish inflections.

Daniel swirled the glass. "My parents were very religious. I've been thinking about that a lot today."

Unease blossomed along every one of her nerve endings. Where was this conversation going? "Oh?"

"Are you a spiritual person?" Fire lit his eyes. Had she really thought him subdued?

"I went to a Catholic church growing up." She stumbled over the words. How to explain the complicated intertwining of church and family, faith and spirituality?

"That's not what I asked." He poured another slug into his glass, taking the shot in one smooth tip of his head. "My father used to beat my mother, and the one time I stood up for her, he beat me. Not very Godly in my mind. It took me years to come to terms with my faith."

Her hands twisted around the mug, and she remained silent. Could she sneak out? Run back to her room and pretend this conversation had never happened.

"I still have the scars." Daniel exhaled, the smell of whiskey sharp and sweet. "Today, I am reminded that the past always holds power over us, and though we believe we are in control, we are not. It's a fairytale somebody told us so we won't go insane in the vastness of space."

Clarity hit her like a cold winter chill. Rage. That's what he was suppressing by a hair.

"That's an incredibly cynical point of view. Are you all right, Dr. Burgess?"

He leaned forward, scooting the bottle of liquor closer to her teacup. "Daniel, remember. Here, you may need this."

Her brows drew together. "Why?"

"General Kaspar has approved your project to start initial human trials."

The chair dug into her back, sharp and implacable like the outrage now spearing through her. All her discomfort at the conversation vanished. "What? He can't do that!"

"Funny enough, that's exactly what I said." He pointed at Eva, glass in a firm grip. "I quoted the Geneva medical code of ethics and everything. Would you like to know his response?"

Eva nodded even though it had been rhetorical. Thoughts tumbled one after the other like rocks in a rock tumbler, any words lodged in her throat.

Daniel continued. "He said, and I quote, 'You all know what you signed up for.'"

"Fuck that. I didn't sign up to do illegal human experimentation or make super soldiers for a corrupt government." Eva never cursed, but the word slid out of her mouth, frigid and ugly. She walked to the sink and poured the tea down the drain, replacing the liquid with Daniel's whiskey. Johnnie Walker Blue. A very American Scotch.

"Yes, but apparently, it's not quite as illegal if the subjects consent to the experiments under certain circumstances."

She couldn't tell if he was being serious. "That's hair-thin, and you know it. The 2034 addendum doesn't cover something like this. We're not ready. Plain and simple. The Shield Serum is still too unpredictable, and there is still no consistent data from the lab animals. You can't rush science, Daniel. When you do, bad things happen."

"We're at war, Eva. Everything is possible when there's a war. Especially a war we're losing. Another quote, just in case you were wondering." He swirled the liquid in the glass.

"It doesn't matter. We're at least a year out from—" She stopped when he raised his hand.

"What if we do the absolute minimum at first? Continue most of the work on animals? Would the data still be valid? I have something else in the works upstairs—something I've been trying to fix for years. It could shift their focus from the serum. It's the counterpart to Shield's final objective. We just need to go through the motions of following orders." He leaned forward again, his energy all over the spectrum, his eyes dark, intense pools. "Can you do it?"

Eva's mind raced. What he was asking…it was impossible. No, not impossible, untenable. "With what? A placebo? Even with that, nobody is going to volunteer their family to be lab animals."

Back and forth she paced. She felt his eyes following her movements like laser beams locked onto a target.

"There are people who would do anything for enough money. The desalination plants can't keep up with the demand for freshwater, and the production of these plants can't be built while people are suffering. A possible nuclear winter is bearing down. Desperation breeds folly. Families will sign up just to keep from starving or dying of dehydration." He planted his hands on either side of the empty glass.

"So, now I'm supposed to capitalize on suffering? *Dios mío*, Daniel. We don't even have enough data to determine the exact long-term effects of Shield. A quarter of the chimps became malnourished, forty-eight percent lost all higher brain function, eleven percent were unaffected, and ten percent died. The reasoning for each outcome can be whittled down, genetic code by genetic code, but that takes time. We're at a six percent success rate, with the positive effects lasting three months before the lab animals need another dose. Testing on humans at this point isn't only unethical, it's unproductive. I say again, who's going to risk their children, their families on what amounts to a long shot?" She threw her splayed hands in the air. "This is insane. *He* is insane."

"Capitalize on suffering," he rolled the words around in his mouth, almost savoring them. Their eyes connected, and she stopped pacing. "I tried to reason. I tried cajoling, logic, emotion, all of it, Eva. The General wouldn't listen. One of these days, I'll tell you how I met the man."

He poured more liquid into both their glasses. At this rate, neither of them would be able to make it to their respective bunks.

"But you're Dr. Daniel Burgess. You used to be one of them. A military officer. Don't you speak their language? There are so many things that could go wrong and invalidate everything we've accomplished so far."

"We have no choice." He rose to his feet, bumping the table. His half a dram of whiskey sloshed over onto its side. "They will do this with or without us. If we're here, maybe we can mitigate the risk."

"There's always a choice." Eva tilted her head at a stubborn angle.

"Choice, like control, is an illusion when it comes to a project like this. If we succeed with our experiment, we could make a positive change, save people, and make them more resilient." His forehead wrinkled, and he planted his hands on the table. "Seriously, just buy me some time, go through the motions, and try to mitigate the fallout. The machine I'm working on upstairs will change everything if I just have the time to get it to work right. It's called the TMRWS device. Apropos, I think."

Eva resumed her pacing, and he grabbed her hand lightly. A spark of awareness traveled up her arm where bare skin met bare skin. Daniel blinked, dropping her hand, and stepped back. He'd felt it, too. Connection.

Unsettled, she flexed her fingers, trying to dispel whatever had just passed between them. "If we fail by moving too fast, we could kill them all."

Regret played across his face. "The decision has already been made."

Plop. Plop. Plop. The puddle of whiskey from his overturned glass dripped in amber rivulets to the floor.

"I'm leaving tomorrow. I can't be a part of this." Government experimental projects always came with an innate understanding that results could be applied elsewhere, weaponized even. Her genetically modified organism research, meant to make plants and animals require less water, was far from making *people* do so. Its application to Project Shield was even farther down the road of science. The General was right, Eva knew what she was getting into when she took the job. But even she had limits, and they taught ethics in medical school for a reason.

Tension thrummed through her, and she walked to the janitor's closet to get cleaner for the floor. The old white analog clock on the cement wall ticked in time with her footsteps.

"When I said you have no choice, I meant it. They locked down the facility an hour ago. No one in. No one out." Daniel's tone was flat.

Claustrophobia sank its claws into Eva, deep and strong. The bottle of cleaner slipped from her trembling grip, bouncing to roll beneath a nearby table. Her lungs seized, silver sparks swarming her vision like shooting stars. She lurched forward, the walls of the cramped room coiling tighter—a serpent swallowing its own tail. In two swift steps, Daniel caught her arm, his steady grip guiding her to a chair.

Head between her knees and heart racing, she heaved in gulps of air. This one weakness always made her feel small and embarrassed. Hell, she'd gotten through med school at the top of her class, worked relentlessly for every bit of it, was invited to apply for this project, and stood up to some of the biggest hardasses in the government. She should be able to fight the stifling anxiety punching her in the gut.

"So, we're prisoners here?" Her breathy words echoed inside her skull. The spinning had stopped, but Eva continued the long, deep breaths. It would be more embarrassing if she hyperventilated and passed out.

"It will work, Eva. We will make sure of it. I'll get Project TMRWS where it needs to be and take the pressure off Shield so we can do it correctly. Ethically. I am so close. Are you all right?" Worry lines creased his forehead, and the crevice between his brows deepened. Eva had the sudden urge to smooth away his distress. She clenched her hands in her lap and squeezed her eyes shut.

"I'm claustrophobic. I need something to drink."

Without a word, he handed her another shot of whiskey. She slammed it in one gulp. Fire burned her throat and worked its way clear to her stomach.

"What about our families? What are we going to tell them?" Eva's parents worked in food processing plants, and her sister, Sarah, was a medical researcher at the remnants of the University of Washington. She hadn't seen them for years as the Puget Sound area remained under Eastern Bloc control. She'd tried to contact them, but contact was limited.

"I'll talk to your team first thing." Daniel stood, smoothed his hair, and buttoned the top two buttons of his shirt. Dr. Burgess, scientist and military liaison, stood in front of her; forthcoming, drunk Daniel was gone. "Can I escort you back to your bunk, Dr. Zapada?"

Eva shook her head, a little taken aback by the abrupt transition. "No. I think I can find my own way, Dr. Burgess."

He nodded. "We'll start choosing candidates in the morning."

CHAPTER 1

From the journal of Dr. Eva Zapada

Project Shield. My greatest achievement and my greatest regret. So many people put their lifeblood into that project, hoping to protect humanity from the drought sweeping the world. So top secret, that even now it's difficult to write this so openly. Back before the Collapse, nobody could agree on whether the drought was naturally occurring or man-assisted. Governments and organizations took advantage of and exploited the issue. In the end, it didn't matter; changes were occurring, streams and freshwater sources were vanishing at a rapid rate, and desalination plants couldn't keep up. So thus, TMRWS and Shield. One in an attempt to control the weather, and one to make living organisms stronger and more resilient. Sounds great, right? But as it usually does when dealing with governments and special interest groups, greed and power consumed the work. Worldwide wars broke out for over a decade before the final Collapse. Everyone called them the Resource Wars in dozens of different languages. Dubbed this because they didn't just happen between *countries but* within *countries. When everyone scrambles for survival, nobody wins. So many conflicts, it's hard to name them all here. Nuclear weapons and bioagents, death, and destruction as freshwater became the new oil.*

Famines, and from those, plagues. What could we do? First World countries raced to develop something that would stabilize the world as long as the resulting world would be under their control. The scientific and religious communities were the only ones seeming to work together —an irony in itself. In the end, we were too late. Way too late....

#

The sterile lab reeked of antiseptic and failure. Eva stood frozen, her gloved hands clenched as the monitor flatlined.

The patient, a wiry man in his thirties and one of the first "volunteers" for the Shield Serum trials, lay motionless, his chest still, no longer straining for breath. His skin, sallow and paper-thin, clung to sharp cheekbones, the rapid weight loss a brutal side effect of the prototype Shield Serum. Patchy tufts of brittle hair jutted from his otherwise bald scalp, while his lips, cracked and tinged blue, gaped slightly, revealing teeth yellowed from the serum's metabolic toll. His skeletal frame trembled with erratic spasms in the final moments, muscles seizing as his overwhelmed heart couldn't keep up with the rapid cell regeneration.

The heart monitor's relentless drone sliced through Eva's conscience like a blade. She'd known the risks, warned General Kaspar, pleaded with Daniel, but here it was: death, cold and undeniable, on her table.

"Time of death, 14:47," Dr. Henshaw declared. The lab techs padded around Eva and the good doctor, unplugging sensors and covering the body. Eva stripped off her gloves, her hands clammy, and backed away. Her parents would be ashamed of her. They might just be better off under Eastern Bloc control, toiling at their jobs in the food processing plants, while her sister Sarah buried herself in medical research. At least they weren't with her to see her downfall.

Her *abuelita's* voice echoed: *No shortcuts, mija. Do what's right.*

But what was right when every choice was a trap?

She fled the lab, the fluorescent lights blurring as she stumbled into the corridor. The colored lines on the concrete floor mocked her, guiding her nowhere. Her parents had raised her to heal, not harm. Sarah, with her relentless drive, would've fought harder and found a way to stop this. Eva's breath hitched, the walls of the MUC closing in. She needed air, but there was none down here, only the suffocating weight of earth and steel.

The mess hall was empty when she reached it, the familiar dim bulb over the counter casting even longer shadows than usual. She grabbed a chipped mug and filled it with water, her hands shaking so badly that it sloshed onto the counter. The image of the patient's lifeless eyes burned behind her lids. He'd signed the consent form, desperate for the money to feed his kids, his family. She'd capitalized on his suffering, just as Daniel predicted. *Dios mío*, what had she become?

The door creaked. Daniel stepped in, his dress shirt slightly wrinkled, a bottle of Johnnie Walker Blue in hand. His eyes, that strange mix of colors, softened a touch when they met hers. "Eva. I heard."

Eva turned away, gripping the mug. "Don't. I don't want your pity."

"Not pity. Never that. Maybe commiseration, though." He set the bottle on the table and pulled out two glasses. "You look like you need this more than I do."

The whiskey's amber glow caught the light, tempting her. She wanted to drown the guilt, but the burn wouldn't erase what she'd done. "I killed him, Daniel. The serum—my serum— stopped his heart. I told that man it wasn't ready."

He poured two fingers into each glass and slid one toward her. "You didn't kill him. The system did. Kaspar did. We're just…caught in it."

A bitter laugh escaped her lips, and she snatched the tumbler. "That's a coward's excuse."

The whiskey scorched Eva's throat, grounding her in its fire.

All she could see was her mother's loving and nurturing hands tending to the garden, coaxing life from the soil. Her father, sorting fruit and giving his all for their small family, preaching integrity and kindness. Their twin presences in her mind entwined together, a foundation of ethics and morals she'd tried her best not to stray from. They'd never understand this gray world she'd fallen into.

Daniel leaned against the counter, his gaze steady. "You're not a coward, Eva. You're fighting a war you didn't start."

"Stop trying to make me feel better." She set the glass down hard, the clink echoing against the metal counters.

"Never." He took a slow sip, his eyes never leaving hers. She hated it—hated how his presence steadied her, even now.

Eva paced, the concrete cold under her shoes. "Tell me about Kaspar. You said you'd tell me how you met him. I need to know who's pulling the strings, who's making me a murderer."

Daniel's jaw tightened, his fingers tracing the rim of his glass. "You're not a murderer. But I did promise." He gestured toward a chair. She shook her head, crossing her arms.

Daniel sighed and sat instead.

"It was right before the First Wave. I was a military engineer, tasked with developing a weather system to challenge the Eastern Bloc's monopoly. An earlier version of TMRWS. It was meant to control rainfall and counter the drought. Noble, right?" He snorted, pouring another shot. "Kaspar was the oversight officer. A colonel, then, all charm and ambition. I saw through him the first day."

Eva sank into a chair, clutching her glass. "What did he do?"

Daniel's voice darkened. "He didn't care about the tech or the people it could save. He saw TMRWS as a weapon—control the weather, you control food, water, survival. Power. That's all he's ever wanted. One night, he pulled me aside, offered me a deal: falsify data to rush the project, make it a military asset. Said it'd fast-track my career."

Her stomach churned. "You didn't."

"No. I reported him. Thought I was doing the right thing." He laughed, sharp and bitter. "He buried the complaint. Had connections everywhere. Next thing I knew, I was reassigned to Diomede, right on the warfront, and he was promoted. Kaspar's a viper, Eva. He'll burn the world for his own gain."

She stared into her whiskey, the amber swirling like her thoughts. Her parents had taught her to stand up to men like Kaspar. But down here, trapped, she felt powerless. "Why do you stay? You could've left, exposed him."

Daniel's eyes met hers, intense, almost pleading. "Because TMRWS could still work. Not as a weapon, but as salvation. If I can finish it, we could shift the war, save millions. I stay because there has to be a way to do better. To use our knowledge for good."

Her chest tightened. The connection between them pulsed, raw, and dangerous. She wanted to hate him for dragging her into this, but his conviction mirrored her own stubborn hope. She thought of Sarah, who'd once said, *Science is only as good as the hands tasked to wield it.* Eva's hands were stained now.

"I can't do it again," she whispered. "Another patient, another death. I'm not strong enough."

He stepped closer, his hand hovering near hers, not quite touching. "You are. You're still here, fighting. That's more than most." His voice was whiskey-warm. "We'll do this together, Eva. Slow it down, protect the others. I'm almost finished. There's just one piece missing, and TMRWS will buy us time to complete Shield the right way."

Eva longed for his words to be right, to lean into the fragile bond forming between them. But the patient's face haunted her, and her family's voices in her head did nothing but judge. She downed the rest of her whiskey, the burn a punishment she deserved.

"I need to get out." She stood, pacing once again. "Not just this room. This place. There's also something missing in my research, and I can't quite pin it down. There's a doctor, a researcher who used to work with my sister. I met him once at a conference. His name is Dr. Amrit Badal. He might be able to help. We need to find him. It'll kill two birds with one stone."

Daniel sat back. "That's a hard ask, especially if he's on the other side of the mountains. We might be able to get a team, but it'll have to be timed just right."

"I need to be on that team. Please, Daniel. He'll recognize me, it might help." She clutched his outstretched hand, so, so close. They hadn't touched since the first night of lockdown, like wary tigers circling each other. Tingles of awareness zinged up her arm. Her grip tightened. So did his.

They sat that way for a long minute, pulses syncing, until somebody cleared their voice near the door.

Daniel pulled his hand away first. All of a sudden bereft, she clenched her hands together in her lap.

"Sorry, didn't mean to interrupt. Dr. Zapada, they need you in the lab." One of the senior lab technicians, Dr. Rani Soto, stood at the threshold. She nodded her head at Daniel. "Dr. Burgess."

"Dr. Soto." He capped the whiskey and cradled it in one arm. "I'll see what I can do about your request, Dr. Zapada. No promises."

Daniel squeezed past Rani.

Rani raised one fine brow at his departing back and turned toward Eva. "What was that about?"

Eva shook her head, heart still pounding like a drum in her chest. "Nothing. Nothing at all."

CHAPTER 2

From the journal of Dr. Eva Zapada:

I can't stop thinking about Sarah. People call her a psychopath, crazy, a murderer, and an Aberrant. The sister I remember was a scientist with a spine of steel, sharp, and hard-nosed. She'd tear through research like a scalpel, no patience for excuses or half-truths. Back in grad school, she'd lecture me on ethics, her eyes blazing, insisting science had to serve humanity, not egos. I admired her clarity, her fire. But like with us all, the war changed her, and after what happened at Hansee Hall, the sister I knew started to fray. Today's young people don't get how it all changed, what we all did to survive. War and loss hollow you out, twist your mind into shadows of yesterday. Sarah's not crazy; she's misunderstood, carrying scars nobody bothers to read. The world broke her, and she's fighting to piece it back together, even if it looks like madness to outsiders. I don't think she ate those people, but I do think in her own twisted way, she thinks by not stopping the cannibalism, she's helping until she can find a cure—and she doesn't trust anybody else to do it. I'm scared I'm heading down that path. I feel the cracks forming, the same ones that splintered Sarah. I need my sister back, her strength, even if it's wild and fractured. If I can reach her, maybe we'll be able to save each other.

September 2044

Eva clung to the Apache's seatbelt, her pulse syncing with the thrum of its muted rotors—a gunship, Daniel had called it, a predator with stealth so silent it ghosted over the woods surrounding Seattle like a falcon on the hunt.

They flew low, treetops so close you could touch. No enemy craft rose to challenge them. So far, the intel had been correct. The Eastern Bloc's forces were spread thin, with most guarding key resources like water, food, and scientists. Too many places to sneak in remained throughout the vastness of the forest and cities surrounding Puget Sound. Plenty of locals sided with the invaders, so they would still need to be careful, but for now, their mission had gone without a hitch.

Nerves frayed, she adjusted the headset. "What trouble should we expect?"

Daniel had worked his magic, and Eva was now on the mission, though both she and Daniel were well guarded. He'd told General Kaspar that she was the only one who could effectively identify Dr. Badal. Not a lie, but maybe an exaggeration. Eva had met the man at a conference right out of med school. They'd shared a meal and a discussion. Eva's research focused on animal and plant genetics, while Amrit was a clinical geneticist working on human DNA mutations. He was the only one still alive in the area—that she knew about—who could cleave and fuse parts of the human genome using a new method from Oxford. His research had fascinated her, and they'd exchanged contact information, promising to stay in touch. Then, of course, the bombs fell.

"The plan will work. We've got the best of the best covering our backsides." Daniel reached across the space between them and grabbed her hand. She let him, savoring the strength. Nightly drinks in the mess hall had become a common occurrence, but nothing else. Too much was on the line.

Four men and two women, all heavily armed and, she assumed, heavily trained, sat grim-faced in the remaining seats. Battle-hardened and weary, she wouldn't want to meet any of them in a dark alley. Enriquez, a tall, buff woman, eyed her with a narrow focus. Goody, her own personal babysitter.

"I'm more worried we won't get out before we're discovered, before we can get Dr. Badal," she said.

The Eastern Bloc had strongholds in most of the major cities along the West Coast, with a few in the Midwest, where China had been buying farmland for years before the California occupation. The First Wave had brought wars on multiple fronts across the globe as food supplies and resources dwindled along with the rapidly vanishing freshwater. Desalination plants along the oceanfronts could only do so much, and any area with underground aquifers was at a premium.

"If we stick to our parts, we'll be fine. One more time, repeat the steps." He released her hand.

She flexed her fingers and crossed her arms. "I approach Hansee Hall, where they're keeping the scientists. Under the cover of night, with blood all over my face, I ask for help. There are two guards stationed at the front entrance, showing a definite lack of security. While they're most likely yelling at me to leave or some equivalent, I make a big scene, weeping and wailing and hoping they don't shoot me. In the meantime, you all are breaching the back and looking for the good doctor. I'll do my part for five minutes before woefully fading back into the woods, where I'll confirm if you snatched the right guy. Did I miss anything?"

Daniel quirked an eyebrow. "A bit dramatic, but that's the gist. What happens if they want to keep you?"

"Do my best to get away, then run and hide at the meet-up. You'll move to Plan B, which is a lot more bloody." Anxiety honed the nerves to a fine edge. What was she doing? She was a scientist and a researcher; she had no military training. Not that the way the world worked these days allowed for that distinction.

"Good. Here, just in case." Daniel handed her a small pistol. "Put it in your boot."

Eva eyed the gun without taking it. "I'll be fine. I barely know how to load the thing."

"Take it. You never know when you'll need it. Just point and shoot." Steel threaded his voice, brooking no argument.

She made sure the safety was on and tried shoving it down the side of her boot without success.

"Here. Like this." One of the female soldiers—Enriquez—twisted the gun, angling the barrel so that it fit snug against her calf. "You got this. We have your back, all you have to do is say the code word if things go south on your end." She tapped her headset to indicate the tiny earbud she'd have attached next to her eardrum during the extraction.

"Thanks." Eva settled back in her seat, closing her eyes and visualizing each of the steps, one after another.

Unbidden memories of her parents and sister crashed through Eva's thoughts. If they were still where her last report indicated, they would be so close—maybe a mile tops away. Daniel's warning from this morning still stung: reaching out was a gamble. "We don't know where they stand," he'd said, voice clipped. She'd shot back, "We won't know unless we try." Eva had eventually given in, logic overriding her driving need to make sure her remaining family was safe. This mission was critical to all humanity, and Daniel wasn't wrong. He just wasn't right.

The helicopter descended toward the camouflaged roof of a low-slung building hiding in the trees. Its multicolored green corrugated sides blended in with the surroundings, and camo-netted Jeeps and Humvees sat parked along one side. In the field next to the building, another helicopter hunkered down, its darkened rotor blades at rest.

Fear and anxiety twisted themselves into a knot in her gut. "You know, I could identify him through a picture or vid feed."

"Not in this case. We need definitive proof the person we're grabbing is him before bringing him into the MUC. You all right?" Daniel's hand again. This time on her knee.

She gripped it. "We'd better get started before I lose my nerve."

CHAPTER 3

September 2044

Eva limped along the walkway, one hand clutching her side, and collapsed within sight of the guards. The other hand clutched the side of her head. "Help…they're coming."

Tears leaked from the corners of her eyes. It didn't take much with the emotions roiling around inside.

The first guard snapped up his rifle and strode toward her. All muscle and shaved head, he aimed right at her head. "Stay down, or I will put a bullet in you!"

His voice was thick with a Russian accent.

The other guard moved past her to stand at the fence line, scanning the woods and gutted-out buildings in front of the dorm.

"I don't know, I don't…I…I was with a group down south. I think it was a deserter; he was wearing a uniform. Please don't shoot me, please!" Eva held trembling hands up in surrender, hunching over in a submissive pose. "They're all dead. All of them."

Sobs shook her shoulders, rattling, gasping sounds full of

phlegm and all the heartache of the past few months. Every piece of sorrow and guilt packed into a performance that felt all too real.

"Good job," Daniel whispered into her earpiece. *"We just breached the back door. Inside now."*

"Bullshit. No deserters in the Eastern Bloc. Nobody's that stupid. Let's try again. What is your name? Where are you from?" The first guard poked the barrel of the rifle into her side so hard it would bruise.

Eva yelped in pain, falling the rest of the way to the ground on her side, arms wrapped around her head to protect it.

"You, okay? What happened?" Daniel again. The rest of the team relayed one to two-word status reports, but not him. He needed to focus, or he was going to make all her theatrics null and void.

The second guard stepped forward, pushing the rifle away. "Hold up. It could be real. She's bleeding like a stuck pig." Perfect English. Not a Russian. He was American, then.

He crouched, eyeing her. "Where was this at? What kind of weapons did he have? It could be a breach, sir. Somebody could have stolen the uniform."

Sobbing in earnest, now, Eva pushed back to sitting with effort. Just a little longer, a few more minutes. "I…just saw rifles. He started shooting, and there were more people in the woods. I ran… didn't see it all. A branch got me in the head." Her voice shook, eyes pleading. "I just don't want them to get me, please."

"We got him. Get the hell out of there." Urgency filled Daniel's voice.

"Maybe…maybe this isn't such a good idea. Maybe I'm better off alone." Eva stumbled to her feet.

"Now, wait. If there is somebody out there impersonating a guard, we need to know more." Guard two grabbed her elbow. Eva stepped back, the first swell of panic gripping her when she couldn't yank her elbow free. She'd acted too well.

"Please!" She fell to the ground again, and the guard lost his hold. Rolling to the side, she bolted to her feet and turned to run back the way she'd come. A figure strolled from around the end of the building. A woman.

"Eva?" Shock filled the woman's voice.

Sarah.

"Honey, you know this woman?" The American guard hauled her back before she could run. Not that the shock would allow her to.

Honey?

Think, think, think. Improvising, she began to cry again. "Sarah? You're here! *Dios mio*, I found you!"

"We're on our way." Daniel's voice was clipped and hard.

The other woman walked closer. Stress rimmed her eyes, and her black hair was pulled back in a tight braid. "What are you doing here?"

"I've been looking for you," not a lie, "are Mom and Dad here? Are you all alright?"

Sarah cocked her head to the side, a cynical skepticism twisting her mouth and narrowing her eyes. Where had her sassy, smart sister gone? "I see. The last I heard, you were working for the Western Coalition."

At this, both guards snapped to attention, each grabbing an arm.

Shock numbed all of Eva's senses. Why would her sister say that? "How do you know that?"

"We hear things, rumors, chatter. Now, why are you really here?" Sarah walked closer.

"I told you, I wanted to find you, Mom, and Dad." She just needed to stall. Just a little longer. Where was Daniel?

Sarah grabbed her chin, examining her face. "You never were a very good liar. Despite that, I will tell you that our parents died two months ago. Some bioagent the WC deployed against the campus. You won't find much sympathy here for your cause, big sister. At this point, we're all just trying to survive."

The world cracked around Eva, grief splintering her view of

the dorm's fractured façade. Memories flowed, one after the other: her sister's laugh, her mother's hands kneading dough; her father helping her learn how to ride a bike. Over and over, images ran, one into another of all that was.

Eva hung limp between the guards.

She hadn't tried to talk them into coming with her after their initial refusal so many years ago. That decision would haunt her forever, now. Truth be told, as long as she knew they were alive, they operated in the back of her mind, distant, compartmentalized.

Her world was shattered, the guilt bombarding her insides.

"Oh, Sarah, I'm so sorry—"

Her sister cut her off. "I don't want to hear it. You said you would find a way to get us out of Seattle, and then nothing, for years. They never gave up hope, but I knew. You've always been able to push us all to the side. Dad called it a single-minded focus, but I knew better. You were just selfish."

That's not what happened. Kaspar had lied to her. Again. All the words crammed in Eva's throat, refusing to come out.

The guards turned her around to take her inside, but the report of a rifle stopped them in their tracks. The American guard next to her slumped to the ground, blood spraying from his throat.

"Move to the right." Daniel's voice in her ear.

She jerked to the side, and the next shot took the other guard in the chest, his body flying back from the high-powered round.

Sarah crouched to the ground, pistol in her hand.

"What've you done?" Sarah repeated the words, over and over, scanning the treeline for a target.

"Don't shoot her!" Eva cried into the night, hoping the earbud picked up the message.

"You killed him." Sarah covered her eyes with the palms of her hands, the pistol now aimed toward the sky. "No, no, no."

Dropping the gun, she collapsed onto the still body of the

guard who had called her honey just moments before. Harsh sobs rent the night.

Daniel appeared out of the treeline like a wraith. His rifle at the ready, searching the darkness behind her. God, people could have been lined up at the door behind, ready to pounce for all she knew. It was eerily quiet.

"Go." Daniel's voice in real life and in the earpiece resounded against her eardrum.

"I can't leave her. Not again." She stepped toward her sister.

"What she said wasn't true, Eva. We did try to get them over the mountain. She refused."

"Liar!" Sarah picked up the pistol and launched herself at Daniel, a sloppy, feral move fueled by grief.

Eva didn't hesitate; she whipped the pistol from her boot and thumped her sister in the head. Sarah tumbled to the ground, unconscious.

"Daniel?"

"I'm not lying. She wanted to bring someone else with her, maybe that man, I don't know. Command said only immediate family. After that, we didn't hear back from her."

"Why didn't you tell me?" Betrayal from all sides tonight.

"You would've wanted to go find her yourself, and General Kaspar wouldn't allow it. You would have tried to leave and... let's just say, you wouldn't have been allowed to do that either." He tried to grab her hand, but she took a step back, arms crossed.

"What if I leave right now? What would you do?"

Daniel stiffened. "Look around you, Eva. Where would you go? Everything on this side of the mountain is either anarchy or tyranny. Society is crumbling. Do you really think you'd be able to survive on this side with what's coming next?"

What was the universe doing, putting Sarah in Eva's path tonight? She hunched her shoulders. "I'm not leaving her, Daniel. I can't. Please. She could be useful."

She hated the pleading and desperation oozing from her voice.

"We have incoming. Hurry it up." Somebody from their team said in her ear.

Her and Daniel's eyes connected, the dim light shining from the downstairs windows reflecting in their stormy depths. He cursed.

"Fine. We have to leave now. Here." He handed her his rifle.

Daniel caught Sarah in a fireman's carry.

"Thank you." She gripped the stock of the heavy gun.

"Don't thank me yet. We just killed her lover. Now, let's get out of here before the residents get up the nerve to come and investigate."

CHAPTER 4

September 2044

Flame and smoke sucked the oxygen from the air. The disorienting incongruity of haze combined with the drone data from her lenses turned Eva's stomach. A chunk of building flew through the air, and she ducked. Somebody grunted behind her.

Shadowy figures scurried all around her in a martial dance, and the *rat-a-tat* of automatic weapons fired at close range rang in her ears.

Panic and chaos enveloped Eva in their cold arms. She covered her ears and hunkered low. Nothing made sense. Where was Daniel? Or Tobias? Or Enriquez?

"Eva, move to the northeast. Now." Daniel's low voice sounded in her earbud.

Eva's entire body froze, her breath coming in ragged gasps.

"I don't think I can." She barely breathed into the mic.

She was a scientist, dammit, not a soldier. Order and scientific method, those were the things that made sense. Not buildings blowing up. Not gunfire so close she could taste the powder.

A large soldier, balaclava and gas mask firmly in place, ran toward Eva from the smoky haze. Adrenaline, hot and fast, coursed through her veins.

Don't freeze now.

She pulled her pistol.

He lifted his rifle.

Eva's hands trembled.

She was going to drop the gun.

Strong arms wrapped around her waist from behind, propelling her into a different trajectory against the wall of an old apartment building.

Daniel.

"Go. We only have thirteen minutes to make it to the exfil site."

Relief at his presence mingled with panic. What if their group didn't make it?

"We'll make it." Daniel again, like he had read her mind.

Tobias hung between two of the soldiers, a rivulet of blood dripping down the side of his face where a brick had gashed it open. The big man clung to consciousness by a hair.

They had twelve minutes left.

Eva gripped her pistol in a sweaty hand. Nobody had told her to holster it.

The two remaining male soldiers had Sarah in a fireman's carry and Dr. Badal bound and gagged. Sweat and soot coated all their faces. It left her, Daniel, Private Enriquez, and the two other female soldiers, Privates Mulligan and Donovan, to guard their retreat.

A mile separated them from the pickup point in Calvary Cemetery, where the stealth chopper would evac them.

God, when had she started thinking in military parlance?

Her night vision glasses streamed location and stats in real time and showed her any upcoming obstacles along their path.

The eerie stillness of the night was getting to her. In her college days, the U District was teeming with life. Cars traveled the streets, and all night, businesses offered entertainment and a break from studying. It felt like the entire city held its breath—and maybe it did.

A crack from somewhere behind them had the group freezing and hunkering in place. Daniel eased out from under Tobias's arm and duckwalked to the rear next to Donovan. The other soldiers did the same with their human cargo, and the trained unit surrounded Eva and the other three.

Ten minutes remained.

They had taken an old asphalt running path from Hansee Hall to the cemetery. Two six-story, beige apartment buildings with every window darkened—an oddity in itself—lay to their right. On their left, a walkway with stairs, bushes, and trees veered off up a hill to another set of apartments. At least being in Seattle had one advantage—a lot of cover.

Another crack, this time closer. Was it sticks snapping? Or bullets farther away? Her untrained ears couldn't tell the difference.

Eva checked on her sister. Sarah's warm pulse thumped against her fingertips, slow and steady. She checked on the doctor. He glared back, above his gag. The small amount of ketamine to make the man compliant was wearing off.

Eva tapped the earpiece to speak to the group. "Anybody have any more ketamine?"

Daniel glanced back at her. "Off the comms."

"The ketamine is wearing off. Amrit might try to run." Even though her voice barely registered as a whisper, it felt like she was shouting in the muted environment around them. Heck, not even a night bird sang.

"Impossible."

Eva gave him was an exaggerated shrug.

Another crack, and this time Eva knew, clear down to the soles of her feet, that it was gunfire.

"Are they shooting at us?"

Daniel shushed her with a sweep of his hand.

She clamped her lips together.

He motioned for the group to get off the path between the two apartment buildings. They dragged the bodies of the three incapacitated members of their party and dropped them against the wall.

Amrit tried to stand but got pushed back down.

She dug through one of the other packs the soldiers had dropped alongside them. Rapid-fire gunshots from an automatic rifle fragmented the night. Somebody returned fire in a different direction, almost on top of them.

Could it be the team they came here with from the Underground Railroad, retrieving people from the university?

Her eyes widened. It wasn't her group that was being followed. Daniel turned, and she saw the light dawn on his face as well. The evac team for the Underground Railroad had an entire group of civilian scientists and doctors they had come to rescue for the Catholic Church.

He tapped his ear. "We need to assist the Alpha team. Enriquez, stay with Eva and the others. Concealment first, but don't let anybody be captured. The rest of you, follow me."

Her right lens changed to a floating map. It showed moving red dots—had to be people— some 200 yards to their west. The drone at work. Another, larger cluster of dots representing a different group plodded in comparison. The rear group was catching up fast.

Daniel nodded his head at her. She couldn't see his face well in the dark, but her stomach twisted.

The brush and trees swallowed the small group of six as they took the winding staircase path across from them.

They had seven minutes left.

"Sorry," Eva whispered to Enriquez.

"For what?" The other woman looked confused.

"You look like you wanted to join them. Instead, you're left here babysitting."

The other woman shook her head, a serious expression in her

dark eyes. "Every mission is important. You say that man there," she pointed at Amrit, "could be the key to stopping the Resource Wars. I would say baby-sitting duty is pretty damn important at this point."

Enriquez focused her attention back to the pathway, her head on a swivel.

Amrit moaned. Louder this time. Hell, she'd almost forgotten.

She dug through the remaining bags. No sedatives.

Eva scrambled to the man's side and covered his mouth.

Enriquez eyed her and Amrit. "Keep him quiet."

"I can't find the ketamine."

The man attempted to get to his feet, yet again.

More gunfire popped, a bit closer now. She shoved him back down, and he kicked out, connecting with her shin.

"Ow, shit!"

Something rustled across the path. Dr. Badal squawked out a grunt around the gag and was met deftly with the butt of Enriquez's rifle.

But it was too late.

The rustling turned into two shadowy figures about a hundred yards down the path, hunkered low, rifles swiveling left to right in a search pattern. The all clear hadn't come over their earbuds, so the figures couldn't be from their team.

Eva grabbed Amrit's legs and heaved, trying to yank him back down the lane between buildings. If those shadows had body heat detectors, her and Donovan were screwed.

Tobias lay slumped against the opposite wall, Sarah beside him, just out of sight.

Heart pumping, arms and legs like rubber, Eva unholstered her pistol yet again to stand guard over the prone bodies on the ground.

Guns, bombs, and bioagents. To say she despised all things that destroyed life was an understatement, and yet, here she was, depending on one to keep her alive. Irony in its finest form.

Enriquez lay prone on the ground now, rifle stabilized with one hand, her elbow planted on the ground, the butt tucked into her opposite shoulder. She tracked somebody with the barrel. In a breath, she squeezed the trigger. An explosion of sound, dulled by the earbuds' noise-canceling tech, rattled Eva's teeth.

A curse from not very far away met her ears, and a bullet shattered a window on one of the second-floor apartments above her. Eva gripped the pistol hard, finger just out of the trigger grip like Daniel had shown her. Enriquez returned fire.

Gravel crunched behind Eva.

She whirled, but it was too late. Something hard knocked her in the head with a glancing blow. Stars filled her vision.

Don't pass out, don't pass out.

Eva rolled to the side and landed awkwardly on her back. One of the people in black stood over her.

"Surrender and I'll let—"

The man didn't get to finish his words. His head exploded like a melon, blood splattering her in the face.

"*Clear.*" Daniel's voice said through the earpiece.

"Copy that."

Eva covered her mouth with a trembling hand. She'd seen dead people. Many, many dead people after the First Wave. But this was different. She couldn't take her eyes off the nearly decapitated man in front of her. Blood and bone, greenish black through her night vision lenses, covered the apartment building wall in an alluvial splatter. One dead eye looked back at her from the mangled body.

Daniel's face appeared in front of her, his hands cupping her face. "You need to snap out of it, Eva. We've got to move, sweetheart."

Sweetheart? She blinked. "Daniel?"

"Yeah. We've got to get out of here, and I don't have enough people to carry you." He handed her the pistol. How had that slipped out of her hand? "Put that in the holster, we'll keep you in the middle of the pack."

Shock numbed every one of her senses. Daniel was so close she could see the small wrinkles fanning out from around his eyes. Crow's feet? Wasn't that what people called them? She covered her mouth before a hysterical giggle could escape.

"Okay."

He helped her to her feet. She joined the rest of the group. Enriquez had blood on her face but otherwise appeared healthy and unharmed.

They continued along the path.

Four minutes to their evac site.

The evacuation took three minutes longer than the original plan, with the helicopter preparing for liftoff right as they reached the cemetery's edge.

Now, she and Daniel sat on their bunks at the warehouse in the woods, hair wet from showers, and MRE remnants on the floor beside them. What she wouldn't give for a nice juicy cheeseburger. Or steak. Medium-rare with a salad, a side of baked potato, and sourdough. Her mouth watered, and she kicked the beige package with the words "pork ribs" in bold, black lettering under her bed.

The two military bunks were only a couple of feet apart along the back wall next to ten others. Some were already occupied at the far end. Boxes of supplies rested in orderly piles in front of them, but there was no other privacy. The two of them had four hours before the stealth chopper could return them to the MUC along with Dr. Badal and her sister—four more hours of what felt like freedom.

"We could just leave," she murmured."Disappear into the woods never to be seen again."

He cocked his head to the side and reached out to thread a stray hair behind her ear. "Could we, though?"

Eva captured his hand before he could pull it away. "I'm not suited for this. Military secrets and missions. Killing. Hell, even rescuing. I'm just not wired that way. I'm a scientist, a researcher. An intellectual."

"Come here."

"What?" She gave him a startled look.

"You saw a person get killed in front of you. For the first time, judging by your reaction. Come here. We both need to get some sleep."

Her stomach flip-flopped. They'd never spoken of the attraction buzzing between them. God, was she going to become a cliche? Sleeping with her boss? But this felt different. Maybe because of being locked down together for so long, or the gravity of their projects. Or a combination thereof.

She rose from her bed and gazed down at him. Daniel scooted over, opening his arms. For crying out loud, they were going to spoon.

In that moment, there was no place she'd rather be.

CHAPTER 5

From the journal of Dr. Eva Zapada

I've hesitated discussing the TMRWS device—Daniel's baby and life's work. Built on the bones of HAARP, it originated from a defunded U.S. military project. Its goal was weather control. The TMRWS gathered atmospheric moisture, stored it in vast underground aquifers, and redistributed it based on regional needs. Daniel said they were scattered across the country before the Collapse—nearly operational. Tantalizingly close to winning the global weather control race. Then the final bombs fell. The main challenge for the TMRWS prototype was determining when to stop accumulating the water–the control part of weather control. That's where sample Tau-159 came in.

This plate-sized meteorite had a tellurium core, a rare, brittle element encased in iron for stability. Its secret? Self-replicating, extraterrestrial organic enzymes, unlike anything found on Earth. Their genome could start and stop cell reproduction with minimal damage. Dr. Badal and I dubbed them "tellurium enzymes," despite their non-tellurium composition, and used them in Project Shield. Badal's breakthrough was incubating and controlling them in organic hosts. Daniel integrated them into TMRWS's AI, creating an organic core to manage the system. It became his control mechanism, but he was only able to manage it for one machine. Then the final bombs fell and everything changed.

#

October 2044

    "It won't work!" Dr. Amrit Badal tossed a tablet stylus on the metal lab table. It clanked against a graduated cylinder and clattered to the floor.

Eva threw her hands into the air. "Well, with that attitude, it won't."

Daniel strode through the door, slacks rumpled and a two-day stubble shadowing his chin. The tenth floor project took more and more of his time these days, and she only saw him at night as they fell too exhausted into the bunk to even move, let alone make love.

"I was going to ask how it's going, but I can guess by the tone, not well." He leaned against the work island in the center of the room. "Why don't we take a break. Get a full eight hours of sleep tonight and start again in the morning?"

Amrit picked up the stylus and tossed it back on the counter. Tensions were high, and even though the doctor had settled in as best as could be expected, he pushed back whenever he had the chance. Eva couldn't blame him, not really. Especially after hearing how he'd lost his family in the First Wave. She might have done the same. Eva's sister, on the other hand, still wouldn't say a word, even after two months.

"Sleep isn't going to help," said Amrit.

Daniel's eyes narrowed on the other man. "Get some sleep, Dr. Badal. That's an order. Dr. Zapada, can I talk to you privately?"

Amrit shot them a knowing look, condescension dripping from his eyes. He slapped his hands against the lab doors, probably heading toward Sarah's room.

Eva sighed. "Everybody knows about us, *Dr. Burgess*. We don't have to put on an act. Just like everybody knows sub-level eight is working on cryostorage for humans, and sub-level four is working on something for NASA. Secrets are like targets for us prisoners."

In an underground community, where all three-hundred and fifty-one personnel for the MUC bunked on the same two floors and couldn't leave, it was easy to see who slept where every night. Daniel had a bit larger bed with no top bunk, and a private bathroom, thus, they slept in his room. Amazingly, with him, her claustrophobia remained at a manageable level and sleep hadn't been a problem.

His face softened. "Yes, but because of that it's even more important to keep work and personal life separate. And who in the world has been talking about sub-level eight?"

"It's not like we all don't have top-secret clearance, Daniel. Don't worry, I just heard a snippet of conversation between Tamara and Ron. Nobody's letting loose with any specifics. What did you need to talk to me about?" Eva skirted the table and looped her arm through his as they walked through the door. They were off duty, right?

He didn't drop her arm but squeezed it closer to his side. "I think I have something that can speed up your timeline with Shield."

Eva froze in the middle of the hallway. "I've lost two patients this month. Please, don't ask me to test something else."

"I might have a solution for that." Daniel tugged her arm back through his and continued down the hall to the elevator.

"Really?"

"Come with me."

"I've got clearance?"

"Just to my lab." He pressed the button to the tenth sublevel. The lit buttons descended in order, counting off as they passed the upper floors. It was the closest to the surface she'd been in months.

"So, what are we looking at?"

"Tau-159. Two years ago, during the third lunar mission, NASA collected samples of various meteorites that had crashed into the moon. One of the larger samples had an enzyme that thrives in vacuum but can survive in atmosphere. This is a piece of that, though where they're storing the main sample is a mystery. I've been trying to help the other team utilize it with TMRWS. The enzymes reproduce at a rapid rate, a little slower in atmosphere but still faster than most terrestrial genomes. I want you to see the results before I transfer the data to your console. It might be the answer you and Dr. Badal have been looking for."

Eva preferred working with plant genomes. Though the number of protein-encoded genes were usually larger than a human's, they were more repetitive. Trying to adapt her research to humans had proven more difficult than anticipated. Humans were just more complicated all around.

"So what you're saying is, we could solve our regeneration problem with an alien enzyme?"

Daniel lifted a brow. "You sound hesitant?"

"Every sci-fi author and movie maker in the past hundred years has come up with very logical and well-thought-out reasons why using anything non-terrestrial on humans is a bad idea. Think of invasive species in various ecosystems around the world. Do we really want to test those theories?"

"So far, it hasn't reacted like an invasive species, but we could test that theory further if it would make you feel better?" He gave her arm a squeeze.

The elevator door opened to the tenth sub-level. They turned the corner to Daniel's lab on this floor. "If it could prevent an extinction level event? Yes, please."

Sterile metal counters lined the walls to the right and locked floor to ceiling cabinets filled the wall in front of her. A level one refrigerator stood to her left, glass reflecting the awful fluorescent lighting above. The mandatory decontamination eyewash station sat next to it. On the work island in the middle stood a sealed glass container about the size of a microwave with gloves facing inward. The glovebox, the most appropriate name if there ever was one, was lit from the top, and in the center resided a platter-sized chunk of jet rock, a fine sheen coating its smooth, flat surface.

"I thought the enzymes could survive in our atmosphere." She moved closer. "That really doesn't look like an average meteorite."

"It's almost solid tellurium inside. We're keeping it there because it reproduces rather rapidly when separated from the tellurium and we don't know the impact of uncontrolled growth."

"How the hell did it survive impact with the moon?" She donned the gloves and ran a gentle finger over the surface. Bits and flashes of metal shone through a dull iron outer layer. "Is it magnetic?"

"Highly."

Eva removed her hands. "Show me the numbers on the enzyme. It lives in the tellurium layer?"

"Between the tellurium and iron, right on the surface, protected. It seems like the enzyme replicates rapidly but controls itself before overpopulating. We've been running experiments to see what part of the genome halts cell reproduction."

A laptop rested on one of the counters by the door, a metal swivel chair in front of it. Daniel tapped out his password. A document appeared on the screen and Daniel clicked out of it. Not before Eva saw the title. *TMRWS (Temperate Magnetic Resonance Weather System): Efficacy and Impact Report.*

That's what TMRWS stood for.

Her thoughts trailed off as he turned the laptop to face her. Charts and numbers filled the screen. Right. Application to their current problem had to take precedence and Daniel wouldn't offer any details on TMRWS, even with her.

She scanned through the preliminary data on TAU-159. There

were redacted documents, graphs and charts galore. "Can the enzyme even be integrated with humans without an immune response?"

"Maybe a viral carrier for efficiency's sake?"

"Hmm, maybe. We could start with the nanoneedle technique and go from there." The numbers and pictures on the screen were fascinating. She'd never seen anything quite like it. Molecular breakdown models were intricate and beautiful, each part flowing into the next unlike anything she had ever seen. Her hand touched the screen, mesmerized by the symmetry. Anybody not believing in God only had to look at such a thing. Nature alone couldn't build such a structure.

Daniel considered her words. "That could work. Dr. Badal will need to be on board. All the way on board."

Eva grimaced, pulling her eyes away from the screen with effort. "Yeah. I'll work on that tomorrow. Being abducted has left him in a foul mood. But hey, at least my sister has someone to commiserate with."

Sarah had shut down, the death of her lover causing her to become more and more withdrawn. Books and food. That's all she'd accept from anybody in the MUC.

"She'll come around. Especially if this works. I'll transfer the numbers to your computer in the morning. Now, let's get those eight hours of sleep." He pulled her up out of the chair, bodies touching along their entire lengths. TAU-159 pushed from her mind for now, she allowed the butterflies to flutter as Daniel wrapped his arms around her.

Thump, thump. Thump, thump. His heart beat against her ear like a metronome, steady and strong.

"Or maybe seven," she said.

###

November 2044

On the morning the final bombs fell and modern society Collapsed for good, Eva missed her period.

Even with all the stress of the project, her menstrual cycle was like clockwork. Two days passed before she realized she was late. Time moved differently in the MUC.

God, how could this happen? They'd used protection. Pregnancy was next to impossible. Right?

Hell would freeze over before she requested an over the counter pregnancy test from topside. After all, she had a state-of-the-art lab at her disposal. A little blood, modify one of the machines to test for hCG, and she'd put this hiccup to rest.

Eva tiptoed out of the bathroom, and dressed. Daniel shifted in their shared bunk and she froze. He didn't move again. She heaved a sigh and proceeded to her lab. This time of day, not many were in the halls. Guards patrolled 24/7 and some of the night owls who worked better when everyone else was asleep were still prowling around. Underground living had screwed with everyone's circadian rhythms.

Eva relaxed as she turned on the lights in her lab. Its sterility kept her sane, each function and piece of equipment a touchstone of order and familiarity amidst the stress of her job. The machines hummed to life.

She retrieved the sample tubes and other items needed to test her blood. God, what would happen if she was pregnant? Would they even let her keep a child in the MUC? *Dios mio*, how would Daniel react?

Gloves donned, Eva snapped a band on her upper left arm and inserted the butterfly needle into her vein. Awkwardly, she filled two vials.

The rest of the process was smooth, and she stared at the final results with equal parts fascination and horror.

Two strong arms wrapped around her waist. "What results are those?"

She jumped, her heart accelerating.

"Daniel, you're awake." Her voice was way too high-pitched.

He peered closer at the readout. "Who's pregnant?"

She had never been good at poker.

He stilled but didn't pull away.

There was that.

"*Your* pregnancy test?"

Tears welled in her eyes and she covered her face. Hormonal response? Or something else? She wasn't normally a crier. "I am so sorry. I don't know what happened. I swear I take my birth control every day at the same time. We're always protected. I don't know what happened."

Daniel enfolded her in his arms.

Why wasn't he saying anything? Throat aching, she controlled the tears with an effort and chanced a glance at him.

An odd look lit his face. Was it fear? No, Daniel was never afraid, even when the world crashed in around him.

"It'll be fine, we'll figure it out." He squeezed her tighter.

"We better. I think I figured out how to stabilize Shield. If I'm pregnant, though...." The thought drifted off. How could this happen now? When she was so close?

She didn't have time to contemplate any of it further.

Massive detonations from above rattled the entire room, and the air raid sirens blared to life throughout the MUC.

CHAPTER 6

From the journal of Dr. Eva Zapada:

The worst year of my life also happened to be the best due to the birth of my daughter, Mia. The Resource Wars, the success of Shield, the TMRWS machines, they're all important, but what happened during that year is vital to what came after. You see, we failed them, those we lost. A beginning in death once again. We failed my sister and the families who signed up to bring hope to world. Sarah should never have been brought into the MUC, I know this now, but you know what they say about hindsight. God, that year. Most of the survivors from the Manhattan Underground Complex started calling it the Year of Hell. It wasn't a clever name, but it fit. We became unraveled in there, in our own Gahenna, buried underground. I witnessed first hand why it's important to have faith in some higher power, because that and being pregnant were the only things that got me through. If Amrit and I wouldn't have figured out the Shield Serum, we'd have all died. Or rather, if it hadn't been for Killian Cooper—the surviving six-year old test subject for Project Shield. I ask myself everyday one question: if we had gotten the Shield Serum working before the world Collapsed… would it have changed anything?

#

ay 2045

Bloody lines slashed through the number seven-teen beside the door of the sub-level landing. Eva got close enough to sniff. The faint coppery scent of blood reached her nostrils and she wrinkled her nose.

The blade of light from the flashlight swept the hallway in either direction, ending back on the crossed out number. The gloom settled like a cloak around her, the open doorway in front of her.

She rested her hands atop her burgeoning belly, the baby inside making her wish for a horizontal surface to rest on.

Daniel stopped beside her and examined the cryptic message. "Sarah and Natalie won't get far. You should go back. This is no place for a pregnant woman."

"This entire Complex is no place for a pregnant woman. And how do you know the other missing person is Sarah?" The baby kicked again, and Eva winced at the solid thump against the wall of her stomach. Another two months of this and she'd be internally bruised black and blue.

Daniel's mouth thinned. "Who else is exhibiting symptoms and has disappeared in the last forty-eight hours?"

Nobody.

Damn it.

"She's my sister, Daniel. We control the eventual way out. It'll take at least two more months to clear the rubble from the tunnel to reach the surface." A lump formed in her throat. Two more months until blessed sunlight warmed her face. "There are not very many places to hide and they'll have to eventually show themselves."

"We can't wait for that. They consumed human flesh, Eva."

She swallowed the bile rising in her throat. Stomach acid burned all the way back down her esophagus. The body had been horrendous, like animals had torn it apart. How human hands and teeth accomplished that level of destruction was mind-boggling—and sickening. So far, they'd kept it from the others.

"What do we tell Killian?"

"He's six."

"He's going to notice his mother is gone. Natalie has seriously overprotected that boy since the Collapse and hasn't been more than a room away since Kyle died."

Died in pain after volunteering to be one of the first people injected with the new proto-type version of the Shield Serum. Health resiliency was the goal of the serum. It's primary versions elicited anything but in their hosts—including Natalie and Kyle Cooper. Even if Kyle's death hadn't been in vain, it ate at her. Now she'd have to tell the little boy his mom was also sick.

Unless they could fix it…

"He'll remember bits and pieces and how he felt but he won't remember the reasons. Trust me. Killian will be fine, I'll—we'll—make sure of it. Now, we need to find Sarah and Natalie's hidey-hole before they do something else."

"You're thinking they found a way into a stable section of this level? Someplace we haven't scouted?"

"Either that or the ventilation. Some of those ducts are large enough to squeeze through and bypass the main cavern."

Eva swept her light once more through the open door. Piles of rubble clogged the hallways and office area, making the room unstable. Through that hallway, there was a workroom and platform for a branch of the underground train track that the old government used to use to move materials and resources undetected.

"Why the slashes? With blood no less." It didn't make sense to Eva. They had marred the number on the sub-floor that would eventually lead to freedom from where they were all buried alive. A message, but why?

"The proto-type isn't allowing them to think straight. They probably don't even know why they did it. Let's go. I'll send a search party to start checking vents." Daniel placed his hand at the small of her back.

Since she'd started the third trimester, Daniel took every chance to touch her. Arm, back, leg. He now guided her back down the man-made tunnel that would eventually lead all the way to Sub-Level Twenty, the lowest and most secure floor left in the MUC.

The two of them stepped across the threshold to a section of Sub-Level Eighteen, shored up on all sides with tables and other detritus from below. Then another small part of intact hallway before another man-made tunnel took them through the main excavation to level Twenty.

Something clanged above them.

She froze and Daniel unholstered his pistol in one smooth motion, yanking her into a crouch beside him.

Luminescence flashed in his eyes, there and then gone.

A reflection? Eva couldn't give it much thought because Natalie now stood in front of them, dried blood caking her face, hands, and clothes, eyes dark pools in the dim light. They laser-focused on Eva's belly.

Daniel shoved Eva behind him. "Natalie, we can help you."

The woman took a step forward, hands clenching and unclenching, head tilting to try and look around Daniel at Eva. Her scraggly hair hung around her head in strings, a hungry look on her feral face.

Eva reached into the back of Daniel's waistband and pulled out his other pistol, checking the clip. She placed her spine firmly against his, dropping the flashlight at their feet. Sarah was still out there.

He tensed. "Natalie, think about your son, think about Killian. He needs you."

Natalie clicked her tongue against the roof of her mouth.

Another dragging step forward.

A shadow moved from down the hallway and Eva narrowed

her eyes. Natalie and Sarah were trying to box them in like pack predators did with their prey.

"It's not working, Daniel. Too much of her prefrontal cortex has been damaged." Eva murmured, not taking her eyes off of the moving shadows creeping her way.

"You don't know that. Another dose of the stable version of Shield could reverse the effects. It's happened before."

Eva's heart squeezed in her chest. "With initial symptoms. Too much time has passed. It's been days."

The shadow avoided the light, the outlines of a human taking shape.

And Sarah appeared. Old blood coated her hands and clothes but her face was clean, hair pulled back tight in a braid. "So, you're saying, sister, that there is no hope?"

Eva startled at the words.

Sarah shouldn't have been able to talk.

"Maybe for you. You're still talking. Can Natalie communicate?"

A hiss, and clattering steps rushed across the floor. Daniel surged forward away from her. It took every ounce of effort not to look. Eva glued her eyes to Sarah, the other woman watching whatever happened behind her back with a cocked head and mild interest.

"Not in any way you would deem tolerable."

Gunshots rang out and Eva backed up until she rested against the wall, kicking the flashlight until it spun, pointing at the melee down the hall. She flicked her eyes to the tableau of Daniel standing over Natalie with his gun, the woman prone on the floor.

Sarah shook her head. "Guess she's not communicating at all, now."

"Come back with us, Sarah, we can help you." Eva tried.

"Listen to your sister. If you're talking, you still have a chance." Daniel didn't look away from the body at his feet.

Natalie twitched. He put a bullet in her head and the thing that used to be Natalie stopped moving altogether.

Sarah peered closer at Daniel, a sneer replacing the mocking smile.

"Aren't you an interesting specimen." She stepped back and Eva aimed. "I don't think I want any more injections today."

Sarah lunged into the tunnel leading back up to Sub-Level Seventeen. Eva made to give chase but Daniel grabbed her arm. "She isn't going anywhere and there's nobody up there to harm."

"But—"

"Think about the baby, Eva."

As if hearing the reminder, the baby kicked her in the ribs. She winced. The tunnel disappeared into dark and gloom. Much like her sister.

She met Daniel's gaze. "Just promise me you won't kill her. Please."

Daniel rested his hand on her stomach, on the life hidden there. "I'll see what I can do. Now, go, get more people up here to help me. We need to contain the body."

She left him standing in the small pool of light from the flashlight, examining Natalie without touching her.

An inscrutable look crossed his face and she wanted to pry his brain open to look inside. He'd been their rock since the Collapse. Holding all the survivors together. It had to be taking a toll, but he wasn't talking to her.

Two more months. And then it will get better. We'll be on the surface.

She glanced at him one more time before descending.

Daniel had never looked so alone.

CHAPTER 7

Eva sat on the hard-packed sandy dirt that dominated the landscape of the Columbia Basin. She blinked away dark spots from her vision as the glare of the sun hit her face. The glorious sun. Tears streamed down her cheeks unchecked as she soaked in its healing light.

Daniel stood gazing out at the landscape, hands on his narrow hips. His jeans sagged, ripped and held in place by a belt that had more holes in it than leather. The t-shirt draped off his once muscular frame in sad folds. The entire group looked like those posters she used to see for the zombie movies except they were all still alive. Blessedly alive. Thanks to the final iteration of Shield.

The baby lay sleeping in a plastic recycling bin next to her. She had named her Mia after her *abuelita*. A fine layer of dust coated the gray government blanket that she was wrapped in. Healthy and pink, she cooed in her sleep, then resettled. Eva rested her hand on the downy dark fuzz that covered the little girl's head, a mix of love and uneasiness entwining like twin flames. She and Daniel had saved her. They had saved as many as they could. More tears leaked from her eyes. She brushed them away. No time for that. The world wouldn't wait for sentimentality.

Weary people emerged out of the rough-hewn tunnel—more mole hole than anything—and collapsed in the warm afternoon sun, dropping any equipment they had brought up as soon as they cleared the entrance. Amrit and a few others helped the weaker ones over the last steep hump. The exit they'd dug from the collapsed train tunnel from Sub-level Seventeen gaped like an open wound in the earth. Soon the one-hundred and two people who had survived in the Manhattan Complex reached the open-air for the first time in almost a year.

The final exodus.

She shivered at the word.

"Where do you want her?" Tobias's voice cut through Eva's rumination as his and Sarah's bodies blocked out the sun, their shadows enfolding her like a shroud.

Bound and gagged, eyes bloodshot and enraged, Sarah glared down at her. Not as far gone as Natalie, but any remnant of her sister had faded–or been buried. They'd soon find out which.

"Over by that pile of boxes should be fine, for now." She averted her gaze and busied herself with Mia's blanket. Her fingers fidgeted with the dusty gray material.

Sarah's grunted protests and expletives met her ears, harsh and tragic. Dust swirled in the air, dancing along with the heat waves radiating over the flat, rocky terrain.

Guilt. A wretched sensation. It dug its ugly claws into her deeper and deeper, fighting with the grief for dominance.

Tobias pushed Sarah to the ground by a couple of plastic bins next to a large rocky outcropping, and tied her legs. If the woman could spew acid from her eyes and spit it at the man, she would have.

Daniel's commanding voice rose above the noise of the group, "Okay people, I know we just got here, but it's time to initiate the plan. Jordan and Alex, you secure the tunnel like we discussed. I changed my mind, though, I want guards 24/7, six hour shifts at first until people get their strength back. Amrit, I want you to go with Ron and his group south, scavenge any medical and food supplies you can find."

"Are you sure? I could do more here." Amrit scrambled to his feet, clearly agitated.

"We need to get our feet under us as quickly as possible. And you know the items we need to replenish the stocks in the lab." Daniel shifted his focus to the next group, and didn't see Amrit's narrowed eyes and pursed lips. But Eva did, and she frowned. *Trouble brewing?*

Daniel continued, "Livvy, you and Aaron do the same heading east. All of you, avoid conflict if you can, but don't hesitate to shoot. Bring back whatever resources you can manage."

A murmur of, "yes sirs" and "copy thats" met the announcement. The two groups milled around, gathering supplies, shouldering high-powered rifles, and saying their good-byes. Their emaciated bodies looked fragile beneath the weight of the gear and oversized clothing, the Shield Serum the only thing keeping them moving and alive.

Mia started fussing, and Eva picked the baby up to place her at her breast. The tiny girl latched on and started suckling. Eva winced.

A shadow fell over them and Daniel sat down, his shoulder brushing against hers.

"How is she?" He asked, the taciturn commander gone as he gazed over at Eva and the nursing child. A few groups had started setting up temporary shelters and securing the entrance to the tunnel, while others lay in the warm sun, too depleted from the long walk to do much else.

"Good. Strong." Eva flinched as Mia rooted around. She switched the child to the other side.

In a rare show of gentleness, Daniel stroked a loving finger over Mia's downy head. "She'll be the best of us."

"That's a lot to put on a child," Eva murmured.

He pulled his hand back from Mia's head. "So, it is. You're in charge while I'm gone. If the heat signatures from SAT-1 are correct before it went down, the settlement lying north of here has several hundred people. Large enough for our purposes and right on the path to what's left of the Lower Monumental Dam and our salvation."

"I still think you need to take somebody with you." Eva brushed a finger along Mia's pink cheek.

He ignored her. "I don't know how far the radio signals will reach, and you'll need to conserve the batteries until we get the generators up and running, but try to call when the teams get back. I'll turn mine on every night at 1700."

Daniel prepared to stand, and Eva grabbed his arm.

"Daniel. Anybody left alive in the area survived the aftermath of the bombs that took us out. Radiation levels are stable this far away from the nuclear site, but you never know. If they see a stranger coming, it could go sideways. Please. Take someone with you." Desperation inflected Eva's words.

He enfolded her face with his hands. "Nobody else can know about what TMRWS really is. I need to find a way under the dam and secure it, Eva. It can allow us to help many, or it can be our downfall. This new world won't allow for any other alternative."

The death and destruction shown on the remaining satellite feed so many months ago was imprinted on Eva's mind like a tattoo. Her stomach churned. Their plan's final objective was to make the TMRWS operational—fully operational—and end the drought in this part of the region. It drove the man in front of her like a Mack truck toward a wall and it ate at him that they hadn't been able to finish it before the world fell apart.

"How do you know? Our people are a lot smarter than you give them credit for."

"Some, but not all." He kissed her lips. "If I'm not back in three days, start phase two of the plan."

Eva reached up with her free hand and laid it against the

scruff on his face. Silvery-white patches of hair mixed in with the dark, making him look handsomely grizzled. The light in the dark, how could a beard be so symbolic of their current situation?

Daniel gently removed her hand, gave it a squeeze, and stood up. He dusted his jeans off. "We need to increase calories for everyone, increase muscle and mass before we can do much else. Three days, Eva."

"I don't like it."

"I know."

"And what do you want me to do with my sister." Acid coated her throat. *Damn it, Sarah. Why you?*

Daniel tilted his head and regarded the woman in question with a clinical regard. "Wait until I get back, see what supplies Amrit collects. There still might be a chance at reversal with a new batch of the serum."

"But after everything she's done...." A lump wedged itself into Eva's throat and she didn't finish the thought.

"Almost anybody can be redeemed, Eva. If we have to put her down, I don't want her death to weigh on you for the rest of your life. It's worth a try. Okay? Remember, it's not your fault. Now, I have to go, the plan needs to be implemented right away before somebody out there figures out we're here." Daniel rested a hand on her shoulder and Eva nodded, a tear slipping down her cheek. He bent, his lips brushing hers in another kiss and then left.

"But it is my fault," she whispered to his departing back.

Aaron Walters, who'd been waiting patiently a short distance away, stopped next to her, two boys in tow. "Would you mind keeping an eye on the boys while I'm away, Eva? They shouldn't be too much trouble."

"Sure. They can help me with Mia and setting up camp." She wiped the moisture from her cheeks and gave the man a reassuring smile.

"Thank you. And if I don't come back...."

"Don't say things like that, of course you'll be back."

Aaron's son Chet and the orphaned Killian Cooper shuffled their feet, both rail-thin and frail. Chet was twelve but Killian had barely turned seven the week before. Both boys had hollowed-out, glassy eyes that squinted in the sun and looked everywhere but at her.

Aaron's wife and Killian's parents had been the first to die when she'd deployed the prototype Shield in the first desperate attempt to preserve their resources after the bombs fell. Volunteers, all of them, they'd given their lives so she and Amrit could perfect Shield. Daniel had his demons. So did she.

"But I want to go with you, dad." Chet crossed his arms.

"Not this time. Stay here and help Dr. Zapada and the rest of camp. I'll be back, I promise." Aaron rested his hand on the boy's shoulder.

"But, you just said—"

"Hush, I didn't say anything. Now be good and help where you're needed." He hugged his son and Killian to his side, then let go, walking away.

Chet looked miserable watching his dad leave. Killian remained silent, his face a mask. He hadn't uttered a word since his parents died. The two boys plopped next to her on the ground.

Mia's mouth had slackened off, her baby hand resting on the top of Eva's breast. Eva laid her back into the converted bassinet.

"Tell you what. You two can be my co-captains, if you're interested?" She tousled Killian's hair. He leaned away and she let her hand drop. Instead, he leaned over Mia's makeshift bassinet and rested his hand on her chest, right over her heart. She fidgeted in her sleep, then grabbed one of his filthy digits in her pudgy fist. A little spark of static electricity passed between the two but didn't seem to bother either of them. Killian relaxed, a slow smile tipping the edges of his small mouth.

Eva regarded them with a wary eye.

"I guess." Chet filtered dirt through his fingers, picking up handfuls and letting it slide down into coned piles.

"Hey, it's an important job. We have to make sure rations get to everybody, and they all have some place to sleep. You'd be helping me out immensely."

"I guess." He looked up at her and let the last of the dirt fall through his fingers without picking more up.

"Seriously, it would be a huge help." Eva kept her tone light. The boy had been through more horror than most. And unlike Killian or Mia, he'd probably remember most, if not all of it.

Chet heaved in a sigh. "What do you want me to do?"

Eva smiled and stood. "Well, we need to take baby Mia to Ms. Rani to babysit, and then we'll get started handing MREs out, how does that sound?"

Chet nodded, and they all trekked their way over to Rani. Rani sat in a huddled group, her usually dark skin pale in the late summer light. She took the bassinet and immediately picked up the sleeping babe. Killian refused to move from Mia's side.

"Looks like Mia has a protector." Rani quirked an eyebrow at the children.

"Yeah, it's really the only person he'll respond to. It worries me. Especially, since, you know...." She let the thought drift off.

Rani shrugged a shoulder. "All we can do is watch, my dear. Give him time and fresh air, fresh food, he'll come around."

Killian ignored the conversation, resting his head on the side of the recycling bin turned bassinet.

Eva sighed. It was probably for the best he stayed by Rani anyway. "Come on, Chet, let's pass out the food. Killian can help baby-sit."

Rani nodded at the unasked question and Chet and Eva started their rounds of camp.

What she wouldn't give for real food. The military Meals Ready to Eat they had been surviving on for months had given them calories but that was about all. Flavor didn't exist. She and Chet meandered between groups of people, checking in as they constructed their makeshift shelters. They accepted the MREs and resumed building. Phase One was fully under way.

#

Sarah slept on a blanket inside a canvas wall tent, her guard sitting just inside the shade near the entrance.

"She hasn't been giving you any trouble?" Eva asked the guard.

The female guard's skeletal face grimaced. "No, ma'am, but she still won't eat. Says it tastes horrible."

Some of the MREs did taste like reconstituted feces but still… Eva hunched her shoulders.

"All right. Don't unbind her without help. Somebody will be here to relieve you soon."

"Yes, ma'am. Thank you."

The reasons for Sarah not eating could be many. Remembered dismembered bodies did their best to push themselves to the front of Eva's memory. With an effort, she shoved them back to where they belonged. *Wait,* Daniel had said. And wait she would.

She flipped the door to her tent open and stopped by a map taped to the wall to take a breather, hands on her hips. Rani played with Mia in the center, sitting in an office chair she'd dragged up from the MUC on one of their many excursions for supplies. Eva's blankets and a few boxes of MREs as a headboard for her makeshift bed were against one wall. Three weapon's crates lined the back wall, Killian in front of them, digging in the sand. The little boy was still reluctant to get too far away from the baby. At some point they'd have to question why, but for now it kept him busy. Chet was out with the only other child in the group playing cards.

"It's been two days. Shouldn't somebody be back?" The air in the tent was stifling. Or maybe it was just her.

The other woman shrugged her bony shoulders and placed Mia back in the bin.

"It would take a day's hike to get down to the Tri-Cities from where we are, especially right now, malnourished as everybody is." Rani made faces at Mia. The little girl smiled and cooed. The woman was a natural with kids.

"Why didn't you ever have kids? You would have made a fantastic mother."

Rani's face shuttered, a sad droop to her lips. "I was too focused on my career. Then the Resource Wars came. Who wants to bring a child into that?"

"Adoption?"

"Why don't we talk about something else? Like how we're going to get some fresh food into everybody's diet. Hunting parties, maybe? We can't rely on Shield and MREs forever."

"I'm sorry. I didn't mean—" Eva placed a hand on the other woman's arm. God, she could stick her foot in it at times.

"It's okay. Now the food situation."

Eva had examined every square inch of the old topographic maps over the last couple of days, tracing the outline of her and Daniel's proposed Territory as if she could make it come to be with a wish and a thought. The northeast section, twenty miles away, showed Daniel's final destination at Lower Monumental Dam.

Eva tapped the map. "We'll have two of the strongest go out and see if there's any game around here and here. I want most people to stick close to camp until the other groups get back."

As if calling it into being with her words, an ear-splitting whistle outside the tent, and the distinctive whine of ATVs approaching, set a shout of alarm throughout the camp.

Eva unholstered her pistol. Most of the senior leaders carried weapons these days. The armory in the MUC had been well-stocked when the group could finally access it last month and now the guns inside were a necessary tool for survival—on so many levels.

Rani nodded at her to go, picking up her gun and scooting closer to Mia's bed. Killian looked up, his solemn, brown eyes too big for his face. She smiled, and he continued to play, content with his roads of dirt.

Amrit, Ron, and the others of their scavenging group rode into camp on two four-wheelers, the back racks stacked high with full bags of what she presumed was food. They stopped the small vehicles and climbed off.

Tracks of sweat ran in rivulets of dust down weary faces, and their shirts were soaked from the day's scorching heat. Unnatural in March. *More signs.*

Some of the weight on her shoulders fell away in relief. "Amrit, it's good to see you."

"It's very good to see you." He wiped a hand across his gaunt face.

"What did you find?"

The rest of the group exchanged glances, but let Amrit do the talking.

"It's not good, Eva. Not good at all. We didn't run into anybody alive. We took as much canned food as we could around the borders of the cities and found these two ATVs with enough gasoline and battery life to drive back. We'll need gas masks or hazmat if we are to go much farther in."

"Nobody?" As soon as her and Daniel had pulled up the old SAT-1 feed she knew, clear down to her soul, that the end had finally happened. That society had finally irreparably collapsed. Being faced with the reality was a different kettle of fish altogether. Could she have stopped this? Finished her research sooner? Would it have made a difference? She closed the door on the thought. No use in "could haves."

"Eva?" Amrit's quiet voice pierced her thoughts.

She blinked. "Thank you. We need to store the food. We'll have to retrieve hazmat the next trip back down into the MUC. I should have thought of that earlier."

Amrit reached out and touched her arm, something he had

never done before. "We all worked as hard as we could, Eva. The world was too far gone. Don't carry all the burden."

His slight accent had soothed her in the past, today it only made his words sound hollow.

"Tell that to the dead." She turned from the group and signaled to one of the tents. The scientists from the MUC included old lab assistants and world-class researchers alike. All of them came out and made their way to the ATVs to grab the bags off the back.

Oh, how the mighty had fallen.

###

The next two days passed in a haze of heat and dismay. Where was the other recon group? And Daniel?

The group fortified the camp, and the supplement of real food lifted everybody's spirits. So much better than MREs, even if it was canned. She sent Amrit and his crew back south on the 4-wheelers to get as much as they could from the fringes of the larger towns. *Increase their mass*, Daniel had said. Easier said than done.

At five o'clock in the evening, four days after they had emerged, she tried to radio Daniel again. Broken static spoke back to her. Even though it would piss him off, she left the radio on for another fifteen minutes, just in case.

Nothing.

Frustration and worry dominated her thoughts as she fed Mia, then herself. People from the camp popped in with frequent reports until finally, she shooed everybody out so she and the baby could rest. Rani had taken Killian for the night, his grunts of protest still lingering in the air as she had forced him away from Mia.

Phase two consisted of resting up and regaining strength; staying put. It also included finding survivors to help them with the third phase.

Before the Collapse, the Columbia Basin was an agricultural center. Daniel always said, if you control the food and water, you control the world. And that's what he planned to do, here, in the old Columbia Basin. It wasn't the world, but they had everything they needed, right here, away from any major city center. Under the Lower Monumental Dam, he had the means to irrigate the thousands of acres of farmland that surrounded them.

His TMRWS machine along with the only organic core and tellurium enzyme used to power it.

To protect it all, they would need a wall and utilize the existing train tunnels created by the military, to do so. Maybe add to them over time to make travel across the Territory more efficient. Not that she wanted to spend a minute longer than necessary underground.

Phase three hinged on what Daniel found out at Lower Monumental Dam and up North with the settlement. Satellite footage had indicated the dam had been left untouched, the re-routing of the Snake River six years prior making it all but obsolete.

The plan would succeed. She ignored the voice that told her she couldn't build life on the graves of the dead. *The past is always present.*

Eva placed a hand atop the gentle rise and fall of her baby's chest. So content. So innocent.

She laid down on her makeshift bed, eyes staring at the stained canvas ceiling.

Somebody opened the flap.

Heart pounding, she reached for the pistol between her and the bassinet and aimed at the shadow framed by the opening.

Daniel stood in the moonlight of the entrance to her tent. Their tent.

"Crap. I almost shot you."

Eva reached over to turn on the battery-operated lantern.

"No. Don't turn the light on yet. I don't want the camp to

know I'm back." He closed the tent flap and came to sit at the end of the bed, no more than a pile of blankets on the ground.

"How did you know this was our tent?" She put the pistol back in its designated spot for the night.

"It's the biggest, and right in the middle of the camp." His voice sounded wry, though she could only see shadowed features in the darkness. "Where else would a leader sleep?

"Uh-huh. How'd you get past the guards?"

"Some of them are ill-trained. I'll fix that. Starting tomorrow. Though I might not have as much finesse as my old sergeant back in my Marine days." He reached across the blanket for her hand. She held on and started to lean into him when another thought crossed her mind.

Eva placed her hand on his chest to stop his forward momentum. "Did you find what you needed?"

"Yes, both in the survivor camp and the dam. The camp's leader is a former Army Ranger by the name of Jack Allen. Can we finish this discussion tomorrow. Please." Weariness saturated his voice, and she allowed him to close the space between them.

Divested of all clothes, they took comfort in each other's arms. Not a word of love had ever been spoken between them, but they depended on each other, consoled each other, and in moments like these, took what comfort they could.

She had watched him every day since that night long ago, where this strange relationship took shape over whiskey and a desperate hope. He never let his guard down around anyone else. Ever.

Daniel curled up around her, the cocoon of his body familiar and secure in the dark.

The peace didn't last long.

Tobias rushed into the tent without announcing himself. Startled, he froze at Daniel's presence in front of him holding a gun, naked.

"Sorry, you guys, I didn't mean to barrel in here, but Sarah's escaped. Somebody untied her."

CHAPTER 8

From the journal of Dr. Eva Zapada:

How do I capture the essence of Jack Allen? According to him, when Daniel first stumbled into his settlement our first day out of the MUC, he nearly took a bullet. Daniel looked like a walking corpse—skin taut over jutting bones, a specter of starvation. Daniel raised his hands and declared, "I know how to protect us all." Jack, ever pragmatic, handed him a can of Spam and a water bottle, half-joking if he'd baked too long in the sun, all while keeping a pistol aimed at his head in case he turned out to be a zombie. Efficient but deadly—that's Jack Allen in a nutshell. Without him, I doubt the Basin Territory would have taken shape. We certainly wouldn't have secured the TMRWS, let alone uncovered the secret buried in the shadowed depths of the Lower Monumental Dam. Humanity's path would be starkly different now, no question. And a lot of that is due to Jack.

#

April 2046

East of where the MUC had burrowed out of the ground like molerats, Eva, Daniel and the rest of the survivors had banned together with Jack Allen's settlement and thrown up a new wall. Pieced together from scavenged farming equipment, tractor trailers, and any other useless pieces of metal junk they could find, it would stop a bullet if fired on. Eva figured that later it would have to be reinforced, but for now it stretched across a canyon between basalt cliffs near a little blink and miss it town. Temporary siding and razor wire looped around the backside of the new settlement until the permanent structure could be finished.

A four-lane highway once sliced through here; now, the overpass and hills provided an anchor point for future expansion of the wall. Jack called it the South Gate. It was a more defensible area than where his people had been holed up, so it hadn't been too hard of a sell.

Six months back, Livvy and Aaron's group had failed to return, another ache that burrowed a hole in Eva's gut. They'd sent search parties, but the pair had disappeared without a trace. Chet refused to leave his bedroom in the house where he resided with Rani for days on end. She felt his grief clear to her bones. Not knowing what had happened, they all had doubled down on securing the new site.

The town, now twice its size, had swelled with survivors over the winter, most scouted from tiny towns across what used to be Southeastern Washington. There were now nearly three hundred fifty people, most of them able to work.

Jack Allen jabbed at the map where Daniel had sketched a tunnel route under the southern wall. "You're nuts, man. That's impossible. Solid basalt for miles—we'd need a ton of explosives just to carve out half."

The cluttered command tent, its walls plastered with maps, tools and equipment lining the walls and a giant pockmarked conference table square in the center, was a testament to the vision they were trying to create. First and foremost, security.

Six months back, Livvy and Aaron's group had failed to return, another ache that burrowed a hole in Eva's gut. Especially when Chet refused to leave his bedroom in the house where he resided with Rani for days on end. She felt his grief clear to her bones. Not knowing what had happened, they all had doubled down on securing the new site.

Daniel ran his hands through his hair, making it stick up in sweaty quills. "What if we shift it a mile this way and anchor it here? Less blasting?"

Eva watched them go back and forth, shaking her head. They were both so hyper-focused they missed the obvious. With a sigh, she grabbed Daniel's pencil and drew a new line on the map. "Or we just use the old tunnel system here, curve it ninety degrees, and run it under the highway. Adds half a mile, but it saves resources and cuts build time in half."

Daniel and Jack stared at her line, brows knitted.

Jack cracked a grin. "Well, hell. That's the move."

Eva swallowed a smirk.

"Good eye." Daniel erased his old marks. "I'll get Ed and Rani to draft it up."

He pulled out a half-empty bottle of scavenged whiskey, pouring them each a shot. "To the Basin Territory."

"To the Basin Territory," Eva and Jack echoed, tossing back the liquor. Jack flipped his glass, amber drops pooling on the table.

"Crews start tomorrow," Jack said. "But we've got spring planting this week for an early harvest. You still haven't told me how we're getting irrigation without steady power. No pumps, no water, no water, no crops—you know how it goes."

Eva and Daniel traded a look. They'd told Jack about Shield, how it kept them alive underground during the Year of Hell, but TMRWS was still under wraps. Scavenged Walmart generators were barely keeping wells alive, and scavenging runs were stretching too far afield. TMRWS had to be repurposed for power—it was their only shot at sustaining the farmland long-term and accessing the underground aquifer.

Eva quirked a brow at Daniel. "Wait any longer, and he'll be more pissed."

"Fair point," Daniel said, downing another shot. "Go for it."

Jack braced himself, stance widening like he was preparing for battle.

Eva leaned in. "We've got an energy source that could power the whole Territory and then some. It was a top-secret experimental device stashed under Lower Monumental Dam. The turbines hid its noise, but that's moot now. A tunnel from the MUC to the dam, which was used by a high speed tram, is blocked by cave-ins from the bombings. We can't get through from the MUC. We'll need to find a surface entrance and dig in."

Jack's eyes narrowed. "Keeping me in the dark doesn't bug me, hell I worked with the old government, I know the deal. What gets me is the half-assed info dumps. When people don't know the full picture they can react in the right ways. That's the kind of crap that landed us in this mess in the first place."

"Greed and fear did more damage," Eva said, sipping her shot.

"Not arguing that," Jack said. "But let's try trust and real talk. What's the full story?"

Tension buzzed between them, sharp and uncomfortable. Eva straightened. If this Territory was going to work, Jack was right —they needed to be straight with him. So, she laid it all out: TMRWS's weather control origins, Shield's role, the whole deal.

"The weather control part's busted, but it can generate serious power. Enough for stable electricity. If it glitches, though, it could be catastrophic. That's why we need more Shielded people working on it," Daniel said.

Jack waved a hand. "Sounds like cloud-seeding."

"Nope," Eva crossed her arms. "Think sucking all the moisture from a thunderhead and redirecting that energy. Simplistic, but it's the best explanation I have. Multiple TMRWS units exist, and they need to sync for full weather control and we only have one power core to make ours mostly operational. Right now, we just need the power generation to work. One more thing."

"Don't hold back now," Jack leaned against the table, lips compressed but eyes intent.

"I'm offering you the Shield Serum. It's risky, but we've ironed out most of the kinks." At the loss of many, many friends. "It means no illness, longer life, regeneration from all but the worst injuries, less need for food and water. For some, it even seems to pause aging."

Daniel watched Jack like a hawk, gauging him. They needed the Basin's survivors as much as the survivors needed what they offered.

Jack's jaw dropped. "You're serious? Why now, not a month ago when you told me about Shield? Or last week?"

Daniel stood. "Because we just found a way to reach the east side of Track Three, right under the dam. And we need your help to get down there."

Eva strapped on the harness and peered into the virtual darkness below her. Somebody had dropped a fluorescent green glow stick in the murky black but it barely made a dent. A headlamp beneath her shone in her eyes and she looked away. Daniel and their engineer, Tamara, sat below with Jack waiting his turn above.

Daniel had tried to talk Eva out of this trip on the grounds one of them should stay in camp for Mia, but she'd declined. This was too important.

Tobias winched her down.

She turned on the headlamp, its glow revealing tubing and pipes lining the curved roundness of the enormous tunnel. She'd been in the subways of many metropolitan areas, and this looked no different except it was beneath the desert in the middle of nowhere.

Her feet landed on the cemented walkway next to the track and Daniel helped her out of the harness. Tobias then lowered Jack.

Shadowed figures silhouetted against the bright sky peeked over the edge and into the tunnel.

Daniel pressed the button on the radio so as not to yell. "We're good. We'll radio when we get there. If we lose contact, wait half a day before sending anybody."

A short, "roger that," from Tobias followed his message. He clicked the radio button twice in acknowledgement and put it in a chest pouch she'd found at a fire station. Both Jack and Tamara carried radios as well, though neither looked inclined to use them.

"Let's get going. It's at least five miles to the dam from this point." Daniel took out a compass, even though the tunnel was probably a straight shot east to west without many curves.

"Air might thin."

"They probably relied on piping it in rather than shafts." Daniel pointed to the many different wires and ductwork lining the tunnel.

"Wouldn't they have a backup?" She coughed into her hand, her body compensating for the lower oxygen levels the farther along the single track they traversed.

"Probably knocked out with the cave in." Tamara pointed a flashlight forward, the beam skimming the edges of black in front of them. Tamara was their only mechanical engineer, a position that vaulted her into goddesshood in this day and age.

After a few miles, the tunnel branched off and there were two choices: Track Three to the right or Track One straight ahead.

"I thought this tunnel ran directly to the dam?" Eva made her way to the far right-hand track and shined her light into the murk.

Daniel narrowed his eyes. "I guess they were doing more down here than they let on."

He took out his compass and pointed to the center tunnel. "We'll try this one first, it heads due east."

A faint clacking from the left hand tunnel grabbed her attention. "Did you hear that?"

Daniel, Jack, and Tamara halted. "Hear what?"

She moved closer to the entrance, shining a light in the shadows. The darkness was so complete, like a creature that fed on the absence of light, threatening to consume everybody in its path whole.

"I swore I heard something." Eva remembered all the monster movies she'd watched in her teenage years. If she said it was nothing, she was sure an alien or a monster would jump out and grab them all with a vicious gnashing of teeth.

"I'm going to check it out."

Daniel's warm hand grabbed her arm. "We need to make it to the dam before Tobias jumps the gun and sends out a search party."

"It won't take long. I want to make sure nobody is down here."

"How in the world would anybody be able to do that?" Jack said, shining his own flashlight around. Long threads of spiderwebs floated from the ceiling like strands of silk. The dirt near the tracks remained unscuffed. *There's still the walkway.*

"You do realize you just jinxed us all, right?" Eva scowled. "Now there is somebody down that tunnel, just because you said that."

"Eva."

"Daniel, I heard something. It could be an animal or something else, but I'm not going to leave our asses exposed. Who knows where that tunnel ends. You taught me that. I'm surprised you're not thinking the same thing." She yanked her arm from his grasp and he heaved a sigh.

"Fine. I'll go with you. Jack, you and Tamara continue on to the dam, we'll catch up." He handed the woman a small pistol in a molded holster.

Tamara looked from it to Daniel and back. "I don't know how to use this. I've been working with rifles."

"This is the safety, don't put your finger on the trigger unless you plan to shoot. Sights are here and here. Now go. Jack can help you if need be."

"Can I?" The other man huffed out a humorless laugh. "You kids be safe."

Tamara's shoulders slumped forward and she clipped the gun to her belt. She muttered under her breath and slunk off into the shadows of the main tunnel, Jack on her heels.

"Lead the way." Daniel gestured into the gloom.

Eva unholstered her gun and walked cautiously down the side of the track. It started curving to the right after a half mile. She examined the ground for any scuffs but nothing looked peculiar.

"We're heading south." Daniel snapped his compass closed, putting it back in his pouch.

"South?" There was nothing of consequence south, just little farm towns and fields.

A flicker of movement had her holding her hand out for Daniel to stop. He held his gun at the ready.

"Shut your headlamp off," he murmured.

She reached to click it off but it was too late.

Daniel's beam of light caught the movement again right before something the size of a small rock clattered to the ground in front of them.

"Run!" Daniel grabbed her arm and yanked her back the way they came.

But it was too late. The force of the explosion knocked them both to the ground.

CHAPTER 9

"Eva, Eva wake-up." A hand tapped her cheeks on either side.

Her eyes flew open, ears ringing, head spinning, and she groaned.

Daniel jerked her to her feet. "Move."

He looped her arm over his shoulder, and they shuffle-stepped back to the main tunnel.

Jack and Tamara had already made it back to the intersection. "What the hell was that?"

"Did you find the entrance?"

"Didn't get a chance. There's a huge cave-in not too far from here. It looks like somebody's been working on removing the debris." Jack looped Eva's other arm over his shoulder, and the group moved out, Tamara in front with her pistol.

Eva's world wobbled. The two men had given up and just grabbed a leg a piece, hauling her down the tunnel quicker than she could have on her own. Shield hadn't kicked in yet, though she could feel a tingle deep in her chest.

"Well, that somebody threw a grenade at us. I need to warn topside to be on alert."

Jack cursed.

Halfway back to the egress, Daniel spoke through his labored breathing. "Tamara, see if you can reach Tobias."

She spoke into the radio, her voice coming through all of their speakers.

Tobias's voice broke through the static, tinny and distant. "I can hear you."

"We have intruders, get everybody within the wall, we'll be at the egress in thirty minutes."

"Copy that." A note of purpose entered Tobias's voice. "Everybody all right?"

"Eva got her bell rung but is fine." Tamara's voice cracked on the last word.

Hoarse rasps of air and the crunching of booted heels on gravel filled the dead calm of the tunnel. Eva's head had cleared but she knew at the moment she'd never keep up with the rapid pace set by the other three.

Who would know about the tunnel system below the Basin? The upper echelons of the Western Coalition for sure, but how many of them were left? She chewed on this thought. Back in the day, all of the projects in the MUC went through Daniel, Daniel to Tobias, and Tobias to the General in charge. Sister facilities were located in other places, though she only knew of Roswell and Kansas City for certain. Maybe Ft. Belvoir in D.C.

Somebody left alive knew what was down below the Lower Monumental Dam. That left three options out in the wild: Sarah, Livvy, or Aaron.

All of them reached the surface, and Tobias had ATVs waiting to take them back to the South Gate.

"Everybody is locked down. I sent scouts out to the north, east, and southeast. Nobody's reported suspicious activity."

"Yet," said Daniel. "Whoever it is, we just FUBARed their operation. I won't let them have the TMRWS, and they know it. We need to be ready. "

###

The wind whipped Eva's tight braid into a wild frenzy. This early in the Spring, the wind in the Basin blew every day. On top of the wall, it was worse. They had placed long metal plank walkways most of the length of both the permanent wall between the cliffs and the smaller makeshift wall around the town located at the South Gate. Later it would expand around an area thousands of acres larger, but for now, it did its job. All their defenses had been beefed up since the attack on Track Three the week prior. Hurry up and wait. That's what they'd been doing.

Until scouts finally reported movement from the East and then a group of twenty people had shown up at their gate, Sarah in the lead.

What was her sister up to? In the deepest part of her soul, the place where the past hid, her heart hurt a little less knowing Sarah had survived her escape. Whoever her companions were, at least she was alive. Hope beat like a drum in her chest. If she could just talk to her, make her see reason.

The bedraggled group of twenty people stood in ragged formation outside the Southern Gate. They didn't look like much of a threat. Was this what had Daniel and Jack in such a tizzy? Starving people in worn-out clothing?

As if reading her mind, a pair of binoculars appeared over her shoulder, Daniel's callused hand holding them. "Don't be fooled. This is what I was afraid of."

Eva grabbed them and scanned the group. At first, she didn't know what she was looking for. Most of the men and women looked normal. Some had necklaces that looked tribal, large rings of something looped together with white beads on twine. One man caught her eye, and she squinted to study him. His eyes protruded out of abnormally narrowed sockets. The muscles on his arms and torso bulged at odd angles, making him appear like some misshapen Hulk. Aaron.

The strength went out of her hands, and she almost dropped the binoculars.

"Holy hell." Their year in the abyss coming back to haunt them in full, blood-soaked glory.

"I counted at least three of them. Look out farther." He nodded out towards the sagebrush horizon.

Eva continued her examination. Nothing stood out to her until she caught the flash of something behind a huge sage. *Where there's one, there's more*—just like mice in the larder. Dread, grotesque and hideous, wrapped it's tentacles around her. Daniel's sayings were always apt.

She handed the binoculars back to him. "We should've searched farther afield for Livvy and Aaron. What are we going to do? The guns will have no effect on them. And how are there more, Daniel?"

His level look told her everything she needed to know. Somebody had gained access to one of the other labs.

"You think General Kaspar's still alive?" It was too much.

He heaved in a long slow breath. "It's a possiblity, he might have escaped the MUC the day it was bombed."

"What are we going to do to fight them?" Images of from the Year of Hell, the death and carnage from gnarled bodies played across her mind. Only the people from the MUC—and Jack—could stand a chance against the mutated monstrosties.

"You know what we have to do." Their eyes connected.

"No. Absolutely not." She put as much steel in her voice as she could muster.

"It's the only way to kill them without getting close."

The horror of his words, delivered in such a cold, emotionless tone, almost broke her.

"What are you thinking? He's a child, not an experiment anymore. How the hell could you even think of doing that to him? He's only seven years old." The fury broke over her in waves. Guards turned towards them in shocked attention.

Daniel grabbed her arm, and she jerked it out of his hand.

"Can we talk about this somewhere else?" A slight crack in his emotional armor seeped through into his voice. The walkway creaked beneath her feet, the force of the wind pushing the large gauge wire against her hip. She gripped it.

"What? So all these people don't find out just what kind of monsters we really are?" The words burned as they escaped her mouth.

"This isn't the time. We could bring Mia. He feels safe with her around."

"Do you hear the words coming out of your mouth?" How the hell could he even suggest it?

Daniel clenched a fist, and Eva tensed. He'd never hit her, she'd never thought him capable, but in that moment...*It's the enzyme.*

He rolled forward on the balls of his feet, muscles tense. She didn't give an inch.

"That's one of the reasons why we used those families as guinea pigs. Why I killed all those people who went psychotic with the prototype so the rest of us could live. Killian has a higher purpose in all of this. You tend to forget that. He's old enough now." The coldness in his voice froze her like ice, and she flinched back as if he really had hit her.

"I've never forgotten. It's burned into my very soul. What you do forget is, we're not God. And you're not touching that child or using ours to comfort him. Find another way. You always do."

"Amrit, go get Killian." Daniel's eyes remained on hers. "And Mia."

When had the other man arrived? God, she was so focused on Daniel's words she had lost track of everything else around her. Amrit skirted them to move towards the stairs leading off the wall.

"You move one more step, Amrit, and I swear to my God and yours, I'll put a bullet in you." Eva didn't flinch or drop eye contact with Daniel. Amrit froze.

"What are you going to do, Eva? Shoot everybody I send?"

Daniel's facade of neutrality broke open, and anger radiated off of him to match her own.

"You're damn right. You're not acting like yourself, Daniel."

Daniel flinched.

"It won't hurt Killian, Eva. He'll be all right," Amrit said in his soothing voice.

"Physically maybe, but not mentally. That child has been through hell. How could we do more to him? And how will you collect enough blood from him to make the anti-serum? We have to take almost a quarter of his volume to make enough to kill those three, and it's never been tested before." She broke eye contact with Daniel and looked at Amrit. "The super-soldier part of the program was halted for a reason, Amrit. We both know it. If you need proof, just look out there at what my sister dredged up."

The wind tangled around them like a hurricane on dry land, drowning out any outside noise. The three of them were now alone on their section of the wall. People had moved down the platform, giving them a wide berth.

Jack walked up behind her. "What's going on?"

"You want to tell him your grand plan? Or are we still keeping him out of the loop?" She couldn't help the sarcasm that dripped out of her mouth. The need to protect the remaining secrets hidden in the Complex had always overridden every-thing else.

"I already know about Killian," Jack said in a low voice. He avoided her gaze. "Daniel told me a while back."

She glared at Daniel. "Equal leadership and equal responsi-bility, huh? Or did you just say that to appease me?"

"Jack needed to know." He said it without inflection; all shut-ters dropped tight, and the military commander in complete charge. "Amrit, go see if you can extract Killian's blood without causing too much damage, and make the antiserum. Tamara can make the .50 caliber rounds to weaponize it."

"No!" Eva protested.

In two strides, his face was inches from hers. "You're thinking with your emotions and not looking at the end result. What'll happen if those monsters are allowed to live? If the monsters who are controlling them—most likely your sister and whoever she's found to partner with—are allowed to keep them? Those are ears and pieces of bone on those necklaces, Eva—dozens of them. Pay attention to something other than your feelings. Our Territory is more capable of handling them; others around us are not. I shouldn't have to explain this to you after everything we've been through. Pull yourself together. Killian will be fine."

Eva slapped him across the face. Jack pulled her back, and she jerked away. She strode down the platform, tears streaming down her face.

"I'll extract the blood. And screw you all."

The children slept, backs pressed against each other, and tear-stained faces dried. As soon as the first needle had penetrated Killian's skin, both children had begun to cry. Eva's own emotions crashed inside of her, trying to escape in whatever manner possible. Amrit settled a hand on her shoulder. She shrugged it off.

"The bullets are complete. The antiserum agent will work, I tested it on some of my own blood. It kills all the enzyme. I'll take them to the South Gate. The children are alright, Eva, Killian's blood volume is already replenishing and his skin is healing. He was just scared."

"Stop. I'll take the bullets to the wall." All the rest of her words had dried up. Never again. They'd find a different method. Killian's skin had tried to heal around the needle, growing and accumulating into the hollow tube, preventing blood from being drawn in the normal manner. She had finally given up and used a scalpel instead. In all probability, it would be easier to draw his blood as he aged and the enzyme's natural stopgap kicked in. She took off the labcoat and gloves, donning her jacket and gunbelt once again.

Mia sucked her thumb and snuggled closer to the older boy, her presence comforting him unlike anything else.

"Before you leave, something disturbing happened after you finished the last cut." Amrit hesitated.

"Just spit it out Amrit."

He heaved in a breath. "A drop of his blood touched Mia's skin, and she *absorbed* it. It's probably nothing, but I thought you should know."

"That's absurd." Eva brushed a strand of hair away from her daughter's face.

"I know what I saw, Eva. We need to run some tests."

Eva shook her head. "Not on my daughter. Ever."

The five modified .50 caliber rounds gleamed steely smooth in the fluorescent lighting of the lab.

"But, Eva–"

"No." She shoved the padded case with the rounds in a rucksack.

"You need to think about it at least," Amrit called to her departing back.

White noise buzzed in her head as she made her way to the track. As long as she lived, her daughter would never become an experiment. And she'd do whatever she needed to do to make that possible.

CHAPTER 10

She emerged at the South Gate to chaos.

Weapons fire filled the air. Somebody had lobbed flash bangs over the wall, and the chemical smoke stung her eyes. She drove her four-wheeler as fast as she could, the wheels carving through the earth with a rebellious determination, a rumble of power and defiance over the rugged terrain.

An explosion rocked the wall. A chunk of an old tractor flew through the air and smashed to the earth beside her. She swerved.

"The North Wall! Somebody breached the North Wall!"

"What *are* those things?"

Screams and the acidic taste of chemical filled the air.

A limb went flying past her face and she almost lost control of the ATV.

She had to find Daniel. He had one of the .50 caliber rifles, and she would trust nobody else with the rounds she carried—no matter how angry she might be with him.

Something rammed her from behind, and her stomach slammed into the handlebars. Her body burned and blood coated her lips. Broken rib. Punctured lung. Air escaped her lips in a whistling gasp before Shield started doing its work. The four-wheeler careened to the side.

Hands wrapped around her throat from the back, and Eva gagged, clawing at them. She threw herself over the side, the four-wheeler rolling to a stop ten feet away.

Flashbacks of that long ago night in Seattle ratcheted to the forefront of her memory. The man's head exploding like a melon in front of her. A life gone in an instant. She hadn't fought back that time.

This time was different. She'd been training with Daniel and Jack.

Eva's elbow landed on something soft, and the person wrapped around her back grunted. Black dots spotted her vision. The person's hold hadn't loosened. God, she was going to pass out.

Stay conscious. Stay conscious.

The stench of body odor enveloped them, the sour smell burning her nostrils.

Eva arched her back, shoving her head as far back as possible, then lurched her head forward towards the fingers—the weakest point. Just like Daniel had shown her in their frequent sparring matches.

The grip weakend She butted her head back, twisted her hips, then tucked her chin to her chest, scooting out of the hold.

The rucksack. Where was the rucksack?

Ahh, still on her back. She crab-walked back as fast as she could and shot to her feet, hands at the ready.

Fists staggered. Chin to chest. Knees slightly bent and feet planted.

A tall woman, dark hair matted and stringy, rolled to her feet. Filth and blood layered her face over a puckered scar, and a maniacal gleam shone from deadened, brown eyes. A necklace of bones rattled around her neck. Were those finger bones? The short hairs on the back of her neck stood on end.

"Sarah?" Eva almost hadn't recognized her own sister.

The other woman lunged.

Eva used her momentum against her and swung her over her hip. Shield strengthened the throw, and Sarah thudded to the ground, all air knocked out of her. Eva kept a hold of the arm and sat, the bones crunching as she broke her arm. The other woman screamed in pain.

Eva unholstered her pistol and put a round into the other woman's chest.

Her sister's chest.

Bile filled her mouth and she rolled to her knees, the pistol loose in her group.

Sarah was dead. She had killed her. Hell wasn't good enough for her now.

Vomit heaved out of her aching stomach. Very little remained from breakfast but the acid churned in her mouth, bitter and hot.

A low, guttural moan emanated from Sarah and seeped into Eva's very marrow.

"Nice try, sister." The voice was still Sarah's but with a feral growl.

She wasn't dead. *Oh, shit.*

A hand touched her shoulder, and she swung around, terror almost making her discharge her weapon in the person's face.

Daniel stood there, sweat-soaked blood saturating his clothes and face. "Never stop in the middle of battle. You got the rounds?"

"Rucksack," she gasped and Sarah charged, seeming not to even see Daniel.

She pile-drived Eva to the ground, the two of them tumbling down a low slope. Eva clawed and scratched, wedging a knee between her and her sister to create some distance. The beautiful girl who had used to braid Eva's hair and dreamed of curing cancer was gone. In her place was a wild thing, savage and vicious.

The prototype Shield Serum had changed her.

Or rather, the Super-Soldier serum. *Call it like it is, Eva. No more lies. It's not a proto-type anymore, somebody developed an entirely different serum from Shield.*

Sarah thudded to her knees, lunging again. Mia rolled, dust and residual chemicals from the flash bang clogging her throat and eyes.

A ratcheting of a round into a large caliber rifle sounded through the air.

Sarah saw Daniel, and her eyes narrowed on the gun. She sniffed the air and glared. She couldn't possibly smell the anti-serum rounds.

Sarah flicked her gaze one last time to Eva before turning and sprinting back toward the wall, shouting orders in a voice Eva had never heard before.

Her sister was gone.

Daniel strode into view, wreathed in smoke, dust, and blood.

His finger tensed on the trigger but he didn't pull. Screaming and gunfire surrounded them like they were in the eye of a storm.

"That's not your sister anymore."

Fury and frustration, misery and anguish warred for dominance within Eva. "I know."

He handed her a high-powered rifle. "Good, now get your ass over to the South Gate."

And he turned and jogged away, the .50 caliber gun bouncing on his back and the rucksack with the special rounds on his shoulder.

Line up the shot. Aim. Fire. Do it again.

Line up the shot…nothing.

Eva blinked. Her shoulders ached, and her trigger finger was numb. She looked through the scope again. Nobody alive remained below the South Gate.

"Jack?"

"It's all good, Eva. We got 'em. The rest are retreating." A note of exhausted satisfaction crept into his voice.

She collapsed to the walkway, covering her face with trembling hands.

Jack's radio chirped, Amrit's voice coming through. "North breach all clear. A handful hightailed it out of here–including Sarah. Daniel is sending Tobias after them."

Other voices got on with various "copies" and "good jobs." Jack included.

Numb and in shock, Eva curled her aching arms around her bent knees and rested her forehead there. Dios mio, *I just need a minute.*

She had killed people today.

Jack slid to sit on the walkway next to her. "You okay?"

"No."

His hand settled on her shoulder. "It'll be alright. Get some food in you, and a good night's sleep. We did good. We defended our own."

"Did we? I crossed a line earlier I never thought I'd cross. With a child, no less. It's not alright. And my sister… God." She dug the heel of her hands into her eyes, trying to rub the day away.

Boots clattered up the metal stairs. She didn't open her eyes.

"I got it."

Daniel.

Jack's hand disappeared, and she heard him retreat farther down the wall, probably to check on the other defenders.

"I can't do this now, Daniel."

"I was able to kill two of them. What remained of Livvy and Aaron. The last one escaped with your sister." He didn't try to touch her, which was good. She might've just throat-punched him.

Eva went back to resting her forehead on her knees so she didn't have to look at him. "He screamed. He still heals too fast to draw any blood with a needle. Painkillers only work for a minute, tops before he metabolizes them. Anesthesia only two or three. At least he's able to heal quickly. We had to cut his legs with a scalpel to get enough blood. You could have done any number of things to contain those…creatures. We were able to during the Year of Hell, we could have this time."

"The Aberrant."

"What?"

"That's what I call them in my head. And in this particular situation, where we weren't buried alive in a contained environment? No, I don't think there was a different option. Out in the open, they were more prone to disappear before enough damage was done; they would've killed more people. In the MUC, we baited and trapped them before pumping them full of so much bio-agent and bullets they couldn't move and then beheaded them. Do you really think that would have worked here?" He gazed out at the people below him, even now cleaning up the aftermath of battle.

"I don't know, but traumatizing a child wasn't the answer."

"A part of you felt differently, or you would have fought me harder."

She whipped her head around, fiery rage burning to her very core. "You didn't give me another choice."

"You could have left with him, left the Territory, and never looked back."

"And where would I have gone?" She glared at the side of his face.

"There are several permanent settlements forming in the region besides ours." He shrugged. "Guilt will get you nowhere fast. We need to track Sarah down before she does more damage. And we need to secure our stores of Shield and the other things we have locked away in the MUC. Too many people are still going in and out. That has got to change. And most importantly, we need to get the TMRWS operational. All of them."

Well, screw him. She rose and stepped over his legs. "I'm staying down in the MUC tonight with Rani and the kids. After that, you need to find someplace else to sleep."

"Eva, wait." Pleading filled his voice.

She continued walking and didn't look back. He didn't follow her.

CHAPTER 11

June, 2046

Cold soaked into Eva's bones and a shiver rippled through her body. The mile-long natural tunnel narrowed for the last hundred feet, and opened into a massive cavern.

After the fight at South Gate, they had explored the track and cleared the cave-in to the dam. Both Daniel and Jack were overseeing the final clean-up before they could access the turbine shaft with the TMRWS encased inside. Tamara and Tobias's new discovery of the cavern fell on her to explore.

"How much farther?" She kept her eyes glued to the ground.

"Not far, now. You should see a faint glow from the emergency lights here around this next bend." Tobias led her along, navigating the uneven ground on sure feet like he'd been born to it. Eva, on the other hand, tripped and stumbled, the bobbing headlamps not offering much help in the dancing shadows.

She'd long since gotten a handle on her claustrophobia but being down in the pitch black with no end in sight still caused her stomach to clench and panic to bubble up like frogs blowing bubbles in a pond. Animal bones littered parts of the cavern, remnants from some predator's midnight snack—how it had entered the cave a mystery. A few crunched underfoot, small fragile things from some rodent or other small creature.

Eva stubbed her booted toe on a rock. "Agh, this is horrible."

"Yeah. We'll get somebody down here to clear the path. It doesn't look like anybody's ever been down here, it was a fluke Tamara even found it."

"You got that right."

"Has she found the bottom of the reservoir yet?" The next thing on Eva's list was figuring out how much water was in there, a necessity when determining which crops to plant; it had to be an overflow from the TMRWS atmospheric collectors, though how it was this full without the device in operation was another mystery.

"Nope. It's pretty deep and there's a drift once her line drops below a hundred feet. She's going to try another method. There's more than enough for what we need it for though, especially if we get the irrigation circles up and running after TMRWS comes online. Then we won't have to rely as much on the deep wells."

The two rounded the last bend and the tunnel brightened near a narrow rift in the cave wall.

"There's the entrance."

"Tamara must have ovaries of steel."

"Come again?" Tobias's mouth gaped.

"Women don't have balls, Toby, they have ovaries."

"I haven't been called Toby since basic." He huffed out a laugh.

"Yeah, well, you look more like a Toby to me. Tobias sounds too formal for the apocalypse."

Tobias snorted and squeezed into the entrance to the underground reservoir only inches on either side of his chest and back. "Whatever you say."

Dios, it's a tight fit.

"You all right?" Tobias had twisted his head, the headlamp's light shining somewhere above her.

"Yep. Just a bit claustrophobic." Eva took a deep breath and plunged into the narrow crevasse before she lost her nerve.

Tobias focused the glow of his lamp on her and moved slower so she could keep up.

"Thank you." Relief rushed through her. They made it to the far side and stepped into an enormous cavern lit by emergency lights, the low hum of their generators echoing against the walls. A dank, wet smell permeated the stagnant air.

In her mind she'd pictured huge stalactites and stalagmites in beautiful crystalline formations. That wasn't this type of cave, though. Here, enormous columnar basalt pillars lined most of the shore of a pool of water black as night. It extended for hundreds of feet in every direction, as big as several football fields crammed together. The rocky ground was rubbed smooth in some places due the nature of the rock. "Does it go under that back wall, you think?"

"We haven't had anybody with the balls—or ovaries—to dive underneath and find out. You wanna give it a try?" He reached out a hand so she could take the last steps over the uneven ground to a cleared out ledge.

"Uh, no, but Amrit used to dive, maybe if we find equipment he'll give it a go."

"Maybe. I'm going to drop off the spare batteries next to the other lights. Be right back."

Eva picked her way along the shoreline, kicking at rocks and filling a water bottle so she could test it later. She sat on a rock and gazed at the inky lake, allowing her mind to wander, the break from Daniel a relief.

He'd gotten worse since the battle, his temper explosive, the change in personality more and more noticeable—at least to her. He said it was because of the lack of sleep and worry, but she wasn't so sure. A few others exhibited the same symptoms: irritability, headaches, and a high sensitivity to light and sound. They were the first symptoms of cell breakdown presented by the people in the study at the MUC before the bombs fell. Her and Amrit had thought they'd had the problem fixed, his technique flawless. The negative effects from the Shield Serum had dropped to minimal risk in a matter of months after they'd introduced the tellurium enzymes.

Eva cradled her head in her hands, eyes focused on the ground below her. She blinked, then peered closer. What the hell was that?

A thin line, almost imperceptible amidst the stone around it, ran in a clean, straight edge to the wall behind her.

She dropped to her knees and brushed the gravel and pebbles away from it, turning on her headlamp and following its path. At the base of the rock wall, it stopped, curved up, and continued to about three feet above her head before making a ninety-degree turn. She followed it until it stopped on the opposite wall and disappeared.

"Toby!" Her voice echoed into the open space. Eva scurried around the rock wall, trying to find what had happened to the cut mark.

A skitter of rocks accompanied his presence. "What did you find?"

"Look." She pointed to the thin line cut into the rock.

"What the hell." He examined it closer.

"I don't think we're the first ones down here after all."

"What was the first clue?" He followed it back the way she had come, all the way to the water's edge, and proceeded to walk the shoreline.

She continued going over the basalt wall, taking her headlamp off to use as a flashlight.

"Got something!" Tobias shouted next to the back wall of the cavern near the north side of the reservoir.

Eva scrambled her way to his side, rocks clicking and clacking in her wake. He showed her where the cut rock formed the rough shape of a door.

"I'll be damned. How the hell do we open it?" Eva craned her head forward, shining the headlamp in all the dark places.

"No clue."

If she were going to hide a switch to an underground, secret door made to look like a rock wall, where would it be? She and Tobias searched the ground nearby until Eva found a control panel hidden in a hollowed out rock. The electrical box with a toggle switch and waterproof case appeared worn, and unused for quite some time. Tobias took off the front casing and wired it to a battery.

"Let's see if it works." He flipped the switch. Sparks emitted from the casing but nothing happened. "Another battery, maybe?"

Eva nodded. Now that they knew it was down here, they'd also start hunting on the surface. There had to be something up top indicating this lurked below.

Tobias wired another battery and this time, the door lurched open, spewing dust and rock.

"That is one fine piece of masonry work." He rubbed his hands along the edge of rock and steel.

Eva shined her light beyond the door.

Another damn tunnel.

She puffed out a sigh.

Tobias cocked his head. "Explore or get help, boss?"

Eva side-eyed him, closing her eyes for a beat and cursing. *Dios mio,* she hated being underground.

"Might as well see what we find. You good?"

Tobias gave her a thumbs up.

She stood in the doorway, a sudden feeling of apprehension unrelated to the claustrophobia flooding her system.

"Eva?" Tobias's brow wrinkled in concern.

Her eyes snapped to his. "You lead the way. I hate the dark."

#

The mile long carved stone tunnel led to a locked metal door. It was a magnetic locking system and would not budge. Where it was getting its power was yet another question. The tunnel hadn't been used for years.

"Time to get help?" Tobias shone the light all around, but nothing stood out. This really was the end of this particular road. For now.

"Yeah." The feeling of foreboding increased. *Listen when your intuition is telling you something bad is about to happen,* her *abuelita* would have said.

"Copy. According to my calculations, we're roughly a mile due west from the dam."

Eva nodded. "That's what I figured."

He nodded and took off back the way they came.

Call it intuition, call it being paranoid, call it a reaction from Shield, but it was screaming right now. Something behind that door wasn't right and was tugging at the very cells in her body.

Eva felt him before she saw him, his presence strong even from a distance. Daniel stopped and reached out to pull her up.

She sat on the floor, legs crossed. Something thrummed behind the door. Something big.

Eva kept her hand on Daniel's arm. "You got it?"

"Of course." He handed her the black box of the code breaker from a canvas backpack and set the bag at his feet. Eva attached it to the keypad alongside the door and pressed a few buttons. Digital numbers flashed across a narrow screen.

"Can you feel it?"

Daniel bowed his head, tilting it to the side like he was listening. "It's not the TMRWS."

"No. We're a mile away from the dam. At least."

Numbers froze on the keypad and the lock buzzed.

The door creaked on unoiled hinges. Pitch black and thin, stale air met them. Daniel handed her the glass night vision goggles and a mask. The googles wouldn't show any drone data, seeing as they didn't have one, but still worked well enough in the dark.

She slipped them on and the green outlines of a room appeared. Two workbenches on one side and lockers on the other. Hard hats, a ripped hazmat suit, and yellowed, curled paper lay on one of the benches. An empty core sample tube and several broken drill bits sat on the other. In the corner, an empty water jug, lone coffee pot and small fridge offered a small break area. One door opened off to the right and another to the left.

The throbbing vibrations were definitely coming from the left. Daniel walked over to the right hand door. "Bathroom."

A hallway twisted from the left hand door like it was following the curvature of something larger and rounder. Several offices opened out to the left, though none of them appeared to hold anything of interest.

The rhythmic humming intensified.

At the end of the hall, another steel door stood before them.

Her and Daniel looked at each other.

She turned the handle. Unlocked.

A solid metal ramp stretched out along the wall of a basalt overhang in an enormous cavern. An observation deck extended out over something she couldn't quite see. To her left, a staircase descended into the pitch black. Eva shuddered. The thrumming came from below them.

Daniel gripped her hand and without saying a word, they walked to the railing of the observation deck.

Below them, energy sparks coursed around like massive fireflies inside a mixer. Only, the mixer was a bottomless pit of black an entire two-story house could fit into.

"*Dios mio*," Eva breathed.

"I don't think God has anything to do with it." Daniel tugged her toward the stairs.

Basalt rock, speckled with some kind of stone—she couldn't tell what color with the night vision glasses, it just looked black with jagged teeth rimming the sides. It was difficult to judge how far across the circumference extended, caverns of this depth had a way of playing tricks with perception.

Daniel gestured for her to follow. She stepped out onto the ramp, legs trembling. Eva may have loved heights, but this was something totally different. Like descending into the maw of an enormous monster.

They tramped down the staircase. It took five minutes to reach the rim.

A drilling rig, water pump, and core barrels lay on top of a platform. Another staircase, this one wood and a thick plastic polymer, descended into the abyss.

"They were drilling rock core samples. But, why?"

Daniel shook his head, brows drawn together in concern. "I've never heard of this place. You would think with it so close to the TMRWS I might have heard a peep. But I didn't hear a whisper. Whoever ran this project kept a very tight lid on it."

"We better see what's down there." Eva grabbed a headlamp and pair of gloves from the cargo pockets of her jeans. "But I have a feeling we're going to want to see without the goggles."

Fifteen minutes later they stood on the final base of a large crater. A strange black rock was embedded into the entire curvature of the pit. It looked familiar, its edges brittle and rough.

Bore holes pockmarked it in places as well, larger platforms bolted to the sides allowing for more access.

The humming intensified and clawed its way through her innards till she gasped. "God, what is that."

Daniel hunched forward, grappling for the railing to steady himself. He ripped off the night vision goggles, fishing his own headlamp from the depths of his pack and turned it on, using it like a flashlight. Eva closed her eyes, shoving the goggles up to her forehead.

She opened them to see motes of something dancing in the light.

"It's flakes of stone," he ran the beam up and down the walls.

With every throb of sound, fragments of various sizes vibrated, sticking to the sides of the crater like magnets to a fridge.

In reaction to their presence?

Eva turned on her headlamp and put her hand in the beam of light. The motes clung to her hand, pricking it like tiny needles, then falling away. She stepped off the platform to stand by Daniel. The dust from the floor clung to their legs like the tendrils of some subterranean beast.

His eyes widened in horror. For the first time ever, Eva glimpsed real fear on Daniel's face. Open and raw. "It's chunks of tellurium meteorite."

A jab of agony knifed through her as particles of stone dug into her skin. She tried to swipe them away, tripped, and fell into the dust below. Her headlamp flew to the far side of the cavern.

Under the new spotlight, a jagged rock rock thrusted up from the ground. With each thrum, like the tribal rhythm of the earth's heartbeat, bits and particles appeared to crawl over it like ants in an ant pile. Tiny motes flew around the cavern like angry lightening bugs, spinning faster and faster, back and forth between the stone and the wall. A tornado of light and rock.

Eva screamed. The pain from the fragments of tellurium meteorite digging into her face, hot pokers of molten stone. Every muscle stiffened, her blood vessels throbbing. Daniel's face clenched behind his mask, the accumulated particles climbing his legs, cementing both feet to the ground in increments. Blood seeped from his pores at the strain of trying to move.

Death was coming for them both.

CHAPTER 12

Once, when she was nine or ten, Eva's parents saved up enough money to take her and Sarah to the Moaning Caves Adventure Park near Sacramento, California. Crystalline stalactites and stalagmites flowed down walls like waterfalls of rock in ethereal aquas, whites, and sea-foam greens. A metal caged staircase wound its way to the cavern floor, exposed on all sides between iron bars, a fairytale world underground.

If that was a fairytale, this was a nightmare.

With each thrum from the tellurium meteorite, the fragments loosened and Daniel dragged himself inch by inch until he reached Eva. Agony wrenched through her, her limbs not wanting to cooperate under the growing weight of the particles.

With a shout of pure torment, he lifted her in his arms, fighting against the pull of rock and dust. Their bodies like magnets with Shield flowing through them. His skin shred beneath the abrasive stone.

Not being able to do much more, he tossed her onto the platform. The world spun, the flashes in the air intensifying at each passing moment.

Like the stone was *alive*.

Eva swallowed another howl of pain. Particles clogged her throat and she swallowed some. Gagging and panting, she rolled over onto her stomach.

Daniel had dropped to his knees, a trail of dirt and rock and blood snaking up his arms. His face leaked red and he mouthed something, a ghoulish movement of lips.

Eva shook her head. His voice was lost in the vibration from the black shards only yards away and the chittering of the particles in the air.

"Go," he breathed.

Tears streamed down her face, making the dust and rock fall away like it was never there.

"No." Eva wriggled until her upper body hung over the edge of the wooden platform and she reached out toward him, her fingertips skimming his arm.

She almost fell, her right hand falling into the glimmering dust on the ground. Immediately, the fragments coalesced on her hand. Eva jerked away with a startled yelp.

Daniel's head jerked from side to side. "Get…out…of… here….."

"I'm not leaving you. Just reach out and I'll pull you in. It's not far."

She couldn't do it. Leave him. This man who'd been through all the trials and hardships with her. Through all the pain and tragedy. He was her partner and confidante, her lover and best friend. No matter how angry she was with him, she didn't want to do this life without him.

"But Mia…" His eyes pleaded.

Tears streamed down Eva's face. Was she selfish for not thinking of their daughter? Indecision rocked her.

Daniel heaved in huge gasps of air, his body folding in on itself under the weight of supercharged dirt.

Eva grabbed for the exposed part of his arm, her fingertips just skimming the fine hairs. He was too far away.

"Please," she begged.

Something shifted in his entire being. A stubbornness. A drive that had gotten him through to this point. All of it bunched up inside tensed shoulders and bulging muscles. Agony ripped along every sinew and with a raw scream that shattered her very core, he yanked his arms from the pile of rock and debris, blood streaming from his abraded palms.

This time, their arms met, clasping together, his blood making their connection tenuous and slippery. Eva strained, gaining a better grip with a force of will she had clawed and scratched for over the years. Wrapping her legs around the bottom of the staircase railing, she yanked and tugged, time slowing as she fought to release Daniel from the fragments of stone.

Daniel held onto her body like a lifeline. Blood formed around his calves as his feet gave away in ragged inches, ripping his pant's legs to shreds. Stars formed in her eyes, her body attenuating to almost unbearable lengths. Shield working over-time to shore up the damage.

Her world became nothing but agony, blood, and her grip on Daniel.

With one final shout, he dragged his lower limbs onto the wooden ramp and the particles from the tellurium meteorite loosened and fell away. He rolled to his back, his wounds seeping and not closing as they should.

Proximity. They needed to get out of here before he bled to death. He needed time for Shield to heal him.

Fighting through the pain and the stars in her eyes, Eva crawled to the staircase, pushing Daniel in front of her. He cried out in agony, only half conscious.

"Go, go." She wrenched the goggles back over her eyes as the light from her fallen flashlight faded.

Her lungs burned, her breath hot inside the mask.

Eva made it up the stairs to the rim of the hole and collapsed.

"Daniel?" She croaked.

He groaned beside her, pockmarked skin only half healed,

abraded hands a ragged mess, calves drenched in blood. Shield had somehow slowed.

"Eva?" The weakness in his voice was a little disconcerting. He was never weak.

"Yeah, I'm awake."

He snagged her hand and squeezed it a few times. "I think we have a problem."

A hysterical laugh burbled up and out of her throat. "That's an understatement. What was that? I thought they found the tellurium meteorite on the moon?"

Daniel coughed, adjusted his face mask, and patted his head with his free hand. His night vision goggles were long gone and there was no way to retrieve them. He gripped her hand tighter. "Honestly, I thought so too. I always assumed they used Lower Monumental Dam for the project due to its proximity to the MUC but now I'm not so sure."

"It was like the rock had a mind of its own. Why the hell were the particles attaching to us?"

Daniel's other arm draped over his forehead. "I don't know. Magnetism, maybe? I...I just don't know."

She closed her eyes, her blood humming in tune with the beat at the bottom of the hole, entire body still trembling in shock.

Daniel finally kissed her hand and let it go, sitting up. "We need to find a way to study it. Just you and I. Nobody else can know about it. That thing is too dangerous."

"I agree with the hiding and the danger part, but are you crazy? We need to leave that thing alone. Bury it. Implode this entire place."

"Bury it? Have you looked around? How the hell did it get down here? It'll take the world generations to recover from the Collapse, Eva. The people coming after us won't have the knowledge base we have to deal with such a thing. At least not for many, many years. You would leave that thing for them to find? God, use your brain."

Eva narrowed her eyes at him, even though he couldn't see it. He could be such an ass. "I am using my brain, *Dr. Burgess*."

His head fell forward and eyes closed. He reached out his hand. "Eva, I'm sorry. It's this place, it's frying my nerves. Can we talk about it topside? Please?"

She considered the outstretched hand for a long moment. "You just don't want to get your ass left down here in the dark."

"No, no I don't. But I am sorry I said that last thing."

Eva stood, pulling him to his feet. "Topside it is."

The two of them made it to the underground reservoir.

The surface of the dark water was ominous but absorbed most of the sound from the meteorite far below them. A definite improvement.

"We need Amrit down here to go for a dive. *If* we can find some scuba equipment." It was an offhanded comment, one meant to be neutral.

"No. We'll place a camera in here to track water, but this entire place is off-limits from now on. Hell, we'll just close down the entire section of Track Three that runs past the place, find the other entrance, and shore up the walls so nobody else can enter."

"That won't last long term. You tell people they can't do something and sooner or later somebody is going to try it. What if our daughter stumbles in here? Get's taken down by living rock? What then."

"What do you want me to do? I'm not destroying this place, Eva. That thing is too valuable."

And there was the crux of the matter.

"Fine. Let's go home, see our daughter. It was a damn close call, today, and I don't want to fight you anymore right now." Eva walked to the crack in the wall of the cave that was the only entrance they'd found so far and turned, holding out her hand.

A suspicious gleam entered Daniel's eyes. "Just like that?"

"Just like that."

###

Blasting crews for wall construction had stashed an entire crate of explosives near the South Gate. Bolt cutters from the MUC opened the lock with a clank. Eva eyed the stash in a disconnected haze. There was something wrong about this. Something important....

The thought drifted away like dandelion fluff on the wind.

She tied the boxes down on the back of the four-wheeler. It would be tricky to get them through the cavern wall but she'd figure it out. The rusted hand cart on the front clanked and rattled over the bumpy road.

Eva had left Mia and Daniel asleep, worn out after a long, harrowing day. Sleep. Hadn't she been sleeping too?

The crate squeezed through the opening in the tunnel wall back to the cavern of water. Somebody had turned off the lights. That was okay. She had night vision goggles. And ear plugs.

Eva fit her face mask in place, the movements unhurried and mechanical. Part of her screamed to stop. Stop now. Her feet halted for a split second and pain rushed through her veins. No, she needed to get this finished.

She lugged the crate of explosives to the door to the mine shaft. Halfway down the hole should do it. Not enough to harm the meteorite, but just enough to cover the entrance. She ran the explosives cord up the side of the shaft and snaked it to the ramp beside the door.

The explosion drove away the numb cloud and she fell to her knees at the impact. A fog of surreality cleared from her brain like somebody—or something—had released the strings of a puppet.

God, what had she done?

"The farther backward you can look, the farther forward you are likely to see."
-*Winston Churchill*

PROLOGUE
COOPER

April 23, 2072

py work after the Collapse was like working with a scavenged bomb—cobbled together, volatile, and one fumble away from oblivion. At one time, Killian Cooper craved the rush, the high that came with slipping into places other people couldn't—or wouldn't. At least he did back when he was doing it for the right people. Now, one wrong move and, bam: dust.

Crouched low, his pistol a cold weight in his grip, he edged past a rusted pipe sagging like a drunkard's spine from the curved roof. Echoes and the play of sound through the tunnel suggested something much more cavernous ahead, but from here, the walls swallowed the light like a grave, the still-intact tracks disappearing into the void. Traintrack to hell. A more modern version of AC/DC if there ever was one.

Cooper flicked on the night vision glasses, one earpiece held together with black electrical tape. Green outlines of the enormous, curved walls and multiple train tracks flickered into view. A hub. Static buzzed across the base of the glass lenses. Like most things requiring electricity after the Collapse, the glasses were just one more thing giving out. Soon, there would be nothing of the old world left, the remnants of that not-so-distant past eroding like water through sand.

Cooper slowed. A heat signature at forty–he tapped the sides of the frames when the numbers froze–no, fifty feet appeared ahead. An unmoving human-sized lump. How had something alive make its way down here? Hell, the air was thin for him, and he was Shielded. The serum may have made him resilient, but it didn't make him immortal.

He crossed the tracks to the other raised walkway about three feet off the ground, the metal trestles firm and unbroken beneath his feet. The tunnel system hadn't been opened to the light of day for quite a while if the musty smell and layer of dust were any indicator. How Sarah had even known about this place worried him. Old government projects and that woman weren't something he liked to contemplate too much if he could help it. He just did her bidding and kept his daughter safe. What else could he do?

The lump heaved itself up.

Through narrowed eyes, his back to the wall, Cooper sidled closer on silent feet.

It had four legs, not two, and its sides heaved; whether in pain or lack of oxygen, it was hard to tell. Its rear-end wiggled in a tentative motion. A dog. A damn big dog and it was wagging its tail.

Cooper jumped back down onto the tracks, scanning the area for any other heat signatures or movement. The dog could be a trap.

He crept closer and reached out a hand. The dog took a painful step toward him and sniffed the outstretched digits, giving them one dry lick. Okay, then. He ran his hands over the rough coat, its skin stretching over jutting ribs, its backend concave. Near its hindquarters, he found a hole oozing blood.

So, Sarah was right. Somebody *was* down here.

Patting the dog on the head, he pushed it back to the ground so it wouldn't follow. If he could, he'd come back for it. Nothing should have to die alone in the dark.

"I'll be back," he murmured to the pitiful creature.

It whimpered but hunkered down with a soft sigh, almost like it understood his words.

He hopped back onto the walkway. Anger seethed through him. Where he came from, one didn't leave an animal to suffer. Well, where he originally came from. The people he was forced to work for now would probably cook the animal up for dinner.

The tunnel narrowed after a pillared brick archway, once again. On the side of one of the pillars, a large number "3" stacked atop the letters MP: KC and EP: MUC offered little in the way of explanation for the track and he was for damn sure not going to get an explanation from his handler. She would have him kill anybody left in this tunnel if it meant she could find more Shield Serum or other top-secret tidbits. The insane woman had a single-minded focus, he'd give her that.

A whoosh and a hum echoed down the track in front of him, increasing in intensity. Holy crap, a train?

He sped up.

The noise pulled away.

At a dead run, he cleared the first bend, the Shield Serum pumping through his veins giving him a quicker edge.

Too late. A bullet-shaped engine was speeding away from him down the track, a very familiar face in the window. A swirl of dust obscured the area.

Dread settled low in his gut.

Cooper tapped his earbud. "Home base, come in."

A click, and then a young woman's voice came over the airwaves. "This is home base. ID?"

"Beta-1-1-3. I need to talk to Ms. Zapada."

Silence and then. "I'll get her right away, sir."

Moments passed, and then another woman's voice, deep and pissy, thundered in his ear. "What did you find?"

"What did you think I'd find?"

"Just answer the damn question, Cooper."

"Track is labeled with a three, train of some kind pulled out of here." He didn't mention the dog.

A sharp curse cut through his earbud, and he winced.

"What's the label?"

He repeated the series of letters.

"Mid-point and End-Point," Sarah said. "You better grab your go bag."

"I'm not going anywhere without my daughter."

"You'll do as you're told." Her cold voice cut through the airwaves like an icepick.

A helpless fury soaked into his bones. He could defy her, go out on his own, and never look back, find a nice settlement somewhere that still had water. Live out his days without killing another soul for this psychotic woman and the twisted organization she worked for. Only soulless monsters would sacrifice a child for their own gain, and though he'd wondered at times, he did, in fact, own a soul.

He punched the wall in front of him, pain shooting through his fist. It disappeared as Shield healed the wound. Claire might not be blood, but Cooper was all she had.

"Where to, this time?" He gritted out through clenched teeth.

"Don't you recognize the initials MUC? You should be rather familiar with them. It is where your parents died, after all." She sounded way too satisfied.

The dread multiplied tenfold. The Manhattan Underground Complex.

The bitch was sending him right into the lion's den. A place he swore he'd never return to.

CHAPTER 1

COOPER

Wednesday, September 7, 2072
5:04 P.M.

Tumbleweeds and sagebrush. If somebody had dumped Cooper bound and blindfolded in the middle of this damned desert, he would still be able to identify it as home.

He scanned the horizon from the back of the cart, rifle across his lap and his dog, Kiva by his side. Heat waves danced in the distance above the dry, desolate landscape. The clip-clop of the horse's hooves and the rattling of the wooden frame filling in the lack of conversation with his fellow travelers. Even the silence was far better than walking alone.

Cooper poured the rest of the water from one of his canteens into a small dish. Kiva raised her head, soulful brown eyes gazing at him. He figured she was a shepherd mix of some kind. He hadn't regretted returning for her in that train tunnel beneath the wilds of Virginia a few months ago. Even if others said he should. Why he split his rations with what amounted to a pet was something he didn't contemplate too much. Maybe he was just getting sick and tired of killing. Of course, it didn't have anything to do with loneliness. Of course.

"Go ahead." He pushed the bowl closer. Kiva sighed and lapped at the water without moving more than necessary.

He readjusted his baseball cap and aviators, scanning the landscape once again. Home represented betrayal and loss. A place he never wanted to return to. Not that he had much choice. *Buck up, buttercup, and get it done.* One of Daniel Burgess's favorite sayings. He had plenty of them to motivate the troops. It wouldn't be a grand homecoming by any means.

"Hey, you guys have any spare water?" He asked the two men on the front bench of the buckboard.

They exchanged a look. A few days ago, Cooper had flagged them down, trading guard duty for a ride under the pretext of negotiating with the Basin Territory. They'd been heading to the same place, so it worked out well.

"We only brought enough for us and the horses to get to the Territory, my friend." Jorge, the younger of the two, craned his neck back. "You wouldn't be out if you cut that dog loose."

He grimaced. "She's a good companion. Catches rabbits, too. Been traveling awhile through the badlands, only a few watering holes about. I might know of an old house coming up. It's in a ravine cross-country, about a mile. If you drop me off at that next rise, I can go scout the place. It'll be a bitch of a hike but worth it if there's water."

"No driveway?" This time the old man, Jerome, spoke up, his deep, gravelly voice tinged with a touch of Southern skepticism. He couldn't blame him for being suspicious.

Cooper turned up the charm.

"Nah. The driveway starts at another road on top of that hill over there." Cooper gestured to a rocky slope, a flat plateau of sage and dirt above it. "I don't think it's been used since before the Collapse. It'll be fine. I'd be mighty grateful if you waited, though."

Jerome raised one bushy, silver eyebrow. "You're sure?

Haven't had much problem with scavengers in recent years, but things happen. Three guns are better than one."

"Isn't that the truth? But I've got it. It's just a water run. And like you said, no scavvies out this way for awhile." He blasted the man with his best, easygoing, lopsided grin.

In truth, it wasn't just for Cooper's benefit, no matter how much he needed to stay on mission. The old man had stumbled off the cart yesterday, and the last thing any of them needed was a geriatric with a broken hip.

Jerome regarded him, the deep brown of his face wrinkled and worn. "Let us know if you find water. Be good to add another marker to the map."

"I can definitely do that, sir."

Jorge halted the horses in the shadow of a basalt boulder half-buried by the hill. The enormous rocky debris littered the Columbia Basin, remnants of an ancient flood that had swept through the region thousands of years ago. Before the Collapse, theories abounded about the cause of the flood. The most interesting had claimed a large asteroid had plummeted to earth during the last ice age, melting the massive ice sheets at their southern border, and causing a violent, catastrophic flood in the region.

Whatever had caused it, some of the leftovers fascinated him. Like the enormous boulders that looked as if a pouch of giant's marbles had been spilled out over hundreds of miles of otherwise flat land, some out in the middle of nowhere taller than a two-story house. Or the craggy canyons and leftover dry waterfalls, prehistoric and mysterious, deep and ancient. It must have been one hell of a rager when it happened.

"If you find any books, grab a few. I've been running short on good reading material." Jorge turned in his seat, a young man of few words thus far.

"I can do that. I'll give two sharp whistles when I return. Wouldn't want you to mistake me for a scavvy." Cooper hopped off the cart and shouldered his pack and rifle. Kiva followed, coming damn near to mid-thigh, her black and tan coat shining in the sun and a blue bandana around her neck. His daughter, Claire would have chosen pink. Maybe he'd have to look for one.

Jerome harrumphed and waved him away. "We'll camp here tonight. See you when you get back."

A slight trickle of guilt pricked his conscience. He hated telling even white lies to good people. Jerome and his grandson deserved better. If his daughter's life didn't hang in the balance, he might feel guiltier.

He nodded his head to the duo. "I'll try to scrounge something up for dinner while I'm gone."

Cooper crouched along the brush line just outside the mouth of the ravine, well away from the old, run-down farmhouse but near enough for good visibility. He waited. Patience, like a fine Scotch, only got better with age, and he had learned a long time ago that most things in this new world required caution. Not that he remembered much from the pre-Collapse years. He'd been almost six when his parents signed their family up for Project Shield and the deep, dark depths of the Manhattan Complex. Immense hunger and thirst clung to edge of what few memories he had of that time.

Life clarified after Salvation. For better or worse.

Kiva waited for his command and hunkered low. He rested his hand atop her silky head.

Leaves rattled in two poplar trees near the house. It stood two stories with a large wrap-around porch. The beige brickwork blended with the sandy soil of the hillside, run-down but still intact. At some point, a branch had smashed through a corner of the porch, though no debris blocked the front door.

A dirt driveway and parking area separated the house from a derelict barn. Red paint peeled in thick chunks from its wooden planked sides, and the back half had collapsed in a mangled pile.

It wouldn't be much longer until the rest of the structure followed suit, a slow irreversible death of the past.

Cooper envisioned the homestead as it had been once upon a time. A time before his parents abandoned good sense for false patriotism and a shattered past. Before their desperate bargain with the devil hiding beneath twenty stories of cement, dirt, and rock. If he squinted, he could almost see the lush fields of green with crops ready to harvest, and dogs barking in the barnyard, The horses and cattle grazing in the pasture, while a lone tire swing swayed in the breeze. Now, all that remained were the lost things, broken and forgotten, scattered to the four winds of this miserable planet. There were no crops, no barnyard dogs, and only the tire remained, sticking up half-buried under years of soil drift.

Fifteen years had passed since he'd last visited his childhood home. The passage of time swift and painful. His thirty-four years settled in his bones like one of those boulders from the ancient flood.

What would he do if somebody had squatted in his parent's old house? Kill them? Or let them live? These days, most of the remaining people lived in settlements where they rationed water and food, living by a strict code and hanging by their fingertips to the glory of a vanished past.

Of course, there were the outliers, but he couldn't see Daniel allowing any this close to the Territory.

The overgrown barnyard remained unoccupied; no horses or carts. Nobody moved about the property. Not even a fly buzzed.

Cooper gripped his pistol, flexing his fingers in the ever-present gloves, and stood, hoisting his pack with the rifle strapped to its side. He snapped his fingers and Kiva jumped to her feet, alert.

He skirted the sagebrush to the road, the fine dust billowing behind him in trackless powder a foot deep. A fallen fence lay on the ground in front of the house, the gray, splintered pickets all but disintegrated.

He circled the yard and headed towards the back where the well-house used to reside. It was still there.

Cooper slammed his shoulder into the jammed door, and it gave way with a sharp crack. The interior was dense with cobwebs and dank with moisture. Dead flies and spiders littered the rough cement floor in macabre piles, attracted to the small oasis. Halfway up the tank, a slow drip pattered onto the cement, a slimy rivulet running under the now broken door.

Bless his father for the installed hand pump—the large metal cylinder attached to the base of the well with a manual crank on the top. A hose made its way from the base to a sealed valve at the top of the tank, and another dirty, capped hose lay on the ground, ready for use. He eyed it as if it were a snake ready to strike, took one more glance out the partially opened door, then entered the well-house. Kiva's ears flicked and she focused her attention on the house. She glanced at Cooper but didn't make a sound.

Cooper petted her and then pumped the handle a few times. Cold water, clear and clean, flowed from the hose onto the ground.

He emptied the two full water bottles still in his pack and refilled the canteens with the new water. Fresh was always better. Jerome and Jorge would be none the wiser that he didn't actually need water after all, the little white lie a necessity for what he needed to retrieve from the house. Heck, in the end, they'd have a new watering hole to mark on their map.

The screen door hinges to the farmhouse creaked, a sound imprinted on his brain from childhood. Kiva stood, and a low grumble issued from her chest.

He stilled, unholstering the pistol once again.

Shadows inside the small building blended with his dark clothing, and he crouched to peer outside, making himself smaller–less of a target.

At one time, his mother had danced barefoot in this back-yard, classic rock blasting from a Bluetooth speaker while she hung clothes on the line. His father always teased her that they had a perfectly good clothes dryer, but it didn't deter her. She swore the machine ate the clothes, one thread at a time.

Movement flashed behind one of the windows that looked out from the kitchen. A flicker of ragged curtain that could have been the wind. His gut, and the dog, told him something else.

He signaled for Kiva to stay and sprinted in a zigzag pattern across the powdery earth of the backyard. No shots rang out. Maybe whoever it was thought he would leave. Or maybe they didn't have a firearm. Ammo was becoming scarce in the wider world.

Back against the wall, he eased the screen door open, then the inner wood door. Dried blood streaked the floor and up the side of the cupboards to the sink. Bones and the smooth surface of a human skull, bits of meat and hair still clinging to its cranial ridges stared back at him from the counter. Shoe prints of various sizes tracked through the rust-colored smudges on the light-colored Pergo laminate.

An island stood between the kitchen and dining room, the living room behind it. The open-concept floor plan offered little to no cover except for the front closet, master bedroom, and staircase leading to the second floor.

"I know you're in there. Come out, so we can talk." Cooper remained by the door, halfway behind the jamb, and kept his eyes moving so as not to focus on any one thing. Peripheral vision could pick up a lot when you let it.

A woman and male teen rose from behind the couch.

"Please, don't hurt us." Scraggly hair, slick with muck and something unidentifiable, fell across hollow cheekbones. A cagey awareness looked back at him.

The boy, no older than fourteen or fifteen, glared at him, vitriol behind his eyes, the blue all but gone in a sea of black dilation. Drugs? Or something else?

Who Cooper assumed to be the mother settled a hand on the kid's shoulder and squeezed.

"What settlement are you from?" Cooper asked.

"None, we're refugees looking for one."

He didn't lower his pistol. "What about Basin Territory? It's only a day's hike from here."

She sneered. "They don't let anybody in there. Think they're better than all the rest of us."

So, Daniel and Eva had closed the border. Cooper filed the knowledge away for later, focusing on the pair in front of him.

"There's a smaller one about eighty miles north. Colville. It would take a bit on foot, but they're always looking for more help in their mines."

Something flashed in the woman's eyes, and a feral grin tipped the boy's lips. They both leaned forward, excitement dancing in feverish eyes.

A shuffling of something scraping the wood on the porch behind him and Kiva's snarl was Cooper's only warning. Adrenaline kicked in, and he whirled around, raising his arm in defense.

He registered the stench of body odor, rotting teeth, and bright blue eyes surrounded by ratty hair. The man held an ax over his head, a necklace of bones around his neck. Faster than any person had a right to, Cooper stepped into the man's inside guard, sweeping his arm in an arc to knock him back with his shoulder. With his other arm, he slammed the pistol against the man's face, knocking him out cold.

Cooper whipped around. The woman and boy froze, shock on their filthy faces.

"Whose blood is that?" He pointed to the sink and floor.

"How do you move so fast? Nobody moves that fast." She hugged the boy closer to her.

He aimed the pistol at the body on the floor beside him and stood on the house's threshold. "Answer my question."

"Ain't your business. A person has a right to feed themselves."

"Wrong answer." And he put a bullet into all of them, neat

and clean in rapid fire succession. A painless death. Probably a lot more than they deserved. Bitterness coated his throat, a long burn all the way to the pit of his stomach. Killing the teenager bothered him, but he'd seen it many times. The young man had been too far gone, gripped in strange contagion eating away people's sanity and empathy one chunk at a time. A creation of a past world gone mad. The new world, where prisons didn't exist and medical care was a foreign concept.

A quick death was the only mercy he could offer.

The necklace of finger bones around the cannibal's neck disgusted him. They would all need to be buried, but he'd bury the trophy bones elsewhere.

Cooper crossed over the threshold into the kitchen, and a stench of rotting meat and blood permeated the hot room. He breathed out of his mouth. Holding the gun at chest level—close for control, just like he'd been taught in Daniel's militia as a teenager—he searched the large room for any other trespassers.

The master bedroom door was open a crack. Bones littered the corner, and a fresh body of a young boy lay sprawled on the bed, one of the hands cut off at the wrist. The bathroom and hall closet were also empty of any other squatters. Cooper resisted the urge to return and put another bullet into the trio for good measure.

He didn't have any answers about the insanity, but if some weren't found by somebody, he had a feeling every unShielded human on the planet would end up like one or the other of the dead bodies on the floor: the eater or the eaten.

Cooper pushed the thought aside. Not his circus. He had other problems to worry about.

Time to find what he came here to retrieve.

His old bedroom looked the same with its full-sized mattress, brown curtains, and sturdy wooden dresser. The only difference, a thick layer of dust that had blown in through the broken window and the chewed holes from rodents.

Cooper removed a plank of the hardwood floor by his bed.

Wrapped in a bath towel alongside a few baseball cards and other boyish trinkets sat the last gift his father had given him so long ago.

The bone-handled bowie knife *shnicked* out of its sheath, titanium-plated with perfect balance. An ideal weapon to delve out justice in the shadows. Or revenge, depending on how you looked at it. At the thought of his handler, Sarah Zapada, he growled. Kiva's ears perked up at the noise. Cooper slid the knife sheath into the top of his boot. It wouldn't be much longer. If he could pull off his plan, walking the tightrope between staying on mission and liberating both him and Claire from Sarah and her crew, then it wouldn't be much longer at all.

The plank on the bottom of his hidey-hole came up with a bit of prying from the knife. Beneath lay the other item he came here for. A black box the size of an old cell phone. He flipped the switch on the side, and a little light on the front panel blinked green. Fifteen years and the damn thing still worked. Gotta love science and nuclear-powered batteries.

Wrapping it in the towel, he shoved it into the leg pocket of his cargo pants and stood.

Step one of saving Claire had commenced.

CHAPTER 2

MIA

Thursday, September 8, 2072
11:52 A.M.

Dank air settled around Mia Burgess like a cloak. A nasty cloak. Full of moisture, mildew, and too many secrets. Everybody else just called the underground track she travelled on the Mainline, but she called it Hade's Railway. Not just for the suffocating humidity but for the oppressive weight that clung to this stretch, like a gaggle of ghosts haunted every nook and cranny. Possible with what the government used to do here.

The double subterranean rail system connected the MUC in the West to Lower Monumental Dam in the East beneath the Basin Territory. Several recent branches, all guarded by security cams, shot off the Mainline to other Sectors and even to a subterranean town in the northwest beneath Sector One dubbed Down Below after some old sci-fi television show.

This section where she stood was closest to the dam and where one of her guards had reported an anomaly—code on the radio for crime scene. Since the dam also held their power source, it required Mia, as head of security, to investigate.

"How much farther, Talia?" Her apprentice sat beside her on the mining cart converted to a passenger tram.

"Tobias said after the entrance to Track Three and we'd know when we saw it. Do you think it's another one?"

"God, I sure hope not." The tram passed around Hub Eleven, one of several large cylinders that routed irrigation and electricity to different Sectors of the Territory, and Mia eased the control back. The cart slowed.

Track Three. Over the years, residents had snooped along the tracks until her father installed titanium plated doors across the tunnel a hundred yards from the hub. Some had still tried to breach it.

All without success.

Those few individuals discovered how fierce her father's temper could be. After the last flogging in regards to the mysterious track, interest had all but dissipated.

Public humiliation was barbaric and horrifying but in this case, effective.

Talia shone the flashlight on the walls and just after Track Three branched off to the left, there it was, in all of its blood soaked glory.

Mia stopped the tram and hopped off, jumping up to the walkway.

We Must All Pay For The Past

The four-foot tall words slashed across the pockmarked cement wall. Two furry, mangled bodies, pinned to the brick with railroad spikes, underscored the furious streak of letters.

"How the hell did they even get this close to the dam?" She swept the beam of her flashlight across the tracks, over the gravel rail bed, and along the walkways that bordered each side. Dim emergency lights burned above her in even intervals, marching away from her position in both directions. Pipes and conduits ran along the crown of the ceiling; vital electricity and water that flowed to all corners of the Basin Territory. Every brick and beam in place, every rivet and screw untouched. Nothing else was disturbed but the marked-up wall.

Talia shrugged, black braid bobbing with the motion. "Emergency exit at Westbound-2, maybe?"

"Unlikely. We just replaced its camera and upgraded the lock." Mia stepped closer and wrinkled her nose. "And what is that smell?"

The younger woman stopped beside her, nose sniffing the air. "God, I don't know, but it sure puts cat piss to shame, doesn't it? I'll get blood samples to the lab before I call in a clean-up crew. Maybe whoever did this poisoned the bodies."

Mia nodded and took a few measured steps back. Either the person who had painted the letters had been very tall, or else they had a ladder. Right. And just how the heck did they get one down here?

There were three entrances to the tunnel in this part of Sector Three: the second Westbound emergency exit that Talia had mentioned was a half mile away, the highly-secured entrance to the old Lower Monumental Dam only five hundred yards away, or the tiny access hatch a grown man would have a difficult time squeezing through over a mile away. None would be easy and all were monitored closely this near to the dam. The first two ingresses could fit a ladder, but the last, not so much.

"The perpetrator wants to rub our nose in how close they could get to something essential." Her father was going to be pissed.

Damn, it.

This looked and felt like Sector Nine. The isolationist group on the outer edge in the northeast of Basin Territory. Their protests had increased in recent months, even spilling over into Sector One. They raised livestock and usually kept to themselves, but parts of their Sector were never content, developing wild conspiracy theories and pushing for a complete lockdown of the Territory. She'd read the old debriefs. Sector Nine chafed under the restrictions of the Territory Council. Their biggest disagreement: their one-time leader of the Basin Territory, Jack Allen, forming an alliance with the surviving scientists from the MUC. The last conflict ended twenty or so years ago when all twenty representatives from the shiny new Council—including the two from their own Sector—refused to give the protesters food and water for an entire month.

We Must All Pay For The Past. Yeah, it sounded like some of their protest signs, trying to revive old rebellious sentiments—but why?

"Like the one yesterday. Containment protocols, again?" Talia murmured.

"Just to be on the safe side. Only the Shielded on clean-up. I don't want to take any chances when we remove the animals. I'm going to poke around a bit more. Keep channel four open." Mia checked her own radio, twisting the dial to the correct channel. The Shielded—or the people who had taken the Shield Serum—would be immune to most diseases or radiation. If somebody had laced the animal blood with something toxic, they would stand a better chance of survival, hazmat suit or not.

Talia did the same, hopping off the walkway onto one of the two tram cars on the track. Its welded door and bench seat were so similar to the pictures of old teacup carnival rides Mia often wondered if they hadn't been the template.

"Copy that, boss. Be careful."

The cart rumbled away.

Down here, silence never reigned. Water swished through the pipes, the TMRWS machine, their power source, hummed, spinning in its turbine, and the distant rattle of faraway carts all funneled through this part of the tunnel. Still, without Talia, the suffocating emptiness surrounded her.

Mia got as close as she dared to the wall, the rank odor of supercharged ammonia almost beating her sensitive nose to death. The first crime scene yesterday had been a skunk nailed to the wall of the Council House. She had thought it in response to her father's edict to shut down the borders to the Territory.

Starting a month ago, no more visitors were allowed to spend the night within the Inner Territory walls. No more refugees were to live here. This current blood-scrawled message was an escalation in behavior, the letters taller, the destruction of food in the form of animals more shocking.

On a hunch, she put her nose in the air and walked to the right, back towards the dam. The rank smell dissipated. She changed directions, heading towards the dim gray of the entrance to Track Three. The scent lingered, milder but present, and Mia followed it like a German Shepherd on a scent.

A hundred yards out, the smell faded. Mia took out the antique brass compass her father had given her as a baby and clicked it open. Still exactly due west of the crime scene.

Something reflective flashed on the ground next to one of the rails.

A spurt of adrenaline shot through her, and Mia hopped onto the rail bed. She kneeled for a closer look. A necklace. Dirt and gravel covered most of the heavy-duty chain, but the corner of a pendant peaked out, shining silver in the light.

Taking out her knife, she scraped away the debris and all the hair on her neck stood on end.

In any other situation, the ouroboros would be just another symbol from the past. Everybody who served the Western Coalition pre-Collapse had some form of it, somewhere; the image used on the alliance's flag.

The message of this particular necklace negated any of its meaning.

About the size of a half-dollar coin, a snake head looped around, biting its own tail in the classic sign of destruction and re-creation. Each scale overlapped in fragile lines, the workmanship careful and detailed. A miniature spike through the snake's eye gave her pause, but the neck of the creature was what alarmed her. It was ripped off, the mouth of the serpent still around its tail but disconnected from the rest of its body. Somebody had painted the jagged edges red, like the message on the tunnel wall.

Mia removed one of her gloves, picked up the necklace with the flat of her blade, and dropped it into the leather confines. She would have to get this analyzed.

Something scraped against the stone behind her. She whirled, crouching into a fighter's stance, hand going to the pistol at her side. A human-sized shadow played against the gray of the wall, running away.

The barrel of her gun cleared the hard plastic of its holster. "Stop, right there!"

The shadow took off on the walkway. No time to boost up onto the platform. She'd have to take the tracks.

Mia flew along the rails, the Shield serum helping to make each step precise, each stride smooth despite the gravel and obstacles. The figure in front of her maintained a similar speed.

Shielded. Had to be to outpace her.

Now, her father would be monumentally pissed. She needed to catch up before the first utilities hub.

Sixty yards. Fifty yards. The distance closed.

Her respiration and heart rate beat in an easy rhythm, elevated but not labored.

Forty yards.

The tunnel brightened as the next hub neared.

Damn, it. She wouldn't make it.

The person she chased wore black clothing and a hood, was of average height, and had an athletic build. The description of dozens of other people.

She fired off a round. It pinged against the cement wall of the tunnel. The person dodged, arms pumping faster.

A metal staircase appeared, and Mia angled toward it, speeding up to the walkway before it curved to Westbound-2 and the entrance there.

Thirty yards.

The person careened around the hub disappearing from

view. Mia followed, circling the huge interchange of pipes and conduit running through a large metal cylinder in the intersection.

A sinking feeling settled in her gut. The other side came into view and the person had vanished.

Crap, crap, crap.

She paused and listened, straining her eyes to catch even a flicker or rustle of movement.

The amount of water rushing through the pipes drowned out any other noise. She jogged back to the hub and scouted along both sides of the smaller branches. Nothing.

How the hell had the person disappeared? Westbound-2 dead-ended several hundred yards on her right and the hatch to the entrance hadn't opened. So, the Mainline was the only possible exit.

Mia unclipped her radio and put the mic near her mouth.

"Talia, you there?"

A moment passed, and then the radio clicked. "I'm here, boss."

"I need you to get a team together and meet me at Hub Ten. Possible trespasser."

"Really?—I mean, copy that. Also, Jack's late, and nobody can find him."

Mia frowned. "Did anybody check his house?"

Make sure he wasn't sleeping one off. She left the words unsaid. Jack Allen may have been part of the Council and her father's best friend, but lately he'd gotten into funks and would disappear into the bottom of a bottle for weeks. With her father out checking settlements, it wasn't outside the realm of possibility he'd plummeted down a rabbit hole. Mia clicked the radio again before Talia could respond. "And check in with his ex-wife and kids. They might have seen him."

Talia gave an audible sigh through the airwaves. "Yes, ma'am. ETA on the search crew is fifteen minutes. Clean-up crew should be at the crime scene already."

"Copy that." She clicked the radio off, a movement in her peripheral catching her eye.

Mia whirled, but it was too late. A sharp, shooting pain clobbered her head, and she fell to the ground.

The last thing she felt before passing out was hands rifling through her pockets.

Voices. A swish of a hand. Swirling headlamps and the clack of a train cart on rails bombarded Mia's senses in a swirl of sound and motion. Head pounding and heart racing, she reached around her.

The glove was gone.

But her compass was still in her pocket. At least there was that. Her assailant had only wanted the macabre necklace.

Talia peered down at her, brow furrowed in worry.

"God, that hurt. What time is it?" Mia rubbed at the healing gash above her eyebrow and sat up. Blood smeared her hand. The world spun and she braced herself against the gravel on the ground.

The other woman held out a hand to help her to her feet. "Almost 8:30. When I couldn't reach you on the radio, I hauled ass back here along with the search crew. You all right?"

Twenty minutes had passed.

"Yeah, it's healing. I want every inch of this tunnel examined. Whoever hit me got in somehow. I want to know how. Pull whoever you need to to get it done." Her voice was sharper than usual.

"Yes, ma'am. And boss, your father was on the radio trying to reach you."

What? "He was? He's supposed to be down in Redmond."

Talia just shrugged. "He needs to speak to you, ASAP. He'll be out at the wall for the next hour. He said you'd know where."

Mia closed her eyes until the world slowed and didn't tilt at an odd angle when she moved. Whoever had hit her had a good arm. "I'll be available by radio if you find something. Even if you have to interrupt the conversation with my Dad, got it?."

Talia nodded, "Copy that. Are you sure you're all right?"

"The ride out to the wall will clear my head." She walked to the exit ladder.

Mia surfaced beside a guard shack and a livestock pen near a cliff. Somebody had brought her old gelding, Rocky. He flicked his tail, content in the shade of the jutting rock. His ears perked up as she emerged from the tunnel. Mia usually drove her side-by-side All Terrain Vehicle—which always reminded her of a cross between a Jeep and a four-wheeler—but had left it back at her house when she rode in with Talia.

She mounted and rode out toward the wall that surrounded the Inner Territory's farmland. Heat waves danced above it, the ninety-degree weather heating the metallic structure and radiating out like a furnace.

To an outsider, the wall looked like a chaotic heap of scrap: crumpled tractor-trailers, broken-down farm machinery, corroded washing machines, flattened cars of every make, and countless Ford and Chevy pickups, all plucked from the wreckage of a lost world. It sealed the inner Basin Territory border like a jagged metal glue, bolstered by steel beams, concrete, and rebar. Sturdy enough to repel a serious assault, it stretched thirty miles across the northern edge of the old Columbia Basin, running unbroken by cliff or canyon. It barred all but the most relentless intruders, human or beast, from the irrigated fields and Council homes within. Only when electrified could it truly block everything.

Her father once said a wall's core purpose was dual: to trap things inside or to shut things out. People always assumed it served one role or the other. This wall, though, had a hidden edge—it diverted attention from what lurked below. A decoy, masking the labyrinth of tunnels and subterranean dwellings woven beneath the Territory's surface.

Mia tugged on the reins of her horse, and the gelding stopped its plodding pace next to her dad. He leaned against his own electric side-by-side ATV jotting something down in a small notebook. Tall and muscular with a full head of dark brown hair, he did not look like a man of sixty. *Thank you, Shield Serum.*

"You're late." Daniel shoved the paper pad in his back pocket and crossed his arms, regarding her over the wire rims of a pair of worn sunglasses. His hazel eyes settled on her with laser focus.

How could her father make her feel like a teenager again with just two words?

"You know I'm twenty-eight years old, right?" She dismounted and tied the horse's reins to the back of the ATV.

His brow furrowed. "Then you should know by now not to be late."

"Somebody defaced a wall by Track Three and then clobbered me over the head. So, not my fault. I didn't expect you to still be around, I thought you were checking settlements." Mia stuffed a hand in her pocket, fingering the cool, smooth surface of her compass. It helped to keep at least one hand occupied.

Her father stilled. "Track Three? What happened?"

After relaying the events on the track, Daniel closed his eyes. She could almost feel the gears shifting and whirring inside his brain. "Another protest by S9."

"It had that feel. Unless we have intruders."

He straightened, hooking the sunglasses on the front of his t-shirt. "Get Tobias on it. He knows that group better than anybody."

"I'll check out the protest if I get time as well. Never hurts to have more eyes on it. No fights have broken out in awhile."

Daniel rubbed the bridge of his nose. "I should have shut it down when it started. Old rights for an extinct world."

She resisted the urge to touch his arm. He hated being touched by anybody but her Mom. "It allows them to blow off steam, Dad."

The two of them stood at the edge of a harvested wheat field, the stubble prickling out of the ground like spines on a porcupine. One field over, a circle of sprinklers extended it's long arm out into a corn field, rotating at a turtle's pace through the tall stalks. It was where her father had taught her how to shoot a gun and ride a horse. The very edge of the inner Territory's northwestern corner.

"There's something else." Daniel shifted his stance. "Jack's missing and he was supposed to take the negotiation this afternoon with Jerome from Colville."

Mia frowned. It was a little late in the year for one of the five remote settlements in the region to be negotiating. Added together with Jack's absence and the killing of food animals, the day was just getting better and better—and it wasn't even noon. "Like actual missing, or hit-the-bottom-of-a-bottle-somewhere missing?"

"I don't know yet, but something feels off. If S9 is really riled up beyond just the protest, we can't afford to take any chances. Jack may have his faults, but he would never miss a negotiation." His tone was contemplative, focused on his inner thoughts.

A niggle of worry fell like a stone in her gut. "Why do you think S9 would have something to do with Jack being gone?"

"What happened to your forehead?" He ignored her inquiry. Wonderful. One step forward and two steps back with the forthcomingness.

"Somebody decided to play baseball with my head. I hit my face on the way down." Mia rubbed the goose egg on her hairline. Dried blood flecked her fingers.

"Damn it, Mia, I trained you better than that." He gripped her shoulders and peered closer.

"I must have forgotten the lesson where you taught me how to fight ghosts."

"Ghosts?" Surprise flashed across his face.

She told him about the fight. "Whoever clobbered me didn't

make a sound. And could keep pace with me. Quick. I don't know how they got down there."

Daniel's jaw twitched. "Nothing else?"

"There was also a smell like supercharged cat piss."

Every single muscle in his body froze. "How strong?"

"Strong. Like sticking my face in a bottle of ammonia."

"Dammit," he said under his breath and then, a little louder, "I'll take this one. I need you to take the negotiation with Jerome. He likes you better, anyway."

"Just like that, huh? What does the smell mean, Dad?" She narrowed her eyes on his shuttered face.

"I don't know. Could be anything." He stepped back toward the driver's door of the side-by-side.

She unwrapped the reins of her horse. "You have an idea, though, don't you?"

"Are you going to ride Rocky back, or do you want a ride to the Brokerage House? We can drop him off at Sullivan's if you want to come with me." Cagey. That was Daniel.

How does he manage to tell me no without ever uttering the word? "We're not finished with our discussion."

Hard steel filled her father's voice. "Yes, we are."

Her arms tensed and the horse jerked its head up. Mia relaxed her grip on the reins. She would table the discussion for now, but if he thought she was forgetting about the investigation, he had another thing coming.

"Right." Sarcasm oozed from the word.

"I'm going to head out to the crime scene. After you're finished with the negotiation, we'll go look for Jack." He turned over the small, electric engine. It hummed in a low whir.

She narrowed her eyes. "I'm horrible at food negotiations."

"You're not horrible, you just don't like the extra B.S." Daniel cocked a brow in question. "Coming?"

Mia could go in the ATV, question her father more on the message, tell him about the decapitated ouroboros—more symbol than necklace—but something held her back, like if she got into the vehicle, he'd hog-tie and stash her somewhere for the duration of the investigation. No. Not happening. "I'm not too far from my house. I'll drop him off there and get my own ride."

Daniel regarded her like he could read her mind, head tipped back. "Suit yourself."

#

Mia parked the vehicle in the back by the rear entrance. The thick door of the security barn, the metal so incongruous next to the red paint, opened smoothly with a whoosh of air-conditioned air.

Apart from a few stalls in the far corner for patrol riders, the converted interior reflected her father's penchant for maintaining heightened security. Daniel liked a good camouflage. In this case, from the outside, the old-fashioned barn looked worn and like something to house farm animals, but on the inside, it included thirty-year-old high-tech security systems and numerous guards. One of these days it would all wear thin, but for now they could still coax life into the old system.

She allowed her eyes to adjust, then moved farther into the room, brushing her black hair away from her face and back into the bun at the base of her skull.

A dozen young guards occupied old creaky office chairs behind sturdy, steel government desks. They were spread in rows atop the cement floor, looking like something out of an old NASA movie. Flat-screened computer monitors took up every square surface of flat space, video footage of this sector—Sector Six—flashing in intervals on the screens. On the front of one of the salvaged grey, metal desks across the bottom, somebody had taped cut out hands made of black electrical tape. It reminded her of Dorothy's house after it had fallen on the Wicked Witch of the West and only her fingers—instead of her feet—remained.

The words "help!" were written next to them. Somebody had a sense of humor.

Power from the underground tunnels running beneath the Territory kept everything running, though modifications over the years kept it secure. The equipment had come later but the cement floor and steel reinforced walls had been built amidst the rapid construction in the years after Salvation.

Salvation. Ironic, really, that a bunch of scientists with various beliefs, faiths and religions, who had rescued themselves from their super-secret, underground military facility would call the day they saw sunlight something as biblical as Salvation, but what did Mia know? She had been a baby.

"Pull up the Brokerage House." Mia stopped behind Corey, one of the guards working at a monitor.

The young woman tapped at the keyboard, enlarging the section. It was a well-maintained house, whitewashed with a large front porch and basement. The Council maintained the single-family dwelling for negotiations because it looked "homey." Mia had scoffed at that image. Her mother would have too, and her heart clenched. Even at her age, she missed Eva's presence with a vengeance. Absence didn't necessarily make the heart grow fonder, it made it ache.

A hazy figure beside a horse and wagon sat parked under one of the few large pine trees left alive in the yard. She peered closer.

"Who's that next to Jerome and Jorge's wagon?" Mia pointed to the man with a baseball cap, and an enormous German Shepherd heeled at his side.

"Chet said his name was Cooper. He wants to trade."

Years ago, the Council had allowed more people at the negotiation table until one ended in a blood bath. Now, they limited attendance to two. "He'll have to wait."

Mia pressed a button to zoom in on the stranger. She couldn't make out any details on the grainy black and white screen, so she reset it to its original size. Having a dog for a pet these days was unusual, though some in the more remote settlements bred them as livestock. Her stomach turned at the thought.

"I thought Mr. Allen had this negotiation?" Corey said.

Mia grabbed the ledger from an old dinged-up filing cabinet, a green, leather-bound book, faded and mottled from age and wedged it under her arm.

She schooled her features. "Plans change. Keep one of the screens up showing the man by Mr. Warren's cart. I don't want him wandering off."

She strode through the barn and exited out into the dusty yard, Chet and Tobias at her heels. The rolling hills of sage and a section of the southern wall about a mile away stretched across the horizon, one of the guard towers in the distance rising above it all.

The hinges on the back door creaked and the exposed pine rafter beams sloped over the converted living room they used for meetings. Stifling air hung thick and heavy. Her father didn't allow outsiders to know how many resources they maintained, so the house didn't have air-conditioning. Mia grimaced. Hot air circulated through the room from open windows but sweat still pooled at the base of her spine and underarms, wetting her t-shirt.

The curtain-less windows of the stark meeting room looked out onto the dry plain of brush. The ticking grandfather clock, creaky metal office chairs, and a long, pockmarked oak table offered the few sparse trappings.

Mia sat next to Jerome. She hated this part.

"Mr. Warren, it's good to see you," she said, and this farce called food negotiations began. It went as expected.

Mia would kill Jack for missing this negotiation.

Disgust swirled through her, a bitter pill. The food her Territory grew could mean the difference between life and death. Denying any of the smaller settlements in their region sat like a hard stone in her stomach, no matter what drivel she tossed at them.

"I'm sorry we're unable to be more accommodating. There will be open negotiations next year. Your first food shipment will be ready in two weeks at the North Train Yards." Was the man going to keel over? "Can I get you something, Mr. Warren? More water, maybe?"

Jerome's face blanched and he grabbed his chest. "I'll take nothing from you except what…I'm…owed."

He skirted the table in choppy jerks, holding his left arm and wheezing. Jorge shot her a dirty look and followed his grandfather to the front door.

"Escort them out, and make sure he's all right," she told Chet. The man nodded and took off after the pair.

Mia shoved the ledger across the table. Anne, the administrative assistant who crunched all the numbers, would be irritated if she tore any of the pages, the figures like gold to the distributors in Sector One, but Mia didn't care. The book spiraled to the edge before tipping over and landing on the floor with a thud.

If you control the resources, you control the world. Her father's favorite saying echoed in her mind. Was that what he was trying to do? Why her mother was gone on yet another trip?

Frantic shouts erupted from outside the window.

God, what now? Mia unholstered her gun and ran to the door. The bright, sunny day threatened her vision as she emerged into the yard. Someone had collapsed to the ground, a small group surrounding him.

Jerome.

CHAPTER 3

COOPER

Thursday, September 8, 2072
12:48 P.M.

As Jerome Warren's rickety wagon rounded the bend this morning and the Basin Territory's wall loomed into view, Cooper's first thought was that the old bastard had done it. Daniel had completed his wall. When Cooper had left, the structure was a skeletal maze of twisted rebar and patchy concrete, farming implements and tractor trailers riddled with gaps where the wind screamed through, carrying grit and the sharp tang of rust, while sunlight glinted off exposed metal rods and pooled in harsh shadows on the cracked, uneven ground.

A mixture of sorrow and pain had punched him in the gut, as unfamiliar and rusty of emotions to Cooper as sentimentality. At this rate he'd be a puddle on the ground in no time, his tough guy image shattered.

But Cooper wasn't on the ground, now. Jerome was.

Cooper eased a glove off one hand and prayed Jerome wasn't Shielded. The last thing he needed was a dying man's presence pinging around inside his head—the unpleasant added side effect only he had developed from Shield.

The old man's pulse fluttered against his fingers, then faded away. Jorge administered CPR, stopping to breathe into Jerome's mouth in even intervals.

The tall guard Chet—and Cooper wondered if it was the same guy he knew from so long ago—kneeled next to them. "He have a pulse?"

Cooper shook his head and returned the glove to his hand. Another decent human gone. Kiva whimpered by the wagon wheel where he'd made her sit. Yeah, he felt like whining too.

The tall dark-haired woman he'd caught a glimpse of earlier holstered her weapon and walked toward them from the house. Her sharp hazel eyes surveyed the scene and settled on Jorge working on his grandfather. Eyes just like her father's. He eyed her closer, a spark of recognition alighting deep inside. Hell, the last time he'd seen Mia she'd been a young girl, and he not much older. Would she recognize him? Cooper was a long way from the skinny teenager he'd been, plus he had a beard, but still....

"Mr. Salva?" she said.

Jorge didn't respond.

"Sir? He's gone," she tried again.

"No! My grandfather is the strongest man I know." He continued pumping on Jerome's chest.

"He doesn't have a pulse. We're thirty miles from medical treatment. He's gone, Jorge," She placed a light hand on Jorge's shoulder. The young man shrugged the gesture away.

A breeze picked up, blowing dust across the yard. A foul stench like rotten meat cooked in ammonia emitted from Jerome's slack mouth. Cooper eased back even farther.

Jorge gave one more frustrated pump to the old man's chest and shot to his feet to face Mia.

"This is your fault! If you had just given us what we needed, this wouldn't have happened!" He leaned toward her, anger and grief carved in every line of his young face.

"We both know that's not true, now back off." Her words were reasonable but her hand settled on top of her holstered weapon.

Cooper stood, Chet doing the same.

"We just needed enough for a handful more people. How could that be too much?"

"This world just doesn't work that way anymore." The woman's words were a quiet testament, not unsympathetic, but not giving the young man an inch, even in his grief. They'd all experienced more grief than any human should bear.

Jorge scrubbed his hands across his face. "Screw that. The world needs to change."

"Why don't you go with a couple of my guards and rest? We have an apartment in the back of the barn. I'll take care of this with the utmost respect to Jerome." She motioned to the barn. Two young men emerged and made their way towards their group. "I promise."

So, the building wasn't just a place to house farm animals. Cooper scanned the area, spotting at least one lens tucked under the eve of the house. They had enough power to run security cameras. Was Daniel's power source still operational?

Jorge clenched and unclenched his fists.

"It might be a good idea, there, my friend. I'll drive you home if need be." Cooper hoped it wouldn't come to that, but he needed to get the shell-shocked younger man out of the way, out of the picture.

Sweat tracks and tears streaked the dirt on Jorge's face. He closed his eyes, then nodded once. The guards escorted him to the barn.

"You know what you're doing?" Chet's lips pursed, directing the question at Mia.

She switched her attention to him. "I'm not going to make him sleep in his wagon after he witnessed his grandfather's death. You'll stay with him tonight."

"Your father won't like it," he said.

"That's my problem." She inclined her chin at a stubborn tilt.

Cooper cleared his throat. He'd remained quiet until then, gathering information like a squirrel hordes nuts. Sometimes listening garnered more intel than being the center of attention. "Excuse me?"

The woman didn't remove her hand from the butt of the pistol. "Would you like to join your friend in the barn, Mr.—?"

"Just Cooper, and they're not friends. Only traveling companions." Cooper didn't offer more, waiting to see where the conversation would lead. He adjusted his ball cap and slid his sunglasses back up the sweat-slicked bridge of his nose. If either she or Chet hadn't recognized him yet, maybe they wouldn't. He had to get in, get Shield for Claire, and enough intel for Sarah about the research on the Aberrant to regain entry to the compound in Montana, and get out. Easy, peasy. He couldn't fail, his daughter was depending on him.

"I see. You…seem familiar. Where are you from, Mr. Cooper?" She narrowed her eyes and tilted her head.

"I guess I just have one of those faces." He grinned. "I'm from farther north. You wouldn't recognize the name."

"Try me." Her tone brooked no argument.

Not that Cooper usually took those hints. On the contrary, he enjoyed a little verbal sparring. This time he played another game, though.

Cooper kept the smile plastered on his mouth. "Riverbrook."

"In Canada?"

"So, you've heard of it?"

"I didn't realize there was still a settlement there. That's quite a ways north." The woman frowned, her brows knitting together.

"Only enough water to support a handful of people. I was going to trade with your Territory for a new pump. I heard you had some." He told the fabricated story with ease.

"Were you now?"

"Not a lot of options these days." He shrugged.

She hesitated. Only for a brief moment but Cooper noticed it nonetheless.

"Well, Mr. Cooper, as you can see, something has come up. I'll have one of my guards take you to the campsite we reserve for visitors and you and I can discuss that pump tomorrow."

With an effort he hadn't had to employ for quite a while, Cooper kept his features neutral. Daniel and Eva's daughter had changed over the years. Not they all hadn't over the years. Now, to lay some of his cards on the table and hope it didn't backfire. *Gain trust, then respect.* Or was that the other way around? He never could quite keep the Daniel-isms straight. "That'll have to work. And, Miss Burgess? Take care when you examine Jerome's body."

"Excuse me?"

Cooper kneeled next to Jerome's head and pulled back his eyelids. "Petechial hemorrhaging usually doesn't cause the entire eyeball to blacken. Even in death. And the air in his mouth smelled foul, unnaturally so. Like ammonia."

Her eyes widened before she could compose her features. Chet grunted. Cooper had almost forgotten about the other man's presence, he'd been so quiet. Being hyper-focused was a dangerous habit to get into.

"I don't know whether to thank you or ask more questions now instead of later, but I think Mr. Warren has been laying here in the sun long enough." She gestured to the barn again and a young woman walked out, rifle on her shoulder, looking dusty and disgruntled. "Talia here will show you to your campsite. And Mr. Cooper? I will have more questions."

###

This day had turned sideways in more ways than one, but if Cooper was anything it was resourceful. He needed access to the Territory, and now he had it—limited though it was with his well-armed escort behind him, silently stalking.

If his sources were correct, Daniel would be nowhere around. This time of year, he and a contingent from Basin Territory checked in with the remote settlements spread around what remained of the old Pacific Northwest on the east side of the Cascade Mountains. Old Western Coalition territory. In Cooper's cynical mind, it was a way to keep them under Daniel's thumb—not that him controlling the entire food trade in the region didn't do that already.

Hell, if Cooper kept away from the more populated Sectors, he might get away with nobody recognizing him–as long as he didn't run into Rani. Or Eva.

Kiva trotted at his side, her ears perked and keeping an eye all around them. Memories of the place flooded back, a part of himself he kept locked away, safe and secure.

After Salvation and losing his parents in the Shield experiments, Cooper was shuffled between foster families until age twelve when Daniel took him, Chet, and other teens from the Basin Territory and established a remote camp away from other survivors. He and Chet had already had Shield running through their veins but the others—well, let's just say the results shocked them. With a shortage of able-bodied adults over eighteen to protect the Territory, Daniel recruited every teenager he could. Cooper didn't resent the age cutoff. Even now, he was unsure if Daniel intentionally aimed to create an army of super soldiers or if it was an unintended outcome of Shield. As an adult, though, he suspected it was the original goal.

Daniel called them his Shielded Militia. They all turned out to be far more than that.

Coming back now had torn some scabs off of old wounds for sure. Not something he'd anticipated.

Needing the distance from the past he forced his thoughts to the conundrum of a dead Jerome.

Surprise was an understatement; any time an innocent was murdered, it sat like bad mushrooms on an empty stomach. Cooper hadn't seen the remains of the old bioagents in years. He wanted to be wrong about the origin of Jerome's blackened eyeballs, but his gut told him he wasn't going to be.

"How far to the South Gate?" he asked the very young, well-armed woman walking slightly behind him. Mia Burgess called her Talia. She kept her mouth shut and held herself like she knew how to use every single weapon concealed on her body. He counted at least five.

"Couple miles."

"Can I ask you a question?" he said.

"Can I stop you?"

"Why do you have so many weapons?" It was a safe question. Nothing to do with Territory secrets. He'd found that the trick to getting somebody to talk was to start simple. "We're inside the wall. You afraid of an attack?"

"No."

"I see. A pack of wild dogs? Alien invasion?" He glanced back.

Talia's lips pursed and she looked straight ahead."Why does it matter?"

He had irritated her. A good start.

"Hey, I'm just trying to pass the time. I noticed the Sig in your holster—very nice by the way, not many of those left out in the wild—the knife strapped to your leg, the back-up piece you have at your boot, and whatever is crammed down the back of your pants under your shirt. With the rifle, it seems to me to be a bit overkill for a territory very few would try to mess with."

Talia's back stiffened, and she stomped forward, stopping mid-stride to pivot. Cooper followed her into her trap on purpose and put his hands out to see what she would do. She turned, swept her arm on the outside of one of his, and secured it in an arm-lock. Cooper didn't react but Kiva barked, growling low in her throat. He waved her back. She sat, hackles still raised.

"'Poor preparation leads to piss poor performance.'" She had missed a few "P's," but the old Royal British Army quote summed up his old home in a nutshell. He was tempted to test the extent of her training—and to see if she was Shielded—but more pressing issues took precedence.

Talia dropped his arm and continued ahead. Rookie mistake, letting him bug her like that. Muddied the mind. He jogged to catch up, now walking beside her. Another mistake.

"Your boss seems very capable."

"My boss?" She clutched the strap of her rifle, her knuckles whitening.

"Mia Burgess. Back at the brokerage house. She seems very capable."

Talia snorted. "You think I'm well-armed? Wait till she comes to talk to you. She learned to conceal weapons at birth."

The young woman's admiration rang clear as a bell.

He started to push a little more. "Does she handle all the food and trade negotiations?"

Talia cast him a suspicious glance out of the corner of her eye. "Why are you so curious about Captain Burgess?"

Captain, huh? He grinned. "Just want to know what I'm up against. She seems on top of things."

"She's Head of Security, she should be. Don't worry, she won't pull your fingernails out or anything. Maybe just a few good punches to get the juices flowing."

He laughed. "Good to know. I'll have to watch out."

Talia relaxed with the banter. Cooper kept talking.

"That barn is pretty nice. I didn't think many of those old barns were left. You know, people have scrapped out most of the unused ones." The barn had appeared innocent, like a building used by the brokers to house their animals. Then, Talia and two other armed guards emerged, and his estimation of security procedure increased tenfold. Planned and protocoled to the hilt. Classic Daniel.

"We have them all over. They can hold a lot of—," Talia hesitated mid-sentence, then continued, "—they can hold a lot of animals."

Cooper grinned. "Among other things. It surprised me how many guards came to help your boss. I would think people would be on their best behavior when coming to discuss food and survival."

Talia shrugged. "Sometimes people don't like what they're told and do stupid things."

He nodded and allowed silence to settle between them. It didn't last long.

"About a year ago, we negotiated with a settlement we don't normally deal with. They tried to kill our lead bargainer. It was a mess." Talia fidgeted with the gun strap.

Cooper had read the report from Sarah's operative on that particular event. The Basin Territory broker's exact words were, "we won't support an unsustainable population boom that could cause another famine," and a young, stupid guy from the opposing settlement tried to shoot the lead bargainer in the head. Tensions with the surrounding settlements increased, though nobody had the courage yet to test the Territory's defenses—they were just too strong for the smaller settlements in the region. A good thing? Only if Basin defended the smaller settlements if the bigger bullies—like Sarah's crew—came calling.

"That's a tough deal."

Talia nodded.

The road they walked along had been paved at one time. Heat and time had pulverized the broken asphalt until nothing but gravel remained. It crunched beneath Cooper's boots.

They crested a hill, and the Basin wall came into view on the Southern border, dominating the harsh landscape with its sheer size. The Southern Gate hunkered under an overpass intersecting a canyon, two basalt cliffs rising to either side. A single guard tower stood watch, built out of an old grain silo and reinforced with welded steel.

For the limited resources, Basin had honed their defenses to a fine edge.

On the horizon, an old four-lane highway, cracked and broken except for one, graveled lane, ran to the gate. The wall's outstretched arms proceeded in either direction on the top of a plateau of rolling hills.

The wall would be damn tricky to breach without tanks and motorized armament. Not impossible—the wall would need a lot more reinforcement for that—but it would be difficult with today's resources. Information he would need to relay to Sarah. Well, maybe.

The woman beside him headed down the hill, and Cooper followed.

"So how is this going to work?" he asked.

"We have a camp under the guard tower for overnight visitors. It's well-lit with a solar generator, so don't get any ideas about slipping away."

"I won't be staying inside the wall?" He attempted to keep the surprise from his voice.

"Nobody from the outside stays inside the walls overnight anymore. It's against protocol."

Mia had allowed Jorge Salva to remain within the walls. The conversation between her and Chet made sense now. She had breached her father's protocol.

Cooper smirked at the thought. He sure wanted to be a fly on the wall when Daniel learned about that little nugget.

They reached the gate. Two welded steel doors, wide enough to allow two wagons to pass side-by-side, intersected the old highway. A normal-sized access door for people on foot stood adjacent to it. Talia signaled up to the tower, and the smaller door buzzed open. He raised his eyebrows. It took a lot of energy for that kind of system. It could only mean the tunnel system had grown along with the wall.

Talia pointed out a broken car under the tower along with a canvas yurt. "That's the campsite. There's firewood in the trunk for cooking and heat. It gets chilly around here at night."

Cooper reached out his hand for a handshake. She hesitated, then reached out her own hand.

Another mistake.

"Thanks for the lift," he grinned.

Talia dropped his hand but smiled. "Whatever. Have a good night. And by the way, nice dog."

Cooper fought the urge to laugh as he walked to the campsite. God, the young woman needed more training. She had potential, the armlock proved that—and her attempt at keeping her mouth shut. A pang of…something rushed through him. What was it? Guilt? Reticence? In the old world, Talia would've excelled in whatever field she chose. Here, she was almost too soft, innocent; she hadn't yet built a callus to the wider world.

The door clanged behind him. He glanced up to the tower. The point of a large-barreled rifle stuck out of an opening towards the top.

Well, then. He'd have to wait till dark, maybe early morning, to sneak away. Food and sleep sounded good.

Large river stones ringed a singed bit of dirt. The yurt had a cot and a sealed plastic container with bedding. Cooper sighed and removed the old hiking backpack. "Better set up camp, Miss Kiva."

The dog laid down, her head on her front paws.

He had stayed in worse places.

CHAPTER 4

MIA

Thursday, September 8, 2072
4:45 P.M.

Mia made arrangements for Jerome's body to be taken out to the lab at the MUC and returned to the conference room in the Brokerage House to look for anything unusual. If it had been poison, as the stranger Cooper had indicated, then it had to come from somewhere.

People died all the time, but this was her first that had a criminal versus a survival element. She reentered the conference room, bending to pick up the ledger. Nothing appeared out of place. The clock still ticked, the chairs still rattled when moved, the empty table still looked like a termite had eaten holes in it. Why her father had kept for so many years was a mystery.

Wait.

Jerome had been drinking water from a glass when she had walked in earlier. Where were the water glasses and pitcher?

She rolled the chairs away, checked under the table, scoured every crook and cranny of the great room. Gone. They were all gone. Nobody had been in here since she'd left when the commotion around Jerome had reached a fevered pitch. So where did they go?

A breeze blew through the room, riffling through the fine strands of black hair that had escaped her bun. Her eyes zeroed in on the bank of windows.

Mia walked over, stuck her head out, and looked down. A pitcher and pair of glass cups lay shattered on the ground. The barn was off to her left out of direct line of sight, but somebody could have still seen something. She glanced up to the eve of the house. The camera was turned outward. No help there. Maybe whoever had entered the building would be recorded on the entrance vid feed?

Whoever was here obviously hadn't had time to do much else with the pitcher and glasses. That told her A) they couldn't carry them without being seen, and B) they weren't worried about being on camera. The only two other people besides Jorge and Jerome that should have been in the conference room besides her were Jack, Tobias, and Chet. She hunched her shoulders not wanting to contemplate the implications of any of those options.

Grabbing a canvas bag from the small kitchen, she took out her gloves and retrieved the broken pieces of glass. On one of them, a fine residue had formed.

Hard water stains, or something else? Blowing out a puff of frustration, she stalked toward the barn. She would question the remaining guards and look at the vid feed then head to Jack Allen's house to meet up with her father. She'd send Rani, her mother's old lab partner, the pieces of glass with one of the young guards. Rani would know what to do with them.

###

6:52 P.M.

Guards rotated every other month to different regions of the

Territory to keep each group from getting too territorial, and the current guards on duty came from Sector Four in the Northeast part of the inner-wall.

Hard-headed and stubborn. All of them. They hadn't seen anything. They hadn't heard anything. Period.

To top it all off, the vid feeds hadn't shown anything unusual either.

Now, she was five miles from Jack Allen's old home. His ex-wife had remained there with the kids after they had split, but Jack could've holed up in the barn—if Peta would have allowed it.

According to a radio call from her father, Jack's temporary, one-room hovel in the tunnels beneath Sector One had come up empty. Why Jack wanted to live in what amounted to town-living in the manufacturing and distribution Sector was like penance for whatever had happened between him and his wife. He had Council housing available in the Inner Territory, nice and aboveground. Then again, self-flagellation was Jack's middle name. Besides, all the whiskey stills were in Sector One.

When Mia was much younger, she spent a lot of time with Peta and Jack and their kids Mikal and Dally. Her parents were often gone, off trying to save the world, or so they told her. She knew the Allen farm like it was her own, the four of them like a second family.

On the border of the property, she halted the off-road vehicle.

Croaking frogs, sprinklers, and the occasional chirp of a bird met her ears. A distant hum of tractors harvesting crops mingled with the sound of the wind stirring the line of trees that offered a windbreak to the fields. At one time, long before the Collapse, farmers had transplanted poplar and pine to the area, seeing as how nothing grew in the Basin but Russian olive trees and sage-brush. Now the faint scent of pine drifted in the breeze like she was in a forest.

Nothing out of the ordinary caught her attention and yet, all her enhanced senses from Shield screamed that something was wrong. She exited the vehicle and slipped into a row of corn. Cool shadows and a slight humidity surrounded her until she reached the boundary to Jack's farm.

No movement stirred around the single story, brick farmhouse. It lay still and quiet. Abnormal during this time of day. Peta and the kids should have been out taking care of their animals, the working dogs barking, chickens scratching. She stepped so as not to crunch the gravel around Jack's old driveway and put her back to the wall of the house. Rough brick yanked her damp shirt up. All that silence contrasted with the virtual cacophony near her ATV. Not even a bird peeped this close to the house.

She took out her sidearm.

Inching around the corner, she peeked at the wraparound porch.

The front door hung open. Just a crack.

Icy fingers clawed their way down her spine. Peta never left the doors open. She despised mosquitoes with an unearthly passion and yelled at anybody who didn't at least close the screen.

Mia crept onto the porch and eased the door the rest of the way with the tips of her fingers. Shield enhanced eyesight but only to a point, and she required some ambient light to check the rooms. Turning on a light now would just alert any strangers to her presence.

The main part of the house lay in shadows before her. All the doors to the bedrooms and bathroom off the main room were closed tight.

Dread churned in her stomach.

The first bedroom had been Jack and Peta's at one time. She opened the door. Empty. Mia moved to Mikal's door and pushed it open. The same. With acid burning in her throat, she moved to the last bedroom.

Dally usually left her door open. The white wooden door had

scuffs where her dog scratched to be let in. She reached for the knob and opened it.

Nothing.

Where the hell were they?

A tinny noise creaked across the kitchen porch and she raised her pistol.

Ch-ch. A gun cocking.

Mia ducked beside the island so she'd have cover for a clear shot.

She whipped her pistol around the corner of the island, and surprise zinged through her. "Jack."

"Hell, child, you about gave me a heart attack. What are you doing in there?" His brown eyes were bloodshot, mousy hair sticking out at odd angles, and too-lean body hunched over as he cradled his left arm against his belly. Blood spattered his shirt, three bullet holes marring the thin fabric. Two in his chest, one in his gut. Shield's quick healing had already begun taking care of them, but still….blood still spread around the wounds, staining the t-shirt in ever-widening circles. It was usually faster than that.

"Looking for you." Mia scanned the porch and barnyard behind him. A haphazardly parked ATV beside the barn caught her attention. He must have been here before her, the side-by-side just out of her line of sight until now.

Mia's brows drew together before focusing back on Jack. "What happened?"

"Long story." Jack rubbed at the bullet wounds in his chest.

"Where are Peta and the kids?"

Something thumped below.

Jack and Mia's eyes connected. Covering his back, Mia followed him out to the large wooden deck, eyes sweeping the barnyard for any movement.

He released a latch on the underside of the boards and it swung up with ease. Underneath was the door to an underground cellar where they stored most of their preserved food. It creaked as he lifted it and the barrel of a shotgun stared him in the face. He ducked instinctively.

The gun didn't go off and Dally lowered the weapon. Three pale faces appeared in the entrance of the cellar.

"Daddy?" She said.

"Thank God. Are you guys alright?"

Peta pushed herself through where the two older teenagers stood at the bottom of the steps.

"What the hell's going on, Jack?" Her fiery temper matched the fading red of her hair. Though Jack was five years older, the lack of a Shield injection and a hard life made Peta appear the oldest. Jack stood up.

"Why are you guys in the cellar?"

"Not until you tell me what's going on. Two kids came at us with shotguns. They're hogtied now, but the way I figure it, you pissed somebody off and now we're paying the consequences. Again. Besides, I don't answer to you anymore." Peta crossed her arms over her chest, a stubborn slit to her eyes.

Jack holstered his pistol and put his hands up like he was surrendering. Mikal and Dally stood by their mother. Both had their mother's red hair but Jack's dark eyes. Their gaze flicked back and forth between Peta and Jack like they were used to them arguing. Hell, maybe they were.

"What? Where are those kids?"

"Not until you tell me what's going on?"

"Hell, Peta, the way things are going, I want you take the kids out of here for a few weeks." He covered the bullet wounds through the stained shirt.

"That's a little extreme. Even for you." Peta shifted her gaze between Mia and Jack. "Does this have to do with that death at the Brokerage House?"

Jack froze at Peta's words and faced Mia.

"What death?"

"Jerome Warren from Colville. Dropped dead in the front yard. Possible heart attack from the sounds of it. His grandson was with him." News traveled like the wind in the Territory. Mia kept her gun out, though pointed the barrel toward the ground. Somewhere, Peta and the kids had hogtied some kids with shotguns. Whatever that meant.

Jack swiped a hand over his face. "Damn it. I should have been there. Natural causes?"

"We're still investigating, but I don't think so." She pictured the broken glass and Jerome's blackened eyeballs and the sickly sweet scent of rotten meat and ammonia wafting from his mouth. "Though, I'm of the same mind as your wife—"

"Ex-wife," Peta interjected.

"Fine, ex-wife. If you know something, Jack. Tell me now. It might help the investigation. For starters, who shot you?"

Jack didn't need to know yet that her father had already absconded with the animal investigations, hiding his own secrets like usual. It would be a minor miracle if those events and Jerome's death weren't related.

His features hardened. He shifted and winced. "I need somebody to help me clean these wounds before they completely close. Then we'll talk."

"I'll help." Dally rushed inside the house to find the first aid kit.

Mia huffed out a frustrated breath. Dealing with this man could be like herding crocodiles sometimes. "Dad and I have been trying to hunt you down for hours. There was another animal nailed to a wall with the message, *We Must All Pay For The Past*. It was right by the dam and the TMRWS machine. So, again, who shot you, Jack?"

"How do you know they're bullet holes?" He countered.

"Jack."

"Later," he growled.

Peta shook her head. "Well, before *I* decide anything, like taking the kids out of the Territory, you both can help get the two idiots out of *my* cellar and off *my* property."

Jack blinked. "They're down there? What were you thinking? You have a perfectly good barn."

"Too far. I'm thinking Sector Nine; Dally recognized one of them but can't remember his name. We didn't know if anybody else would show up so we stayed down there with them. They're zip-tied and gagged. No need for guns. They're not going anywhere." Peta put her hands on her hips.

Mia gazed into the depths of the shadowed stairs and tromped down the steps. His family had been trained well and both young men were not moving.

"Help me get them up to the house." Mia leveled her pistol at the two sets of angry eyes peering up at her from the cellar floor.

Little more than teenagers, they appeared to be in their late teens, early twenties. Mia jerked one to his feet. The man-kid gasped around the gag. Jack grabbed the other one with his good arm and the two of them frog-marched the duo up the cellar steps.

Mia shoved one into a chair in the kitchen and tied his hands and feet. Mikal and Dally did the same with the other and backed up to stand by her. Peta shoved gags in their mouths. The two young men struggled against their bonds and glared at them with a ferocity that surprised her.

"I said off my property," Peta said.

"Go pack your clothes and some rations. I'm sending you to Colville," Jack told his kids.

Peta shoved her face in front of his. "I say where they go."

Mia chose the better part of valor and stayed out of the couple's argument.

Jack held his ground. "You can do whatever the hell you want, but these are my kids too and something's going on. I want them out of the Territory so some asshole doesn't try to use them against me. Now, get the hell out of my face."

"Fine time for you to start acting like a father." Pain and fury infused every one of Peta's words, not altogether unfounded in Mia's opinion, especially lately.

Mia took the kids back out to the porch. Maybe to the barn? No, she needed to hear Jack's side of the conversation.

"Stop making this about us. Somebody tried to kill me today and sent people after my family. You figure it out," Jack grated out.

"I can take care of myself and my children." Pure, stubborn Peta.

"Our children. Damn it, Peta, please just get out of the Territory for a while. This is bigger than you and me. Hell, there hasn't been a mess like this in a long time." A chair scraped across the wood floor, then Jack groaned as he sat down.

Silence reigned for a moment. Then, Peta's cold voice spat out words that perked Mia's ears right up. "This is about her, isn't it?"

"Probably."

"When me and the children get back, I want you gone. For good."

Mikal and Dally cuddled closer to Mia's side even though they were fourteen and fifteen. Their parent's separation had been tough on both of them. She knew the feeling.

Jack grunted. "I'll have the kids get the side-by-side loaded. Be ready in ten."

"What are you going to do with them?" Peta asked, nodding toward the guys.

"Whatever I have to."

Mia squeezed the kids's shoulders and returned to the kitchen. Jack sat in a chair, Peta prying a bullet from one of the half-healed holes with a set of tweezers. Huh. It should have been fully closed by now. Something on the bullets?

Fear shone even brighter in the young men's faces. In the small amount of light coming from the lamp, she could make out features. One had blond hair and blue eyes. He looked fitter and healthier than the other one, and veins popped out from his neck in strain. The other one sat hunched in his chair, a sweaty mop of dark brown curls sticking to his forehead. His brown eyes wouldn't quite meet hers.

Peta finished up with Jack, then herded her kids into their rooms to pack up what they needed.

Mia crossed her arms and regarded Jack with a gimlet eye. "What 'she' was Peta referring to?"

"Your mother."

"My mother?" Mia took a step back. She really hadn't expected him to answer.

"Yeah. Eva's back. I saw her sneaking into her house last night. Keep these guys quiet for me. We'll question them together."

"You're not Head of Security anymore, Jack. I am." It was like he had punched her in the stomach, and then stomped on her for good measure. Her mother was back and hadn't contacted her? Mia pursed her lips, "It's good to see you sober."

Jack huffed out a humorless laugh. "I'm an alcoholic, Mia. Sober is not in my vocabulary. Though, no, I'm not drunk at the moment."

Mia was numb. "At least you can admit it."

"Oh, I admitted it a long time ago. Booze is the only thing these days that keeps the nightmares at bay."

Jack helped his ex-wife and kids pack all the gear into the side-by-side and he jumped in to drive. "We'll question them together. As a Council Member, I'm making that an order. Wait until I get back."

Mia shook her head and watched them drive away in the dwindling light. Just like that, he dropped a bombshell and left.

CHAPTER 5
MIA

Thursday, September 8, 2072
7:59 P.M

Mia rummaged in the pantry. Back when she baby-sat Mikal and Dally, Peta taught her how to bake cookies, cakes and all of the sweet treats that were seen as extra and therefore unnecessary and wasteful. Peta would just smile and wink, telling Mia it would be their secret.

She smiled a wistful smile at the memory and tossed a loaf of bread on the counter. The two young men glared at her over their mouth gags. Mia added a hunk of cheese and a couple of pieces of chicken from the small refrigerator.

"Jack may have issued me an order to wait on questioning you but that doesn't mean I can't think out loud. Let's see, you're Sector Nine. I only know of about half a dozen people who have sons around your age out there, and I can think of only two men who would want to stir up old rivalries and maybe the settlements that have some semblance of power to do so: Hector Ramirez and Tyler Wice." The bread sliced and cheese cut into thin pieces, she slapped a chunk of chicken on and folded it into a sandwich. God, she hadn't eaten since forever.

The two men thumped around in their chairs, but the bonds had been tied well. They weren't going anywhere. Jack had sat them facing each other, stating, "don't want them to think they have each other's back. I want them miserable and scared by the time I return."

It just might have been working.

Mia leaned a hip against the counter and took another bite of her sandwich. "Now, my next question is, why? Why start up old fights? You're all fed, have water for your crops, a fair amount of autonomy. It just doesn't make sense to me."

She took another bite of her food, watching their reactions. The blue-eyed young man glared, the vitriol strong enough to light a fire with one look. Man-child number two still wouldn't look up. Was he trembling? Hmmm.

"Well, it should be interesting when Jack returns. I'm sure—" her words were cut off by the shattering of Jack's front window. Terrified grunts emitted from behind the gags and the chairs rattled as they clacked against the hardwood.

A canister of smoke rolled toward her.

Instinct kicked in, and Mia dropped the sandwich, skirting the island.

She reached Dally's room and ripped the blankets off the bed, shoving it under the door. This room had a window looking out to the front porch. Flowery curtains framed the double pane of glass and Mia crawled to the base of the window to flick them aside, unholstering her gun at the same time. A shadowy figure ghosted along the covered porch from the other side. If she didn't hurry, they'd be inside the house, and she and Jack would lose their one chance at questioning the two men.

Mia busted out a window and fired a shot.

A yelp. Bullseye.

She fired off another round and whoever was outside took off towards the field on the south side of the property around the barn.

Mia yanked the window open, a cool breeze blew the scent of ripe corn into the room.

Something thunked against the side of the house near the window, another immediately following it.

Bullets.

She slithered out the window onto the porch, making sure to go the opposite way of where the bullets were hitting. Footsteps crunched through the gravel between the house and field. The waning gibbous moon gilded the trees in silver light. Irrigation circles hummed, the sprinklers in their long, wheeled rows eking out rations of water as it moved in a slow, steady crawl through the cornfield.

Two people?

Another round shattered the window into the kitchen. So they hadn't seen her leave.

Mia sprinted for the field on her side to the North of the property. She'd circle around after she spotted where the gunfire was coming from.

Another report from a rifle.

The sound came from the circle hub about a hundred yards out, it's pumps moving water into the irrigation pipe from the tunnels underneath.

Deep shadows played in rows of corn.

A dirt path had been worn into the ground from the wheeled irrigation sprinkler. Mia ghosted along it, pistol at the ready. Another volley of rounds and then more silence. She made it to the end of the row and stopped. Tall stalks of corn loomed on either side of her. On the one hand, they'd provide cover, but on the other hand, her line of sight would be compromised. She didn't see any way around it.

She made her way through the corn. The ratcheting sound of a cylinder driving a round into a rifle chamber told her she was close.

Time for answers.

"You put another bullet in my friend's house, and I put a bullet in you."

The man brought his rifle around and took aim. A stocking balaclava hat obscured the face and identity but the body was familiar.

No time to think.

Mia kicked out, catching the shooter's hand. He clung to the rifle and rolled with the kick. She aimed at his leg and pulled the trigger.

The bullet went wide, and the man lunged to his feet with a grunt. This time he brought the rifle around like a bat. The air rushed past Mia's face as she ducked. Years of training kicked in. She put her hand to the ground for balance and kicked out with a leg sweep.

Her opponent was able to lift one of his legs but not the other and stumbled backward, dropping the rifle. Lying with his back on the ground, he yanked out his back-up pistol and pulled the trigger, no hesitation.

Mia's ears rang and a sharp burning sliced its way through her left shoulder. She gasped and returned fire. He groaned, but she couldn't see what she had hit. He took a wild shot, rolled to his feet, and plunged into the corn.

She gave chase.

Warm wetness soaked the sleeve of her shirt. It would have to wait. Shield already worked to staunch the blood, the itchiness almost distracting her.

The cornfield ended, and a fallow field opened up in front of them both, silver-bright under the glow of the moon. He was just in front of her, a slight limp slowing him down. He turned to take another shot. Mia fired first, and this time he fell to the ground on his knees.

He brought the pistol up, but Mia was close enough now to knock the gun out of his weakened grip and throat punch him for good measure. As he gagged, she ripped the balaclava from his head.

Mia stumbled back in shock, bringing the pistol back up to bear.

Chet.

"Why?" The word lodged in her throat, broken in disbelief.

The man coughed and gargled out a humorless laugh. He reached behind his back and pulled out a small, single shot hand pistol.

"Don't make me do this." Years of hard training was the only thing keeping her together. She'd known this man her entire life. He'd been in the MUC when she was born, had survived the Year of Hell with the other MUC survivors, had watched each of his family members succumb to the negative effects of the initial Shield Serum one after another. But, they'd all lost people. Each and every one of them. Did he blame her parents, for some reason? For not saving his? It was the only reason she could think of why he'd be going after Jack's family—or retrieving Sector Nine's people for them.

A harsh, desperate laugh broke the night air.

"It was done years ago, darlin'. Time's just catching up." He raised the pistol to take aim.

Mia was trained to never hesitate in moments like these.

She put two rounds center mass.

Mia's muscles strained as she hauled Chet's body into her ATV. Her arm burned where the bullet had entered and then exited her shoulder. Blood spattered the front of her shirt. It was already healing but would take at least an hour for a through and through.

The side-by-side bumped and shifted over the lumpy soil, the headlights jumping around like a frog in a jar. She dropped him in the barn next to a rusted metal work bench and covered him with a canvas tarp. Chet's Serum levels had always been unstable, even as a young man. Subsequent injections hadn't improved the outcome over time. Most people reacted with enhanced senses, super immune systems, and strengthened musculature. Chet was an outlier–not aberrant, but never fully Shielded. Sometimes he showed abilities but many times, he didn't. There was a fifty-fifty chance Shield enzymes would heal his gunshot wounds. Other Shielded had a lot higher probabilities of recovery.

She handcuffed both of his wrists to the bench. Just in case.

An approaching ATV from the driveway zoomed into view. Jack? Mia unholstered her pistol and waited right inside the barn door.

Jack got out and froze, looking at the busted windows on the back of the house. He hunkered down and drew his weapon, head swiveling.

She yelled out the door. "It's all clear, now. You have a visitor handcuffed to your workbench in the barn.

His eyes landed on her shirt. "You okay?"

"Yeah. Chet. I think there was somebody else, too, but they hightailed it out of here after I shot them." The words felt like they were coming from someone else. A numb kind of reality had taken over, one where her trusted friend had just betrayed her and now she had to figure out why.

Jack's cursing filled the air. He shoved the canvas tarp away and stared in shock down at the body. "Nice shots."

"But it's Chet." Shock still vibrated through her. Never, in a million years would she have pegged Chet as a traitor. And she'd had to shoot him. Her hand found the compass in her pocket and she took it out, clicking it open and closed, the action centering her once again.

He closed his eyes for a beat and let the tarp fall back in place before turning to face her. "Your first betrayal is always the most difficult. Don't let it change you, you had nothing to do with his why."

"His why?"

"Things eat at people, Mia. Sometimes for years. If things in our pasts are never resolved, it can transform us into somebody unrecognizable. Trust me, I've seen it happen. That something turns into a why, why they do what they do. Obsession works like that too. Don't let his why change you too." Jack settled a warm hand on her shoulder as he walked by. "Let's go question those yay-whos up at the house. Maybe they'll tell us something useful."

Heart heavy, she pocketed the compass and straightened to follow Jack back into the house.

He'd dragged a dining room chair and straddled it so that his arms, one hand holding a pistol, draped over the back. She returned to her spot at the island, leaning against it and crossing her arms. Last year, the Council had made her Head of Security in Jack's place, switching him to Lead Negotiator.

When Jack was sober, he was very good at any job he put his mind to. But when he was drunk…all bets were off. His behavior had grown too erratic, the binging out of control. She should have stepped in to take over the interrogation but wanted to watch him at work.

A tiny voice in the back of her head questioned that train of thought. *Step up, you can't truly be the Head of anything if you're always giving in to your parents and Jack.*

She squashed the voice.

He walked to the brown-haired intruder and ripped the tape from his mouth.

"You first."

The kid groaned.

"Who sent you?"

"No-nobody. We came to discuss—"

Jack walloped him upside the back of the head. "I've been interrogating prisoners since before you were born. Don't bull-shit a bullshitter. Now, who sent you to harass my family?"

"He'll kill me." A sob escaped the young man's lips.

"Who'll kill you?" Mia took a step closer.

Jack sighed and waved her back. She puffed out a breath of frustration.

Jack regarded the other boy. The blond-haired kid, his blue eyes slit in defiance, glared back at Jack. Lean muscle strained against the bonds. Fear tracked in his eyes but also anger.

Jack yanked the tape off his face and watched the young man flinch.

"And what have you got to say?"

"Screw you."

Jack crossed his arms and tilted his head. "Two things can happen here, kids. One, I shoot you both for trespassing and attempted murder, then wait to see who shows up for your bloody corpses. Or, you can tell me who sent you, and I stuff you in a hole for a few days. That should be enough time to get this all figured out."

The brown-haired boy shook his head in quick negation, his sweaty hair sticking to his face in thin strands.

"It'll never be figured out, traitor." The blond-haired kid struggled in the chair, making the legs clomp on the wooden floor.

Traitor?

Jack's entire body stiffened and his brows drew together. "What makes me a traitor?"

"You consort with the Infected. I even heard you defiled yourself as well." The boy spat at him. A glob of spittle landed on the floor mere millimeters from Jack's shoe.

Mia's face twisted in disgust. "You want me to just shoot him, now?"

"For spitting? Nah, then we'd be the bad guys. Now, who are the Infected?" Jack yanked the kitchen chair back over and sat down like he had before.

"Go to hell!"

Mia kept thinking of the young men in front of her as boys, kids. She placed their age at a few years older than Jack's children but not quite her age. These two could fight and die for the Territory—and attempt murder on innocent bystanders.

They were not kids.

"What are your names?" said Jack.

"Screw you." The blond-haired one reiterated. He needed a better vocabulary.

"Fine, I'll just call you Dipshit and Asshole." He turned his lips up in a cold smile. "Can you guess which one you are?"

The blond-haired asshole glared at him.

"My na-name is Colin." The brown-haired Dipshit stuttered out.

"Shut-up, coward." Hissed Asshole.

"I'm not dying for this."

"Your dad's going to get you, anyway. He should have never sent you with me."

"Your dad is the one—" Colin caught himself and flushed, clamping his lips closed in a thin line.

Jack sat back and appraised both of them. Mia repressed a humorless smile. There was a reason why some interrogators placed multiple suspects in a room together. Sometimes, magic happened.

Jack shook his head.

"Here's what I see. I see two young men, probably from Sector Nine, who don't know what the hell they're talking about. Why that Sector? Because they are the only ones who have ever called me a traitor. Isolationists hate change, even after thirty years. This Infected thing, though, that's new. I have a feeling somebody is riling your people up for some reason and I want to know why." He pointed the gun at each of them. "And who. Am I getting close?"

Colin's face blanched.

"You don't know anything," said Asshole.

Jack nodded and stood, reholstering the pistol. "You may be right. What I do know is one way or another, you're not leaving here anytime soon. Why your fathers ever sent two incompetent pieces of crap like you for a job like this is beyond me."

"You were supposed to be gone. They were supposed to kill you." Colin's lips thinned, and his chest heaved.

"Is that so? So you were sent to take out innocents? How is that better?" Jack walked to the refrigerator and took out a syringe. At the sight, both men's eyes widened, and they struggled in earnest. Fear permeated the air and a urine smell wafted toward her.

"Jack." Mia straightened from the counter. She didn't know what he had in the syringe, but back in the day he used to keep tranquilizers in there for the bulls, just in case.

He waved her off, yet again. Dammit. Why was it so hard to get through to him? *Just like your father.*

"No. No, no, no. Please, I won't struggle. Please, don't Infect us." Colin's whole body trembled.

They had to be talking about the Shield Serum.

Jack inserted the syringe in a vial, drawing out the process. The man-children struggled in their chairs making the legs chatter on the hardwood floors.

"Don't come near me with that thing. I'll gut you." The whites of Asshole's eyes bled red, and the veins in his forehead pounded in time with his heartbeat.

Jack hummed an old tune and filled another syringe. He went to Asshole first and plunked the needle into the exposed bicep.

"I'll kill you, I swear—" And lights out.

Colin quavered, every muscle straining at the terror of being injected. Tears streamed down his face, and a wet spot appeared on the front of his jeans. Jack popped the needle into the kid's bicep, and Colin's neck lolled to the side within five seconds.

"Creating unity with stubborn people who have definitive ideas about policies and procedures has always been a problem. Somebody is taking advantage of that. Sector Nine's always been the weakest link in the Territory." He threw the two syringes on the counter. "Time to circle the wagons."

Mia frowned. The image of the message on the tunnel wall flashed through her mind—and Chet's words. *It happened a long time ago.*

Jack's assessment might be accurate but it wasn't everything.

"What can I do?" Mia said.

"Send me some guards. Somebody else will come for these guys and I want to be ready. And send somebody out to talk to Carmen at Sector Nine. She's usually the most reasonable of the lot." Jack hoisted Colin in a fireman's carry.

"What are you going to do with them?"

Jack grimaced. "Stick them in a hole for a while."

CHAPTER 6
MIA

Thursday, September 8, 2072
10:32 P.M.

Mia signaled the guard in the watch tower and a spotlight shone down on her face, blinding her for a split second. She put her hand up to block out the light and a loud, "Sorry!" drifted from the tower window. The locks clicked open on the other side of the door and it swung open on a long squeal to the beginning of the tunnel to the MUC.

She hated this part of the trip to the Manhattan Underground Complex. It always felt like she was descending into the pits of hell–a counterpart to Hade's Railway. Knowing what the government did in this part of the region back in the day, she probably wasn't that far off.

The passenger cart sped its way through the ten miles to the old underground lab. This passage connected to the original, Track Three, and was one of only two ways into the MUC from the Basin Territory. There were too many secrets locked away here; her dragon family hoarding old scientific experiments like gold.

The sharp drop at the beginning of the tunnel smoothed out

to a gradual descent. Support beams criss-crossed above her and shadows danced on the wall as the headlights bobbed along. Double beams of steel and rebar reinforced the wooden beams of the supports and metal plating further shored up the tunnel beneath the section under the wall. An occasional dim emergency light punctuated the darkness.

As soon as she'd returned to her side-by-side, she'd called in more guards to support Jack and a code four to her father.

Code four. It was her and her parent's code for 'major emergency, meet at the MUC.' Not that her mother had used it in the past year, off doing Lord knew what. Another sore point for Mia: her parents didn't trust her with all their secrets. How could she get out from under their shadows when she didn't even know where half of them were?

The tunnel started to lighten as she neared her destination. Two large outdoor lights lit the man-made cavern in front of the entrance. The cavern had been dug out next to a metal shaft that shot up through the earth to the surface above. At a ninety degree angle from her current position, another tunnel shot toward the east, angling up towards Track Three on the seventeenth sub-level; the MUC survivor's escape route after being buried alive.

Mia slowed the cart at the entrance to the MUC and rested her head in her hands. Rani's report on Jerome's body would no doubt be thorough, but would it have any answers? The weight of responsibility settled heavy on her shoulders. And now she had to confront her father about her part in the investigation—an investigation he didn't want her working on.

"What are you waiting for? You called a code four, get to it." Her father stood in the doorway to the underground facility, its large reinforced steel hatch scratched and dulled with time.

A halo of light shone over Daniel Burgess's silver-flecked dark hair. At six-foot-three he stood tall and proud. Silver and black whiskers shadowed the lower half of his face.

She eased out of the cart. "More trouble."

"What happened to your arm?" His narrowed gaze zeroed in on blood-spattered limb. The drive hadn't helped. She needed a pain killer, and it wasn't healing as fast as it should. There had to be something on the bullets.

"I need to sit down, Dad."

Daniel indicated the doorway, standing to the side to allow her to pass.

This part of the facility used to be a large conference room. It still housed an oblong black and steel table, cushy, high-backed office chairs in various states of disrepair around it, and a white-board for drawing. Somebody, probably Rani, had written the words 'Happy Day' across it in flowery script.

"Somebody ambushed me at Peta and Jack's house. One side of their house looks like Swiss cheese." She peeled away the upper sleeve of her t-shirt. The edges of the wound puckered together, so it'd stopped bleeding but it should have been a pink scar by now.

Daniel froze, his neutral look turning to a narrowed focus. "Who?"

"Chet. It was a sloppy attack. I don't think they expected me to be there. He could've killed me, but I shot him instead." Soon, the numbness at her actions would fade and the full impact of shooting Chet would wash through her. But she wasn't there, yet.

"Well, hell."

"That's an understatement," Mia stated.

Her father examined the wound, turning her arm over gently. No emotion played across his face except for the wrinkling of his forehead. The lack of outward feelings indicated to Mia just how pissed and worried he really was.

"It's not healing very well," he said.

"Nope. Could the bullets be laced with something?"

"Possibly. Let Rani test the skin and do a blood test."

Mia nodded, the same thought had rattled around her head on the trip out to the MUC. "Where *is* Rani?"

Daniel helped her stand. "Back in the main lab. She'll get you cleaned up and then we'll talk."

The one other door in the conference room opened into one of the main hubs of the MUC. Four hallways spoked off the rocky, cavernous hub; two ended in cave-ins and at one time, the excess dirt from the excavation out of the MUC had been stored there. The other two led to research labs and the emergency exit stairwell that led to the surface. Rani maintained everything with a compulsive need for cleanliness.

They entered the small courtyard, it's rocky, cavernous ceiling towering above, rounded the central electrical supply relay that ran through the entire facility, and continued straight to the lab.

Rani sat at her computer, glasses perched on top of her head at an odd angle. She lifted startled eyes to Mia's when she walked in.

"I have some initial results from Jerome's autopsy, but I'm still running tests on the glass you sent down." She turned and saw Mia's shoulder. "What happened?"

The petite older lady rose and gripped the hurt arm. Her wrinkled brown hands reminded Mia of pictures she'd seen of her grandmother. *Wiseness in form, richness in history.* The words from some forgotten letter or journal entry.

"It's all right. It's healing. Just not as fast as it should."

Rani pushed her into a chair and zipped around the lab, grabbing a blood and sample collection kit, and gloves without being asked. "Let me look at it."

Most of the pain had subsided but a twinge still remained. Rani took samples and drew blood, glancing every now and then at Daniel's dour presence sitting on a counter in the corner.

"Chet shot her," he intoned.

Rani dropped the sample. "What?"

A look passed between the two. Was it sorrow? Or something else?

"Is there anything I need to know?" Mia lowered the bloody sleeve.

Daniel rubbed the bridge of his nose. "I told you to stay out of the investigation on the mutilated animals. Now I want the same on Jerome's death and whoever is shooting at my people."

"Excuse me? Something is happening here that threatens the Territory, and you need my help, especially if one of our most trusted people are in on it. It means there's a security breach. Maybe more than one. And I am Head of Security, put in charge of keeping our people safe." Anger warmed her cheeks and she stood from the chair. Rani scurried back to her computer, her wary eyes shifting from Mia to Daniel.

"You'll be able to do that better from here."

"No, this is my job. My responsibility. A friend—no, family—shot at me. I have every right to investigate." Hands on hips, she pursed her lips.

"That's why you shouldn't. You're too close. Jack and I will handle it. Stay here and help Rani in the lab."

Did he know how condescending he sounded? It was like earlier. He still saw her as a naive teenager, young and eager to please. "Like you're not close? What if whoever is behind this is targeting Council Members? Targeting you? Don't be so damn shortsighted!"

Daniel clenched the back of one of the office chairs. The wheels screeched in protest. "I've been targeted before. I'm trying to protect *you*."

"No, you're trying to protect your own self-interests. Did Jack tell you he saw Mom last night? Sneaking into her house in the middle of the night." Mia walked her first two fingers through the air like a pair of legs.

Daniel froze. "What?"

Rani's chair squealed and thumped against the desk.

"You heard me. Peta thinks it has something to do with her, why she's been gone. Does it, Dad? Is there something you're not telling me?"

A muscle twitched in Daniel's jaw and he took two steps toward her before stopping. Mia had the sudden urge to flee at the look on her father's face.

"This is bigger than Territory business, Mia, somebody has access to old horrors and they shouldn't. Rani found traces of an old bio-agent in Jerome's system. It was used leading up to the Collapse. I keep ours hidden under lock and key for a reason." Tension still crackled all around him.

"Shield will protect me. And you still haven't answered my question. Why is Mom sneaking around?"

"You're not protected from this." He avoided the question yet again about Eva.

Mia clenched her fists at her side. Her parent's shadows loomed large and suffocating. No matter how hard she tried, no matter how well she did her job, she would always be less than them somehow. Coddled. Protected. Never an equal.

She'd never break free of the cage of their past exploits. "Why won't you answer the question about Mom? What don't you want me finding out?"

They glared at each other, neither giving an inch.

Rani walked through the door behind Daniel. Mia hadn't even noticed she'd left.

"Uh, not to interrupt, but Talia's on the radio. Says Jorge tried to leave the Brokerage House, and she had to rough the boy up a little getting him back in. Who wants to take it?"

Crap.

Daniel's entire body stiffened even more—if possible—and Mia strode past the older woman. "I'll take it."

"Jorge's staying the night inside the walls?" Anger punctuated every one of her father's words. He grabbed her arm.

"I was showing him a little compassion. Plus, he's a witness to his grandfather's death." She jerked her arm back and picked up the pace.

"Don't talk to me about compassion. Compassion can get you killed. What were you thinking?"

"There are black out curtains on the windows and standing orders not to go near the place tonight. And now I will have two guards posted at his door instead of one." Temper spurred her on.

"What about *my* standing orders to not to have *any* visitors stay within the Inner Territory?" Daniel blocked her progress down the hall and she halted.

"Under the circumstances, I was not going to send him out into an uncontrolled environment with a virtual stranger as his only companion." Mia kept her voice calm even though every pore in her body wanted to strike out at him, engage like they were in one of their old sparring sessions.

Her father's face was cold, a sure sign of the rage boiling beneath the surface.

"Who's the stranger?" He said it evenly with no inflection and without looking up.

"We allow people to stay out at the yurt all of the time." Mia shot back.

"Where is he from?"

"Up north. Canada. He's here to trade."

"What else have you found out about him? What does he want? Who are his people?"

"All I know is he wants a pump. And he has a dog." The words bitter in her mouth.

"Is this man a suspect in Jerome's death?"

"He's a witness and I still need—"

"So, for the night, Jorge would have been perfectly fine staying with this person? You allowed the kid to stay inside these walls unvetted or signed off by me." He stood straighter. "You put the community at risk. I thought I'd trained you better than that."

All the air left her, the words something he'd tell her as a teenager. "You're overreacting. And using this as an excuse to hide something."

"Even if I was hiding something, you're in way over your

head." He turned his back on her, stalking down the hall. "I'll take care of the Jorge situation."

Mia stared at the empty passage. Suddenly dead quiet.

"He's protecting you." Rani's quiet voice broke the silence behind her.

"I don't need protection, I need honesty. First, my mom mysteriously disappears last fall on yet another mission in the wild, and now this." She wheeled the errant chair back to its place at the table.

"Both of them love you."

"Let's talk about that poison, and then I need to get out to the gate and talk to Cooper before my father does." Mia followed Rani back to her desk where molecular breakdowns spun circles on one of the computer screens. A small stylized ouroboros sculpture sat on one side of the monitor and framed pictures of her family sat on the other. Mia had always figured it was that loss more than anything keeping Rani from leaving the MUC. A lot of grief lived in these walls, soaked into the cement like a sickly disease. And Rani surrounded herself with it like a cloak.

The old woman eyed Mia. "You want me exiled to one of the settlements?"

"Come on, Rani, he'll never find out."

"Your father is pathological in his need to know everything happening in this Territory." She tapped something on her computer then offered a half-smile. "But I did a bug sweep this morning and we're all clear. For now."

"Thank you." She kissed the other woman on the cheek. "For everything."

"Your father will kill both of us if he finds out what I'm about to tell you, kid. I have it narrowed down to three possible poisons. None of them are any good."

"When is poison ever good?" Mia said.

"Well, what makes these so bad is both were synthetic compounds used in two different wars before the Collapse. They're almost impossible to just stumble upon these days."

Rani pulled up a screen on the computer. "The first possibility is called *Flor del Diablo* and was used in the Cartel Wars in Old Mexico. The second was a bio-engineered nightmare called *Deuce*. It was used during the beginning of the Second Wave by the Western Coalition to take out specific populations—mostly anybody with Russian or Chinese DNA. The last is the worst, *Oblivion's Curse* or *necrotizing putreflorum*. It's liquifies the organs within twenty-four hours. Eastern Bloc used it to control its subjects. There's a counter agent, if given daily, that can neutralize the effects. Eighty percent of the time, Shield can fight it. All three can fry the vessels and turn the blood to sludge. I'm still running tests on those glass pieces, but I am sure he was poisoned. I should know which one soon."

"You said they're *almost* impossible to find these days?"

"Samples were kept in some places, including here. Also in our sister facility in Virginia." Rani shifted in her chair. "And in Montana."

Where Sarah reigned.

CHAPTER 7
COOPER

Thursday, September 8, 2072
11:36 P.M.

ilver stars twinkled in the night sky, the Milky Way a cold, distant beauty. The contrast between the sweltering temperatures of the day and the chilly air of evening sent a shiver down Cooper's spine. He donned a long-sleeve shirt and built a small fire in the stone ring. A luxury not often enjoyed out in feral places, its light and smoke beacons in the night.

He had snared a small rabbit earlier. Along with the sealed rations the Basin territory gave him, portions wouldn't be a problem tonight. There had been some nights when he had gone hungry.

Cooper strung the skinned and gutted creature across the small fire and propped himself up on his backpack to wait for it to cook. Kiva dozed in the campfire's light, keeping as close to the cooking meat as possible. The fire emitted enough glow he could work on a Sudoku puzzle book he'd scavenged on the journey west, his enhanced vision helping.

The ghosts of the old house couldn't fault him for stealing

one yellowing book, could they? His daughter would have told him not to worry, that their were no ghosts. Claire was well-grounded—a minor miracle for a ten-year old. The settlement where he'd found her hadn't been secure. Hadn't been secure at all. But, was the situation he'd gotten them in now any better?

He leaned over to turn the rabbit on the spit when the clang of a door from the wall caught his attention. Kiva's head popped up. Who would it be?

Mia materialized on the other side of the fire, face grim in the dim light and a flannel shirt buttoned up to her neck. Kiva's tail gave a couple of thumps, then returned to her doze. He eyed his dog.

Mia examined the beast roasting on the fire."Nice rabbit. No third eye? No extra appendages?"

He raised his eyebrows, "I tend to not cook the irradiated ones, so no."

"Then stay away from the Western side of the Territory."

"Duly noted."

Juice sizzled onto the campfire from the spit.

"Doesn't campfire etiquette dictate you offer some?" Mia's lips tipped up in a half-smile.

"You threatened to shoot me. I think I'll keep my rabbit." His lips twitched, and he tried hard not to grin at the look she threw him. Dang, this woman was trouble. And for some reason, the thought amused the hell out of him.

"I only would have shot you in the leg. Maybe a toe."

Their eyes locked. A little shock of awareness ran through Cooper. *Well, I'll be damned.* It had been a long time since that particular feeling had reared its head.

"I guess that makes it better. You want some?" He held her gaze.

She grimaced and shook her head, breaking the moment. "No, I'll leave you to your rabbit."

"Wary about being poisoned?"

"Maybe. What else do you know about it?" She directed all

her intense focus on him. Tension lines creased her brow and fanned out around her lips. She held her left arm against her stomach as if it pained her.

"What makes you think I know more than what I've told you? I just offered my knowledge of such things. That's all. Thought it would benefit my negotiation." He sat back against the old car parked forever next to the yurt and propped his arms on top of a bended knee, feigning relaxation. Something had rattled this woman's cage. Something beyond Jerome's possible poisoning.

Mia took a seat on the ground across the fire from him and laid her rifle within reach. Her pistol was holstered in a well-worn gun-belt. He scanned her for a knife but didn't see one. There were also no other bulges indicating extra weapons. After what Talia had said, he wondered where Mia concealed her back-ups. It might be interesting to find out. Like a treasure hunt.

"Call it a gut-feeling. Very few strangers I know would have even noticed Jerome's symptoms let alone told others. Very few strangers would offer assistance for nothing. I think you're not who you seem." She tilted her head slightly to the side, and he shifted under her direct scrutiny.

She was an attractive woman, not traditionally pretty, but well put together. And those eyes. So like her father's it was eerie. He remembered them from their childhood. Not that the two of them played much together, their six year age gap just wide enough for them to be on different tracks. But he'd seen her around a few times. Those memories stirred and he all of a sudden craved strawberries—something he knew she liked as a child. Huh. Had to be careful that direction. Dredging up old memories.

Added to the fact he'd always been attracted to women in charge, he had to be careful. He would be well-served not to underestimate Mia. Any daughter of Daniel Burgess and Eva

Zapada wouldn't be easy to fool—or easy to win over. Charm offensive or not.

"That's a theory. It could be I'm just a nice guy wanting to earn points toward a good trade," he said it as disarmingly as possible, adding in a grin for effect.

She snorted. "Something tells me no. You're too watchful. Too quick on your feet. I could still just have you shot you know. Who do you work for? Cordova? Hensley? Zapada?"

He blinked at the names of the two warlords and Sarah. Hensley ruled the food trade in the southern part of the Midwest, and the other did the same on the western coast in what used to be Eastern Bloc-ruled territory.

"Now where would an isolated territory hear names like those?"

She paused before answering.

"The first two sent people over the last couple of years. We turned them away. Politely." She said it without a trace of irony. "The other, well, we've had a few skirmishes with her."

More forthcoming than he thought, but still not saying a word."Since you're all still alive and well, I take it they didn't come back."

"We told them all we don't negotiate with domestic terrorists, and if they came back, they'd regret it."

"And they believed you?"

"Oh, they believed us." Mia adjusted herself on the hard ground but didn't elaborate. All his instincts told him it would be a damn good story. And insightful. He'd been away a long time.

"So then why ask me if I came from their territories? I told you, I'm from a small town in Canada. I just need a water pump." he lied.

"You never know how stupid people can be when they've been slighted." She picked up a twig and threw it in the fire. Her left arm remained rigid and stiff in her lap.

"Well, I've met a lot of stupid people." If she only knew how stupid. Like him getting mixed up with her psychotic aunt. Now, that was stupid on a whole other scale. A stupid that got Claire in trouble. Cooper still didn't know where Sarah had acquired the old bioagents she was using to control the families under her thumb.

He turned the stick holding the rabbit to roast the topside. The savory smell of roasting meat made his mouth water. It had been a while since he'd had fresh meat. Mia eyed it. A faint growl emitted from the vicinity of her stomach.

"Are you sure you don't want any? I guarantee no poison. If I kill somebody, it'll be face to face, no subterfuge."

"Is it bad that I believe you? That I'd trust a stranger with my food more than some of my own people right now?" She threw more twigs in the fire. She hid it well, but fury simmered right under the surface.

Her choice of words intrigued him. *I trust a stranger more than my own people.* Probably not something she should admit to a stranger. What was going on? It took a lot more for that to happen than just one murder of an outsider.

Spidey-senses tingling, he asked, "So, you think one of your own poisoned Jerome?"

Mia's eyes met his, and her lips pinched together. "Who else would have access to the places where the murder occurred?"

"Your wall is huge, but not impenetrable."

"Yes, but it's also well guarded."

Cooper turned the meat one last time then checked it with a fork. Juice dripped off the carcass, clear and greasy. "The only reasons I can think of to kill somebody these days are for power, food and water, or revenge. You figure out which one applies here, and you've narrowed the suspect pool."

"Those are the only options, huh?" She let out a deep breath and rubbed the bridge of her nose. Daniel used to do that quite frequently.

"What other possible motivation is there?" He pulled out one of the tin plates from his pack and handed her some of the cooked rabbit. She took the plate, eyed the meat for a few seconds, then gave in and started picking it apart with her right hand.

He tossed part of his portion to Kiva. Unlike most dogs, she was dainty with her food. She picked it off the bones piece by piece.

"I don't know. Maybe because they find pleasure in killing?" She took another bite, watching Kiva absently.

"That's a little macabre." He'd shot his share of cannibals in the last few years but took no pleasure in it. Their faces still haunted him. Not that he'd ever tell anybody that. Tough guy image and all.

They munched in silence for long minutes, each caught up in their own contemplations.

Mia broke the silence first. "Tell me about your trip here with Jerome and Jorge. Anything unusual? You meet up with anybody on the road?" She rubbed oily fingers on her jeans and set the plate aside. Her focus again squarely on him.

Besides the scavvies at his old family farm? "What would that have to do with the murder? You already believe it's somebody from your territory."

He finished his own food and placed his plate by his pack to clean later.

"Just covering my bases," she said.

"It was an uneventful trip. I met Jerome and Jorge a day from their settlement. Offered to ride along as a guard for rations. Hasn't been too many raiders on the roads these days this close to the Territory, but they still pop up every now and then." Cooper gestured for her to hand him her plate. The odd domesticity of it gave him pause. A couple eating around a campfire with their dog. He shook himself, disturbed by his own thoughts. "We didn't run into anyone. They mostly talked about their settlement. Nothing out of the ordinary."

He stacked her plate with his.

Mia let out a long sigh. "That's what I thought." She twisted another twig in her hand. He wouldn't have pegged her for a fidgeter.

He let the silence encompass them, once again. The crackle of the fire and night sounds of sprinklers and crickets crept in. He added another log and waited. After years of mapping out other people's secrets, he knew when to be patient.

"There were three possibile targets for that poison." Mia started, without looking up. "One, the targets were Jerome or Jorge—or both—and somebody wants to rile up the settlements. Two, I was the target. Nobody knew I'd be there until I walked in but it is possible. Three, the head of the food brokerage office who was supposed to be there. He didn't show up to the Brokerage House this morning, and I had to step in."

She turned the twig over and over in her hands.

Cooper leaned forward. "Why are you sharing this with me?"

She avoided the question. "Did you have anything to do with the poisoning?"

"I already told you, I'm not that subtle. I don't even shoot people in the back if I can help it. You still didn't answer my question. Why the hell are you telling me all this?"

"Let me tell you what I see when I look at you." She clasped her hands together in front of her, not a fidget in sight. "I see a man who practically oozes 'I'm a badass, and I know things you don't.' You knew my name when I'm pretty damn sure nobody ever told it to you. You helped a dying man, not out of compassion, but because you wanted access to our Territory. I see somebody's minion. Not Cordova or Hensley but somebody else. Maybe Montana? I don't know. I don't get cold-blooded killer vibes off of you. This I can work with. I'm relatively certain of your motivation, and I'm ninety-seven percent sure it's not poisoning people in my Territory. I want your help with the murder investigation. I need my own minion who doesn't live within Territory borders. You understand?"

"You think I'm a minion? Really?" Damn it. Did he really not get her name from somebody? He thought back to the afternoon and realized, no, he really hadn't gotten her name from anybody. He'd taken one look at her and just knew who she was. Damn rookie mistake.

"Oh yeah, Mr. Cooper, definitely a minion." She nodded her head. "If you can't help, I could always ask Jorge. He wanted to help find his grandfather's killer. I doubt he'd be very effective, untrained as he is, but at least he's motivated and not unintelligent."

Cooper shook his head at the thought of the skinny young man doing much of anything helpful in a murder investigation. Jorge needed people to lead and chickens to count. "I get one item of my own choosing. No evasion. No questions."

"Why would I do that when I could just send you on your way? And anyway, you already offered to help."

"Yes, I did, didn't I?" He'd have to be on his toes if he was going to work with her. "Like I said, I want one item of my choice from the Territory."

"Is that a yes?"

She met his eyes, and the damn zing of awareness strummed between them.

"How's this going to work?"

For the first time since he glimpsed her rushing out of the brokerage office that afternoon, she smiled a tired smile. "I'll let you know in the morning."

He returned her smile. "Right. Does this mean I get a room?"

"I may need some backup, but I'm not inviting the wolf all the way into the henhouse. I'll see you tomorrow." She rubbed her shoulder.

"Partnerships are built on trust, Mia," he responded.

"I trust you didn't have anything to do with killing Jerome, Cooper. That's as much as I got for you tonight."

"Fair enough. Tell me what happened to your arm, partner, and I'll let it go."

She had a great poker face, but pain flickered across her beautiful hazel-gray eyes. "Apparently, the past is catching up to us."

He blinked in confusion. "The past? Is it something I need to know if I'm going to help you?"

"Probably, but it can wait till the morning. I *need* it to wait until the morning." She dragged herself to her feet.

He stood up and Kiva did too. "Are you sure you don't want me to come with you tonight?" His tone was dead serious now.

Mia closed her eyes, and she swayed a bit. Cooper was about to ask her again when she responded. "I can't."

"Well, you know where we are if you need us." His hand rested on Kiva's head.

"I can't believe I'm going to say this, but thank you." She reached down with her good arm and picked up the rifle. *Don't let your rifle out of your hand in enemy territory.* He remembered that lesson well. He bet it was the first time in a long time she'd let her training slip. Either that or she didn't think he was an enemy.

Guilt stabbed him in the gut and he ignored it.

"So, does this mean I'm not going to get shot by that rifle in the tower," he said to her back as she started walking towards the gate.

"See you bright and early, Mr. Cooper." Mia didn't turn around, just waved her unhurt arm in the air.

His grin turned to a frown "Well, Kiva, I think that's the most intriguing thing to cross my path in a very long time."

She eyed him, then went back to chewing on her rabbit bones.

This was getting all sorts of complicated.

The gate clanged shut in the distance. He was left with the clear night sky, the scent of dry sage and smoke, and the disturbing thought he'd just met his match.

CHAPTER 8

COOPER

Friday, September 9, 2072
3:32 A.M.

Cooper jerked awake at the now familiar clang of the door by the gate banging shut. He reoriented in the dark, the light from his campfire now nothing but coals.

He lifted himself from the cot, the door to the yurt open. Kiva lay just below his cot. A small light bobbed and weaved its way towards him. Mia wasn't supposed to come until later in the morning. He loosened the pistol in his gun-belt and stood in the shadows to wait for the next visitor.

The dog growled low in her throat. No happy tail thumps with this one.

Two men materialized on the other side of the stone ring and he stilled as he recognized both of them; one tall with salt and pepper hair, the other shorter with black hair in wild disarray. Jorge.

"Mr. Cooper, I presume?" Daniel Burgess said in a cool calm monotone.

At the sound of the man's voice, the past came crashing in

around Cooper like debris following the destruction of a tornado.

###

May 2053

Daniel ran his finger along a small highway on the map. It had taken Cooper and the rest of the team over a week to get this far on the side-by-side ATVs. At least they hadn't had to walk, the solar adaptations Tamara had jerry-rigged worked well.

"If we travel along this route, we avoid the main interstate. The side-by-sides will be able to get around any abandoned vehicles." Daniel folded the map up and handed it to Jack. "Jack, you got the lead. Amrit, you ride drag, watch for anybody or anything following. I'm going to take Killian and Layla on a little scouting trip to the University tonight after we set camp. Don't spread out more than a half mile. Got it?"

The two men nodded and gathered their people. Killian—though he preferred his last name these days—tried to forget the horrors of the last settlement outside Couer d'Alene. Twenty dead bodies—all recent. Body parts torn apart and gnawed on, strewn in an ugly warning of what barbarism humans were capable of.

The few settlements through Eastern Montana had been wary but not inhospitable. All were armed to the teeth behind razor wire and makeshift walls. Then the Basin group had turned southeast on old I-90, the freeway cluttered and already starting to crack. The closer to Butte they came, the more they saw the kind of devastation they had found in Idaho. Daniel skirted Missoula, like they had Spokane, both cities rife with decayed corpses. Bands of scavengers patrolled the area, predatory humans that shot first and never asked questions. Shielded or not, Daniel and Jack didn't want to tangle with such folks—most having turned feral.

Jack stuffed the map inside his coat and zipped it. The late fall air had a nip to it this early in the morning. "You heard the boss. We're going to stop about five miles out of Butte. If that refugee outside Helena is correct, then that's where we'll find the assholes who are slaughtering people, so stay alert. Remember this is recon and equipment retrieval, not engagement—unless we absolutely have to. The recovery crew goes to MTU to get the mining and science equipment and the rest of us are identifying the threat level. Saddle up."

That night, they camped in an old dairy farm. The brush had grown wild in the eight years since the last wave of famine had swept over the world in the Collapse. The ever-present drought had dried up the smaller waterways while bombings and pre-Collapse politics rerouted rivers or shifted them underground.

"Killian, Layla, we're moving." Daniel threw a rifle and a pair of the glass night vision goggles to Cooper. Layla, one of the teens who'd been with their unit for two years, shouldered her rifle strap and secured her own goggles. She was tough, smart, and cute—a tall, athletic brunette a year older than him, but Daniel had a strict code about any of his militia members fraternizing. He wouldn't deny them their teenage libidos—hell, at sixteen, he was horny all the time—but no fooling around with each other. Apparently, it blurred the lines.

Until Daniel, Cooper, and Layla returned, the rest of their scavenging team would hunker down and rest. They had covered their small vehicles with brush but left the panels on the top exposed to pick up the next day's sun.

Three sentries stood guard around their camp. The rest of the group lounged against trees and ate rations. They had scavenged houses along the way and would have to again soon for their return trip. Jack forbade any fires this close to their target. He didn't want any stray scouts to locate their position.

Cooper could feel both Daniel and Layla in front of him, his Seeking powers at work. He liked the name; it reminded him of the comic books he'd found on their last scavenging trip. They were his superhero powers bestowed upon him by the power of Shield. He chuckled to himself at the description. God, he could be such an idiot.

The three of them ghosted through the brush, leaves slapping against their clothes with a soft whap, whap. *On the other side of the* bushes, the ground and brush dried out, crisp and crunchy as they got farther away from the pond.

The three of them skirted the patches of brush in a classic search pattern, spread out but in line. Cooper opened his senses and got a blast of information. He felt the other two's presence, their faint heartbeats added to the mix. Insect sounds intensified, and a distant hum as if many voices in one place. He thinned out the extra-sensory stuff. Control of it was vital or it would take over all other thoughts. As far as he could tell, his superpowers were even more superpowery than the other members of their militia, even the adults. He kept it to himself. Well, except for Eva and Daniel during one of his frequent check-ups.

Layla's presence became erratic. Cooper rushed to where the girl was at, Daniel's spark following.

The girl was kicking some guy's ass. She had him by the throat, Shield giving her strength. He reopened his senses. No other heartbeats.

Cooper and Daniel circled the two fighters in case Layla needed help but let her take the fight for herself.

"Left hand," Cooper murmured. She must have heard him because she kicked out the guy's knee, grabbing the knife from his left hand as he fell with a grunt to the ground. She plunged it into his throat.

"Nicely done. Next time, you might not have Killian for the assist, though. Never stop at the throat before you gain access to the limbs."

Her eye twitched, but she nodded. "Yes, sir."

They made it to the west edge of the Bert Mooney airport in the south part of Butte without further incident. Razor wire surrounded the compound. What they needed was up at the Museum of Mines and the mining tech research department at the Montana Technical University. Cooper had no clue what Daniel wanted there, but it wasn't his business to know. His job was to guard the scavenging groups. No questions.

He and the other two dropped to the ground and army-crawled through the skeletal remains of evergreen trees.

Car-sized piles of rocks and clothing littered the old tarmac.

Daniel and Layla stopped beside him. The other man's mouth thinned to a fine line. He put the scope to his eye and scanned the *compound beyond the fence. He cursed under his breath, tapped their shoulders, and they all retreated. What the hell had he seen?*

"What was it, sir? Are they mining something?" Cooper whispered it even though he couldn't hear any other heartbeats but theirs.

"Mining?" Daniel frowned.

"Yeah, the rocks and stuff on the tarmac?" Was the man blind?

Daniel shook his head, brows furrowed, and the tick in his jaw even more pronounced than usual. "Those were bones, Killian. Human bones."

#

"We'll place lookouts here and here." Daniel pointed to the home-made map. They'd sent in pairs to scout the perimeter of the Butte settlement over the course of four hours. Soon, the settlement would miss their sentry, and they couldn't afford to have them forewarned. Nobody occupied the university. Who knew if the research facility beneath the main quad was still intact after a decade. They'd soon find out.

"Are we going to engage the settlement?" Cooper stood across from Daniel. The other scouts had reported women and children being brought in and out of several buildings in the center of town. Tobias had murmured something about it probably being a brothel. Cooper's stomach churned. What were they doing to those poor people? Maybe they were being used as livestock as well.

"Even with Shield, I wouldn't want to test our chances against so many. We need to get in quick, grab the equipment we need, and get out."

"But there's innocent people in there." Cooper took a step forward.

"The young man's correct, Daniel. We should try to save some of those people." Amrit strapped on his gun belt, Layla at his side.

"And just how are we supposed to transport them? Get out of here without being followed? We don't have enough firepower or people. I sympathize with their plight, I really do, but my answer is no. Our

mission is more important." He turned on his heel and slung a rifle over his shoulder. "Now, get the entry teams ready."

They waited until nightfall to initiate their plan, Daniel's statement like a boulder in Cooper's stomach.

Montana Technological University had a compact campus compared to other universities of the past. Its backdrop of wild, rocky peaks and craggy valleys was a direct contrast to the order of learning and high-concept engineering that had taken place there. The focus of Jack and Daniel's group was the Science and Engineering Building—or rather, what was housed underneath.

Jack signaled to Cooper, but he'd already cleared the right of the SE building. They soft-stepped to the sub-basement door, scanning the area under a moonless night.

New concrete bricks and wood planks bordered the existing door, a half-finished reinforcement of some kind.

Cooper popped the hinges, and they entered. A dim light shone along the narrow hallway lined with piles of dirt and man-sized holes in the foundation.

They crept down the passage, slower now. Jack glanced around the corner of the L-shaped hallway. One guard leaned against the wall that opened into a larger room, her back to them. Jack caught Cooper's eye and signaled.

Cooper double-tapped the guard with a silenced pistol, and they halted outside the room. It appeared to be some kind of storage. Wooden boxes lined the walls and were stacked in the middle of the room. A single bulb dangled from the ceiling; the rest of the lights remained unlit.

"Generator?" Cooper mouthed to Jack.

The man shrugged.

Another lone guard stood outside a door on the other side of the room, and Jack dispatched him with quick efficiency.

Cooper opened one of the boxes. His eyes widened.

Jack joined him.

"Holy crap," he said under his breath.

The entire box held automatic weapons. The next was a washer-sized metal case. He opened it. The padded storage held rows of grenades. He glanced at the rest of the boxes in the room. It was a damn armory. Why hadn't it been better guarded? Were they so secure in their dominance around here that the leaders didn't think they needed more than a few guards? Idiots.

Jack tapped his earbud and murmured, "Daniel, there's an armory down here."

Cursing followed the statement. "We'll blow it. Don't have enough people to carry anything else. Put it on a timer."

Jack took a charge out of his pack and placed it on a crate in the center of the room.

What the hell?

Cooper placed his mouth near the other man's ear. "Non-combatants?"

Jack showed him the wireless detonator. They wouldn't put a timer on this one.

The next room was clear, and a short staircase marched its way up to the other levels. A noise came from above. A long, painful wailing.

He and Jack hit the stairs at a controlled jog.

When they entered the main floor of the SE building, they hunkered down.

A tall woman, her reddish-black hair tied back in a tight braid and bandana wrapped around her forehead, held Layla by the throat. A rifle crossed the red-head's back, and a pistol was holstered at her side. Daniel and another one of their people, Ron, pointed their pistols at the duo, the rest of their team scattered behind them, guns also drawn.

Around twenty people huddled next to a broken display case in the corner across from them. A ripped and tattered Western Coalition flag hung behind them on the wall featuring its ouroboros with a red streak across its neck. All were unarmed and malnourished, haunted, with hopeless looks shadowing their eyes. Two guards bookended the group, their focus solely on Daniel.

Where was Amrit?

"You made a mistake coming here, Doc. Should've stayed in your own territory. This one's ours now."

Jack caught Cooper's eye and signaled for him to move around the other side of the foyer, not quite to the group of people but near enough to take the guards out if need be. He needed to save Layla. She had been his best-friend and partner through a lot of scavenging trips.

"What you're doing to these people is atrocious, Sarah. You need to come back, let us help you."

"What you did to us down in that hellhole at the MUC was atrocious." She squeezed Layla's neck tighter. The girl's face turned purple. "Tell me, Doc, have you warned people about the possible side effects of your little experiment before injecting them, or are you still betting on my sister to save your ass?"

"You left of your own volition; now let go of the girl, and we'll be on our way."

Why didn't he just take the woman out? Save Layla and the rest of them?

"Do you feel it yet? The power, the anger, the blissful lack of emotion?"

Daniel's eyes narrowed. "So that gives you an excuse to use people? To create monsters?"

Concrete bricks had been placed around the edges of the glass door entrance. Sandbags, parts from various unidentifiable machines, and other paraphernalia had been piled along both sides of the floor-to-ceiling windows. A staircase to the next floor was blocked off but the balcony was reinforced. Multiple balcony walkways lined the walls up several floors. He couldn't see how far. The entire wide-open space left him twitchy and unsettled. More people could be above them with guns. Daniel stood just out of the line of sight from above, but one misstep could put him in the line of fire.

Cooper hunched behind a broken display case and maneuvered himself, so he had a clear line of sight to the woman. He knew he could take her.

A slight movement from the basement door on the other side of the staircase caught his eye. Amrit eased around it, invisible to the woman and two guards. His army pack, empty when they'd arrived, now bulged, a piece of parachute chord wrapped through the buckles keeping it closed. Daniel's chat session now made sense. He and Ron were a distraction.

Jack signaled to Cooper. He nodded, and in tandem, the two of them moved from behind their cover and double-tapped the two guards. Screams echoed throughout the building. The group backed away from the approaching men, too weak to do much else.

Jack pointed his pistol at the redhead's back. "Drop her, and I won't shoot you in the head."

"Now, you sound like the Doc." She snapped Layla's neck, putting two bullets into her head for good measure.

Cooper screamed, shooting at the woman with more anger than he ever thought possible. She took two in the chest and leaped off the platform. Horror blossomed inside him. She was Shielded.

The movement from above increased. More people.

Jack shot the red-head, the side of her skull exploding in a spray of red. She crumpled to the floor.

Daniel froze, mouth pressed into a narrow line, his eyes riveted to the woman's body. "That was unnecessary."

"Not from my point of view. She has caused us too many issues, I don't care what Eva says. Time to go before our visitors from above make their way down here." Jack frowned at Layla's body, throwing her pack to Cooper.

"You're not in charge here, Jack." Anger radiated from his every pore and Daniel shoved his face in front of Jack's.

Cooper's eyes widened, his heart hammering against his ribcage. This wasn't happening. "You guys, we need to get Layla's body and get out of here. Shield could still fix her."

"Leave her. She's gone." Daniel's harsh words cut Cooper to pieces.

"She might not be dead," he pleaded.

"Even the Shielded rarely survive a headshot." Jack put a hand on Cooper's shoulder.

More shots pinged off the metal railing along the staircase, the sound of footsteps on the stairs.

Cooper fired his gun upwards. Amrit broke a large casement window, and the rest of the team filtered the civilians out into the night.

Daniel's face hardened into a mask. He gave Sarah and Layla's bodies one more look before he leaped over the shards of glass.

They didn't stop until the tree line along the edge of town. A crumbling overpass provided cover. The night stars shone on the shadowed figures of their team.

The bedraggled crowd they'd pulled from the building huddled together, some so young they looked no older than ten or eleven. Cooper stood guard, scanning the night for anybody approaching the group.

"What's your name?" Daniel's voice rasped. He'd zeroed in on one of the younger people standing in front who appeared more alert than the rest.

"R-Rose."

"Rose, you need to get these people out of here. There's a hole in the fence that way. Leave if you wish, but we're blowing this entire campus to hell. You understand?" Daniel didn't break eye contact with her. "The basement entrance covered, Jack?"

"Affirmative," Jack answered.

Rose spoke a little louder. "There's more people in the upstairs with a couple guards. Are you going back to get them, too? Are we coming with you?"

A hard knot formed in Cooper's gut. Extra people didn't play into Daniel's plan.

Daniel hesitated. "Find the hole in the fence. Move about a mile outside the perimeter. We'll try to find you."

Rose grabbed the hand of one of the youngest kids, wide-eyed and pale, his clothes hanging off of him in dirty folds. Others shivered, no coats or boots in sight. The rest leaned on each other for support, and they limped toward the hole in the fence.

"We're going to have to find a different route if we're going to take those people with us, Daniel. They're not all going to be able to fit on the ATVs, and the people here will follow us if we go north." Jack paused by the rest of the group.

"They're not coming with us. I meant what I said. We're blowing as much of this place to hell as we can and then leaving. I set charges

on my way to the front of the S&E Building. They're on remote detonation."

"We can't do that!" Cooper protested. "What about the others in this building Rose was talking about? We can't just leave them."

In two strides, Daniel was in Cooper's face. "We have eighteen people left. They have at least two hundred, and lord knows what else down at that airport. This time, we had the element of surprise. As soon as they get organized, they'll be up here. We got what we came for, and now we're blowing this place to hell to cover our retreat. Is that clear?"

Cooper glared at Daniel. "Then we're no better than they are."

"I've lived with worse."

"But I won't." Cooper took off at a fast lope back towards where they'd come.

"We're not waiting," Daniel called to his retreating back. Heart racing with what he was about to do, he flipped Daniel off and kept moving.

"We can't leave the kid," he heard Jack say.

"Cooper hasn't been a kid for a long time," Daniel replied.

And fire lit the night sky in front of him as Daniel hit the detonator, stopping Cooper in his tracks.

###

Friday, September 9, 2072
3:33 A.M.

"Are you listening?" Frustration chilled Daniel Burgess's voice even more.

Jorge stood miserable beside him, a woolen blanket cloaking his shoulders, holding an electric lantern in his hand.

He deepened his voice on purpose. "What can I do for you gentlemen this late, or rather, early, in the day?"

CHAPTER 9

COOPER

Friday, September 9, 2072
3:33 A.M.

ooper's arms hung loose and ready at his sides.

Jorge plunked himself down by the fire and set the lantern to the side. He leaned to put a log on the coals and stoked it to blazing again. Cooper took a step back, farther into the shadows.

Daniel dropped a leather bag next to Jorge.

"I'll have this one's cart brought out at dawn. Do you think you can keep him alive long enough to make it back to his settlement?" He dropped a backpack alongside the other bag. "Enough food and water for two to reach Colville. And that water pump."

Cooper contemplated the food and the man who had dropped it on the ground.

"And who are you?" He wasn't going to make the same mistake twice.

"Daniel Burgess, Council Leader of the Basin Territory. But you already know that, don't you, Killian?"

Cooper cocked his head to the side and let his lips tilt up in a humorless grin. He doubted Daniel could see his reaction in the dark. Or his face. Though with the crap the old bastard had messed with back in the day, it wasn't out of the realm of possibility.

"You just got it all figured out, don't you, old man?" Amused interest colored his voice. All his senses remained on high alert.

"You spy types are all the same. I've dealt with enough of you over the years. Who are you working for these days? I know it's not those monsters in Kansas or California. I taught you better than that," Daniel held his hands folded at chest level, the common stance for those used to doing violence with guns or hands in dark alleys or tunnels.

Cooper snorted. "Spy? And it's just Cooper now. I've settled down, looking to trade. Hitched a ride with Jerome and Jorge here, and you're the largest major territory this far north."

Daniel didn't even try to hide the incredulity on his face.

"My daughter came and talked to you this evening. What did you two talk about?" The blunt directness prickled Cooper's rebellious streak.

"What a lady and man discuss in the privacy of a campfire should probably be kept between them, wouldn't you say?"

Daniel stepped closer, tension evident in every line of his body. Jorge glanced between the two of them in alarm. He scooted back to remove himself from the verbal crossfire.

Smart man.

"I don't appreciate smartasses, son. I didn't when you were a teenager, I don't now. One signal to the tower and I could have you shot where you stand. Answer the question."

Cooper chuckled. "That's what your daughter said. You're sure a violent bunch. Good thing I left when I did."

Daniel reached for his pistol. Cooper was quicker and drew his own, leveling it right at the other man's head.

"Reflexes are getting slow, Daniel."

At this point, Jorge had stumbled back from the fire and

backed himself to the yurt. The young man held a struggling, snarling Kiva back. *Thank God.* He'd hate it if she got hurt.

Cooper kept himself carefully between the tower's line of sight and Daniel's body.

"Still quick enough. I thought you were dead."

"A lot of people have tried and failed. You put some good shit in that potion of yours." He narrowed his stance and stood with the right side of his body facing Daniel. Bullets could still take him down, just not for long.

Daniel focused on Cooper with a single-mindedness that left no doubt where his daughter got it from.

"I could just kill you now. The bullet might not do it, but science will. You want to die, Killian Cooper? Is that it?"

Cooper let loose with a genuine smile. Daniel had been too focused on him to pay attention to what he took as the weaker opponent. Arrogance.

"Not anytime soon, no. Too many things to do." He grinned. Jorge pistol-whipped Daniel in the side of the head, and he dropped to the ground like a stone.

"Damn, kid, I didn't think you had it in you. Why'd you do that?" Cooper hurried towards his stuff to pack the few items he had lying around. "I hope you realize you just forfeited your horse and cart."

"Yeah, well, I couldn't stand to watch anybody else die today, and he looked like he really wanted to kill you." He folded the blanket and picked up one of the backpacks with the food and water.

A zinging shot whistled past Cooper to thud into the yurt. He shouldered his backpack and grabbed the other one full of rations. He whistled for Kiva, the dog sniffing at Daniel's unconscious body. They'd have to head south. "Time to move."

The distant gate door clanged, and he, Kiva, and Jorge started to jog.

"So, you know Daniel Burgess?" Jorge said between labored

breaths. More bullets overshot them. Whoever was in the tower needed to target practice.

"That is a long story, my friend." Cooper turned to run backward for a few steps to check for pursuit before facing forward again. "A very long story for another night. It doesn't look like they're following us yet. Best to keep this pace for a while though. You good?"

Jorge didn't answer, just kept his head down and nodded, breath labored. He just *had* to get stuck with a malnourished settlement kid. Kiva scouted ahead in the darkness, nose in the air.

Well, it could be worse. He could be back at the campsite having a shoot-out with Daniel—and this was his last clean t-shirt.

4:45 A.M.

When they stopped, Jorge collapsed into a wretched pile on the ground next to a large old-growth sagebrush.

Cooper had taken Jorge's backpack with the water thirty minutes earlier, and it had helped some. He handed the young man a bottle and some of the food from the supply.

"We head out in a half hour. Get a bit of rest. They may not follow us if they think we're leaving." Cooper placed a beat-up metal bowl of water on the ground for Kiva. She lapped it up, then dropped to the ground, panting.

Jorge coughed and then drained his bottle of water in one long pull.

"I'm so out of shape," he said. "Are we going to go all the way around to East Palouse Road, then? That adds a whole day to the trip on foot." Jorge sat there and continued to hack up a lung.

"When was the last time you ate a full two thousand calories in a day?" Cooper inquired, pulling out his own water bottle and snack.

"Two thousand? Really? I haven't seen two thousand in years. We're sitting at around seventeen hundred for most adults straight across, more for the teenagers and mothers. If you're getting two thousand, I want to go where you're going." Jorge chewed on the dried fruit strip and then alternated it with the chicken jerky.

Cooper shook his head, "Your settlement is going to need you, Jorge."

"I know, man. I wasn't being serious—mostly. A whole 'nother meal a day *would* be nice. Then maybe I wouldn't be over here half-dead after a nice jog." He finished the food he held. "So which way are we going to get me home? Not many options with no western route and now no northern one." He glared mournfully at where they had just come.

Cooper contemplated the young man. The nuclear mess left over from wars past lay between them and the Cascade Mountain range west of them. The radiation wasn't constant, but its sporadic nature was almost worse—you never knew when it spiked beyond safe levels.

To go through the old nuclear reservation would be like playing Russian roulette with an unShielded kid in tow. Their only options were directly east through canyons and old riverbeds, a tough climb to be sure, or south along the old roads, adding days to their trip.

"I made a promise to a lady I mean to keep. You can come with me, or I can take you halfway back to your settlement on the East Palouse Road and then come back. They don't want you." Cooper still had to recon the area, now more than ever after seeing Daniel again.

"Does it have to do with my grandfather's death?" Jorge stood.

"It would be better if you just went home, Jorge. I'll lend you Kiva and a gun in case you run into trouble. I don't want to have to wait on tenterhooks to see if you're going to unravel at some crucial moment."

"But you just said I could come with you." Jorge took a step towards Cooper.

"But Jerome was your grandfather. People tend to lose rational thought when it comes to family." *Isn't that the pot calling the kettle black?* Cooper let his arms hang loose at his sides. He didn't think Jorge would do anything, but you never could tell. The kid had been pretty worked up earlier.

"That is exactly why I should come with you. I have a vested interest in finding his killer!"

"Vested interest, huh? Fancy term for a settlement kid." Cooper grinned, trying to diffuse the situation. Charm offensive.

Jorge clenched his fists. "I'm not a kid. I'm twenty-four, and my grandfather made sure I had an education. I am not stupid, and I know I can help."

Cooper squinted at him. "What if we find the killer? What then? You going to fly off the handle? Try and kill the person?" Cooper said. He relaxed his stance.

Jorge tensed his shoulders even more and looked at the ground. A few long seconds dragged by. He finally looked up at Cooper.

"My grandfather kept all of us alive for years. Almost everyone in his generation had died before I was born. He sacrificed everything so our settlement could survive. He always found a way, and now he's gone." Tears welled up in his eyes. "I want to know who did this. I'll follow your lead, but I want a say in what happens to the killer."

"I'll be honest with you, Jorge. I don't have any control over that. I only told Mia Burgess I would help. I still say the best thing for you is to go home and take care of your people." Cooper watched as the young man struggled with a range of anger, grief, and pain. He didn't have a good poker face.

"I'm coming with you." The stubborn tilt to his chin brooked no argument. Motivated, Mia had said. The young man was definitely that.

Cooper heaved a sigh. Having Jorge along complicated matters but also left him with an extra set of hands. They would have to be even more careful after knocking Daniel out, but it wasn't impossible as long as Mia still wanted their help—or rather, his help.

"We'll loop around back to the gate and wait a safe distance to see if Mia comes back. I doubt she will after her father's little show, but you never know. She does seem to be able to think for herself." Cooper put his empty water bottle back in the pack. After this, they would have to conserve the rest; there weren't many places nearby to fill them. "We'll need to find a place to scale the wall if she doesn't show up."

He hoped it didn't come to that. The wall looked like a crummy thing to try and climb.

"Why are you doing this? Does it have to do with how you know Daniel?" Jorge followed Cooper's lead and put his bottle and used packaging from the dried food back in the bag. Dawn light crested the distant sagebrush-dotted hills. A world of contrasts. Beauty and death.

The kid wasn't stupid, Cooper had to give him that.

"Something like that. Now let's get moving before its full sunrise." Cooper led the way as they headed east through scraggly brush and sandy soil. They'd have to walk for a bit before they could loop back around to get a good vantage of the gate.

Cooper ignored the unfamiliar anxiety that settled in his gut at having Jorge with him. He hadn't had a partner besides Kiva in a very long time.

With any luck, Jorge wouldn't end up like his last one.

CHAPTER 10

MIA

Friday, September 9, 2072
6:03 A.M.

Mia awoke at dawn to the smell of bacon drifting through the corridors of the MUC. Rani woke up early most days—if she even slept—and cooked for Mia when she spent the night.

Three hours of sleep. Fantastic. She had tossed and turned for the majority of those hours while images of Chet's face as she shot him intermixed with Cooper's watchful gaze. Both disturbed her for vastly different reasons.

She pulled on her jeans from the day before, and made her way down the hall to the kitchen. Due to her almost agoraphobic need to stay in the MUC, Rani had food delivered on a weekly basis. Her father also made sure the older woman had other things she needed but Mia still worried.

"Good morning." Mia slid into a chair. A cup of black tea waited for her, and Rani stood at the stove, finishing the bacon. Apples from the Basin's extensive orchards were sliced in a bowl on the table in front of her. She grabbed a slice.

"Morning." Rani shuffled to her seat, her worn slippers

peeking out beneath a long bathrobe. Since visitors were limited, she sometimes didn't get dressed for days on end. Mia tried not to read too much into that. She hated to think Rani might be depressed.

"Have the results come back on the glass?" Mia grabbed a piece of bacon.

No hesitation. "It's *necrotizing putreflorum.*"

"What does that mean?"

"It means even the Shielded can become sick, though the necrotizing effects might be weakened."

"Oh. Could it be used on bullets?" Mia dropped the half-eaten bacon back on the plate.

"Yes. God, your mother was right, they should've destroyed all those old bio-agents ages ago, but your father wanted to keep them for insurance. I really need to talk to him before I say anything more, my dear."

"Rani, I'm about done with all the secrets. We have S9 riling pinning food animals to walls and leaving cryptic messages, my father is acting more domineering than usual, and my mother's sneaking around after being gone for almost a year. Now, Jerome's dead, which could get the settlements pissed at us. Something is going on, and you know what it is. Tell me or I'll just go digging around on my own. Hell, without guidance, who knows what I'll find? I've already shot Chet and talked to a stranger about Territory business. How much worse could it get?"

"Don't threaten me, child. Your parents don't want you hurt. Neither do I."

Mia gave her a withering look. "Rani? He's in as much danger as I am. So is Jack, so is everyone involved. And if we have a traitor, we need all hands-on deck."

The older woman heaved a sigh of resignation. "Fine. But I'm not telling you all of it. Your father and Jack think Eva is the traitor. She's been gone for over a year when she was supposed to return after six months, and they think she's working for the enemy. I don't, but my opinion doesn't seem to matter."

"That's ridiculous. She'd never turn against the Territory. And what enemy? Nobody's threatened the Basin Territory for years." So ridiculous it almost rang false. Her mother a traitor?

Rani wriggled in her seat, folding the edges of the bathrobe over her flanneled legs and not meeting Mia's eyes. "You really need to talk to Daniel. I shouldn't have told you what I did."

"Rani."

"Mia."

"You heard him last night. He doesn't want me anywhere near this."

Rani's chin angled up at a stubborn level and she crossed her arms. "Then maybe you should listen."

Mia rose, grabbing another slice of bacon and an apple. "Fine. I'll figure it out myself."

Mia drove around to patrol Sector One and its neighboring perimeter with Sector Nine on the way to her mother's house.

Dozens of protestors still lined the one street leading to the manufacturing district and their warehouses. Signs with the words, "Fair Food for All!" and "Food and Water are Basic Rights!" were the norm. Or, her personal favorite, "Control the Greed, not the Feed!"

Today, one sign in particular, held by a young person she'd never seen around before, read, "Stop the Infected."

She jerked the wheel, guided the side-by-side off the road, and slammed it into park before hopping out. The spot where the strange protestor had been was empty.

They were gone. She pushed through the crowd, the threats and shouts bouncing off her. Who had that person been? And who were they calling the Infected?

A pop and a hiss met her ears and she spun around.

Black smoke was roiling from her side-by-side's engine compartment.

She shoved back through the crowd. A feral excitement shone in their eyes as they shook the signs at her, their shouts intermingling to form incoherent words.

"Who did this?"

"Leave!"

"You're part of the problem!"

"We want equal decision-making in who gets what food!"

The cacophony of voices followed her all the way to her broken ATV.

The Control the Greed guy, a Sector One warehouse worker named Deion, had dropped his sign and eyed her warily. "I didn't see a thing. But, there have been strange people hanging around lately. Maybe it's one of them. That's all I'm going to say."

Mia narrowed her eyes at him. "You sure?"

He looked away, shouting his motto. Mia rolled her eyes to the sky. Why they thought her father would ever change his views on uncontrolled food and water distribution was beyond her.

She looped her hand around the frame, the heat bearable only because of the windshield, and snagged her radio from the front seat. The nearest guard station answered, and she told them what she needed. They'd bring her the spare side-by-side they kept at the North Gate in fifteen minutes.

She walked away from the protestors and her burning vehicle towards the boundary with Sector Nine. The largest—and most desolate—of the Sectors, the center of it was located ten miles away in what used to be a little blink-and-miss-it town pre-Collapse. How they'd gotten even a few dozen of Sector One's citizens involved spoke of their influence.

Mia walked across the field and gazed out into the rolling hills. A dust trail rose in the distance, traveling away from where she stood. She watched it leave with a growing trepidation.

###

The drive to her mother's house in the spare ATV left Mia with way too much time to contemplate Rani's words. And Cooper's.

His insight at the campsite had been straightforward: motivation and opportunity. Basic investigatory procedure.

On the one hand, she agreed with her mother. The older generation screwed up the world beyond recognition, and now her generation had to deal with the aftermath, a weight she felt all too often. Any weapon of mass destruction, like the bioweapons left over from before the Collapse, really needed to be destroyed so the world could truly start anew.

But, she also saw her father's viewpoint.

If there was a hostile force out there coming for them, they needed to be able to fight back with whatever they had available to protect what the Basin Territory had built.

An untenable situation.

If there was a traitor, all bets were off. No amount of philosophy and political views could justify betrayal. Not when lives were on the line.

Her mother's house was the last one this far in the northwest above, where the manufacturing and food processing facilities still operated in Sector One near the old town of Othello.

Mia turned into the driveway and parked the side-by-side near the front door. She waved at the security camera. With any luck, her being here wouldn't attract too much attention until it was too late.

She eyed the padlock and turned her back to the camera, getting out the lock-picks she kept on hand. It opened with a click after a few tries. Relief warred with a strange sense of guilt. Privacy was hard to come by in a Territory this size. Hopefully, her mother would forgive her—if she ever showed herself.

The living area smelled musty, the sparse furnishings covered with old sheets. Dead flies littered the floor, and dust coated every surface. Open curtains revealed dust motes floating in thin rays of light. Mia opened all the windows, allowing fresh air to circulate.

What would her mother need from the house? If all of it had to do with her, maybe a clue would be here in the house.

First stop, the office.

A lone metal filing cabinet was wedged between a bookshelf stuffed with ragged paperbacks and jacket-less hardbacks and a sideboard table. She opened it without much expectation and confirmed her feeling: They were all empty.

Eva's desk also proved fruitless, even the so-called secret compartment elicited nothing, not even a random piece of sentimentality. Not that her mother had much sentimentality in later years. Old pictures in a lone album her mother had saved showed a happier version of a woman surrounded by love and family, tradition, and a rich culture. A war and years spent struggling to survive had sapped that out of her, leaving a hard, pragmatic woman who rarely showed her softer side, even to her daughter. The only time affection surfaced happened at night, long after everybody was asleep, and her mother would read to her by lantern light. It was like she needed the shadows to hide this one bit of joy.

Eva would read Mia biographies of long-dead people, memoirs, science-fiction, fantasy, realistic-fiction, anything she could get her hands on, really. All those stories occupied a space in Mia's head that flowed with a warp and weft into memories of her mother. She couldn't separate the two if she tried.

Dust topped the volumes and Mia ran her fingers through it, scanning the titles and allowing a touch of nostalgia to creep in. But just a touch.

Inspiration struck.

When she was ten or eleven, Eva had read her a story where the main character stored trinkets and memorabilia in a hollowed-out book. She couldn't remember the title, but remembered wanting to have a book like that of her very own one day.

One by one, Mia yanked the books off the shelf and opened them, flicking through the pages for any notes, or for anything. Book after book until they were all stacked next to her. Nothing. What had she expected? Her mother leaving her a secret message in a book?

Shaking her head, she stood and headed for the last two rooms of the house. They also had nothing but sheet-covered furniture and insect-covered floors. A bug trapped in resin, forever waiting for Eva to return.

Giving up, she returned to the office and started putting the books back. The top shelf was almost full, and she pushed aside a copy of *Dante's Inferno* so she could stuff one more in, when her fingernail caught on something sharp. Cursing, she sucked on her finger, the small wound already healing but still hurting like a son of a bitch. What the hell had that been?

She shone a thin flashlight over the inside of the bookshelf. An inch-long, round piece of metal ran along the top side of the shelf, hidden from sight and built into the wood.

Mia pushed and pulled at it. It gave way, and something clicked next to her foot. A plank from the floor flipped up to reveal a one-foot by three-foot compartment.

Well, I'll be damned.

Mia peered over the edge.

Three cracked, leather-bound journals with bookmarks of some kind to mark pages, a pistol, a box of ammo, and a map were stuffed in the small section of the floor.

Mia retrieved all the items and sat down at the desk, the old swivel chair squeaking in protest.

The map showed a printed copy of the old United States. A dotted line from New York to San Diego bisected it horizontally. Another line traveled up from Kansas City to the MUC. Several lines with question marks ended in Chicago, Roswell, and Dallas/Ft. Worth. Other places were marked with a star, others with a skull, and the letter OB. Some of the stars seemed random, near no city or major landmark, and the skulls were in known current population centers. A large star appeared next to a military base in Virginia. What was her mother searching for?

The first journal started in 2045, right after the cave-ins. A skull and crossbones graced the cover, sketched in her mother's sure strokes. The second journal started nine years after Salvation, and the third one was a bit more recent.

Mia flipped to the last entry of the third journal.

She ran a soft finger over the faded words, written in her mother's blocky script. No swirling cursive for her mother, the scientist. Mia rubbed at the poignant ache in her chest.

From the journal of Dr. Eva Zapada:

I'm worried about Daniel. He won't ask for help, and I know he desperately needs some. My symptoms have diminished, but I'm not so sure he believes me. I'll have to leave again soon, try one more time to reach Virginia before we run out of fuel. Ft. Belvoir is key, but virtually impenetrable. We have to find a way around General Kaspar's defenses, or we're all doomed. I know I need to go while he keeps order here, but I don't want to leave him. Most people can't read the man, but even at his most taciturn, he emotes more than anybody I've ever known. It comes off of him in waves. He's rattled. The tests on the weather controls of the TMRWS machine aren't looking promising. Without fixing the one in Virginia, they are all failing. They were created to work as a system. It's taken years to fix the rest of them, and time is running out. Rani and Amrit have discovered that we need them, not only for the water, but to distribute the cure for the Aberrant and the unShielded contagion spreading fingers of enzyme throughout the settlements shutting down people's empathy—or worse. It's slow growing, but one trigger could blast it into the atmosphere. The damn stuff is wily, and we still haven't discovered the location of the last origin stone, though I have my suspicions.

General Kaspar? Her father's old commanding officer? The entire passage made the puzzle come together. She'd seen the parts but not the whole. Why wouldn't they just tell her about the risk? Hell, about the threat level. Her mother made the enzyme in Shield sound almost sentient. Conscious. It affected them all. It was her father's influence at work no doubt: control and order at any cost.

And what the hell was an origin stone?

Mia peered closer. Scratched at the bottom in unfaded pencil. *Mia, ask Rani about what we have hidden on Track Three. 020145032813*

Mia frowned. Her and her mother's birthdays strung together like a code. Not very helpful. Besides, Rani was more afraid of her father than her mother. She would keep her mouth shut.

If this was about the past, maybe she needed to go further back. She opened Journal One.

It was named *The Year of Hell*, like the title of some horror book.

May 4, 2045

So far, the bottom levels are mostly unaffected. Three hundred and fifty-one souls all huddled together in what has become our grave. How the hell did this happen? No warning, no emergency alarms beforehand, nothing. Daniel looks grimmer than usual. And scared. We all are. A team made it to the seventeenth sub-level but the train tunnel there has collapsed to the point it would take several years and heavy machinery to remove the rubble. Tamara thinks we can tunnel out of the conference room on the twentieth sub-level based on the composition of the soil and thickness of the wall and connect it up to Track Three behind the cave-in—as long as we can find where the cave-in ends. Apparently, the conference room is the oldest part of the structure, built first and not remodeled in the last update. She thinks six to nine months if we can modify enough tools. I am hopeful.

May 10, 2045

Food stores have been inventoried. We have, at most, five months of rations. Amrit has finally seen the light. I do believe I've found some-

body just as claustrophobic as me. If we can get the serum to work, even for just a few months, we'd require fewer calories to survive, less water. I know I should probably terminate the pregnancy but… I just can't. I can almost sense this bright soul shining within me even though it's just a heartbeat at this point. My upbringing at play? Or is it because it's something Daniel and I created together? We'll be able to test the next sample of the Shield serum in another week.

May 18, 2045
Success! My god, the cell reproduction is finally doing what it's supposed to. We still have to test the efficacy but Amrit sees the potential and is hopeful.

Mia flipped through pages of entries detailing the initial testing of Shield. And then a page caught her eye. Her mother had drawn the figure of a woman, a baby nestled in the womb. Below it, she wrote the name, *Mia*.

June 12, 2046
I found out I'm having a girl. Bittersweet with what we're considering. Mrs. Cooper is showing some unusual symptoms, though I'm hopeful it will pass. Usually calm, she's been irritable and slapped her son across the face today. We're monitoring. Sarah stays holed up in her room all day. What does she do in there? At least she talks to Amrit.

August 14, 2046
More anger and irritability seems to be happening among the initial test subjects. Due to Shield or from simply being buried alive? Those of us who took Shield later, after we stabilized the enzyme, don't have the same symptoms, but everybody is hyper-alert.

September 1, 2046
Taylor and Oja are missing. The remaining intact facility is not that big, we should know where they went within the day. Mia is a strong

kicker. I swear my insides are being pummeled. Should a baby only five months gestation be big enough to kick me that hard? Overachiever already.

September 2, 2046
We found them. Dead. Their tongues cut and their bodies dissected. Do we have a murderer on our hands? Have to. Is it Shield? Without it we'd die. Tunneling operations are slow but steady, Shield has helped with strength so it's going faster. Tamara Foster is a gem and the only engineer left in the facility. Without her, where would we be?

October 18, 2046
I can't. I just can't. They're monsters. All of them. Daniel and Rani did what they had to do but now the reek of death permeates the entire twenty-second floor. We're down to three hundred and one. And Sarah is calling us the monsters. Can't she see what's right in front of her face?

November 5, 2046
Our current population count is two hundred and seventy-two. What have we done?

November 30, 2046
Two hundred and five. The tunnel collapsed today, we're halfway there but this will set us back weeks. Tamara is hopeful as long as we can access the seventeenth sub-level's storage facilities and the building supplies there. There's a team working on it.

December 20, 2046
Rani found a half-eaten corpse in the storage room on the eighteenth sub-level. Fresh kill. Only a couple of days old. What is causing these symptoms?????

December 25, 2046
Christmas. It's supposed to be a day of light and joy. My only joy is the

baby within me. What am I going to do? Daniel wants an amnio, and Amrit has the skill to pull it off. He wants to make sure that the Shield injection is not affecting Mia. It would be good to know, though we have so many other things to worry about. We finally got the infected contained on the seventeenth floor, and it's strictly off-limits. Sarah has volunteered to run rations up to them every other day. At least she's getting out.

The entries in journal one ended, and she didn't have the heart to open the second.

Mia hugged the leather books to her chest and swore she could almost hear her mother's voice whispering from the pages. Nobody ever talked about that year. She didn't blame them.

She would gather Cooper and investigate Track Three. Rani wouldn't tell her, but maybe she could find out on her own.

8:34 A.M.

Mia arrived at the wall a half hour ahead of shift change. For her own sanity, she wanted to drag Talia out to the campsite with her to talk to Cooper. Backup would be nice against that easy smile.

She parked the side-by-side next to Talia's and pushed the button to access the guard tower. The old, converted grain silo had three stories. The main level held a kitchen area complete with an old refrigerator, a stove, and a sink. They lined-up right in a row, following the curve of the wall. A sign above the sink proclaimed, "Pigs Don't Live Here Anymore, Keep it Clean." Four wooden-slatted chairs encircled a rectangular oak table in the middle of the room. A staircase wound its way to the mid-level and beyond.

The second-floor housed gun safes and a card table. A reinforced window looked out at basalt cliffs broken up by a sage-brush desert. A young guard sat in a chair, sipping a drink from a thermos, and when Mia walked into the room, he stood at attention.

"I take it Talia's in the Bird's Nest?"

"Yes, ma'am." He nodded, and Mia resumed her trek to the turret.

The turret room had a three-hundred-and-sixty-degree view of the surrounding land. A railing surrounded the narrow plat-form. The roof kept the worst of the sunlight off whoever was unlucky enough to draw the Bird's Nest. Talia had her rifle in the crook of her arm and stood gazing out at the fields and houses dotting the Territory.

"Talia?"

"Mia!" The young woman startled.

"Hey, everything end up okay with Jorge, last night?"

Talia grinned. "Oh yeah. He underestimated me and I put him down with that Judo throw you showed me last week. Bam, right to the ground."

Mia quirked an eyebrow, smiling despite herself. Oh, to have the enthusiasm of a teenager. "Good. Hey, I need to speak to Mr. Cooper and I want you to accompany me."

Surprise flickered across Talia's face. "Didn't anybody tell you? Cooper and Jorge lit out of here after a scuffle with your father real early this morning. Then apparently they found Cooper and took him out to the dam. Jorge's in the wind."

Mia struggled to maintain a straight face. "Talia, don't tell anybody else you saw me today. And tell that boy—is it, Stew-art? I can never tell the twins apart—to do the same. That's an order. Not even Jack. Can I trust you to do that for me, please? At least for the rest of the day?"

Talia nodded, her eyes wide. "Can I come with you?"

Mia regarded her. "Not right now, but I may need your help later. For now, just keep Stewart quiet. Can you do that?"

Talia wrinkled her nose but nodded.

CHAPTER 11

COOPER

Friday, September 9, 2072
6: 32 A.M.

By the time the sun had started its slow crawl across the ocean-blue of the sky, Mia still hadn't shown up at the front gate. Cooper touched Jorge's shoulder and they retraced the path back to their piles of gear. He stuffed his binoculars in his pack and picked up his share of the load.

It was time to course correct.

If he knew Daniel, they wouldn't send out search parties, they would just post people at various egresses. He had few options if he wanted to get eyes on Lower Monumental Dam for Sarah, find out about a train engine they might have, and get a sample of Shield for Claire.

Jorge hadn't said more than a handful of words to him since their discussion at dawn and Cooper would give his day's rations to know what thoughts were consuming his surly companion.

He slipped a folded picture of Claire out of the side pocket of his pack. Taken with a Polaroid Insta-camera, her teeth gleamed in a huge grin, a small trout held out in front of her. She was only eight years old in the picture, taken two years ago in one of the few remaining lakes in Oklahoma. He touched her smile, his resolve hardening, and returned it to its spot.

"Who's that?" Jorge upended a canteen into his open mouth.

"Nobody you should be concerned about. Ready?"

Jorge studied him but didn't say more, just nodded his head in the affirmative.

After twenty minutes of hiking, the remnants of an old farm appeared. Nothing of the house or outbuildings remained with the exception of the concrete foundations and exposed pipes. Water seeped out of an old well-head and he and Jorge refilled their canteens. Rule one of life after the Collapse: never leave a canteen empty if you could help it.

The area didn't look well-traveled. No tracks. No other signs of traffic. Cooper would have looked for a better site for a cache, but time was not on their side. It would have to do. He buried the supplies near the foundation and stood.

"Ready?" He asked Jorge.

The kid sipped from a canteen and had almost finished another piece of jerky, exhaustion evident in every line of his body.

"Yeah, think so." He pushed himself up.

Cooper regarded him. He was tempted to leave the young man here with his dog while he scouted the eastern guard tower next to the Dam. Knowing Jorge, he would just follow and more than likely bring unwanted attention to their plan of operation.

How did he get himself into these situations?

"I need you to be sure. This isn't a game. If we get caught, I don't know what Daniel will do. Are you sure you don't want to stay here and rest? Kiva will stay back to guard you."

Jorge narrowed his eyes at Cooper and straightened his back. "I'm not backing down. Somebody in there killed my grandfather, and I'm going to find out who."

Cooper admired the guy's courage but hesitated at his ability. Bravery could only get you so far.

"Well, if you get killed, don't come back to haunt me. I did warn you. Now, we're going in slow and at a distance. Follow where I go. Do what I do. I don't want anybody to know we're looking the place over. This is the most highly guarded section of the wall. If the old topographical maps are correct, there's a hill about a half mile out. We should be able to get a good visual without attracting any attention." Cooper took his smaller backpack and put the refilled canteen in alongside the binoculars and other travel paraphernalia.

"Why are we scouting a part of the wall where we have no chance of getting in?" Jorge narrowed his eyes.

Cooper hedged the question. "We need to scout their defenses."

Jorge frowned. "I'd rather get over the wall and start looking for my grandfather's killer."

"We'll get there. This is a priority; either come or stay." Cooper didn't wait for Jorge's response. He took out his compass and headed north. The kid needed to follow his lead, or he'd be useless in the coming days.

Jorge let out a frustrated sigh and followed him. Cooper kept his back turned and contained a small smile. They hiked in silence, Kiva sniffing the ground ahead.

The hill he aimed for had once been a part of a farmer's field. Nothing remained but chunks of cracked earth and long-dead grass. The ever-present sagebrush grew in clumps with limited cover at the top.

He stowed the map back in the pack and pitched his voice low, "If you can't follow directions, I don't want you up there. No talking. No arguing. No doing whatever the hell you want. I say jump, you say how high. We clear?"

Jorge nodded his head, only a hint of stubbornness in the set of his jaw. "Yes, sir."

"See? That wasn't too hard, was it."

Cooper gave Jorge's shoulder a companionable nudge and started up the hill. The young man made more noise than Cooper as he scrambled behind but not as much as anticipated. Maybe there was hope for the kid yet.

Cooper dropped to all fours and army crawled as they breached the crest of the slope, aiming for a clump of dead sagebrush. The wall and the easternmost tower lay before him, ramparted and heavily guarded. Where the main wall had gaps and was mostly used to dissuade people from entering, this was a different beast entirely.

The dam hunkered over an almost dry riverbed, a creek-sized stream of water trickling in the bottom of what used to be the Snake River. Desert hills rolled away to the east, more of the wall and rocky basalt outcroppings to the west.

He tapped Jorge's shoulder to move out when something rustled on the other side of the hill. Kiva growled a warning.

He and Jorge froze.

Cooper gestured Jorge to move back down the hill with Kiva and eased his gun out of the holster to cover the kid's retreat. The binocular lenses had no reflective surfaces, so it couldn't have been that. A patrol?

A low crack.

Something or somebody was coming up the hill. Not like a herd of elephants, but it sure wasn't far off. Cooper eased himself to a crouch and shoved his backpack with the case well under the brush.

Another short crunch. This time, nearer.

Cooper tucked the pistol close to his body, ready to fire if needed, when a deer popped its head over the crest of the hill, a third antler shooting to the sky like a unicorn's horn. It froze when it caught a whiff of him. Cooper lowered his gun. The animal snorted and loped back down the hill into the canyon.

Damn deer.

Cooper checked Jorge's progress but couldn't see him or Kiva anymore. He took a breath and holstered his weapon. Adrenaline still coursed through his veins. He moved to grab his pack.

"I'd get down on the ground if I were you," a male voice said behind him.

Well, crap.

Cooper put his hands behind his head. The man came around. Cooper recognized him as one of the guards with Mia at the brokerage house yesterday. A long, thin scar marred his hairline, but he looked familiar.

"I'd just as soon stay where I'm at if it's all the same to you. Who knows, you might have an itchy trigger finger."

The man shook his head. "No, sir. We try to question intruders before we shoot them. We only kill the difficult ones." The man came closer and threw a set of handcuffs at him. "Two-finger that pistol and throw it over here. And put those on."

Cooper contemplated the cuffs and his options. He still had his knife in a boot sheath. *No, I might need it later.*

The man stayed just far enough back that getting the gun from him would be difficult. He could try a draw but at this point, that would just be stupid. Besides, the guard was probably Shielded. All of Territory's militia were. Or at least, they used to be.

He wanted to enter the eastern part of the Territory. This would be one way to get there—if he could get back out. He would need to *improvise, adapt, and overcome.*

At least Jorge and Kiva got away. Now, the kid just needed to not do anything stupid—like try to go over the wall or attempt a rescue. Cooper's powers of regeneration made him difficult to kill, a fact the kid was unaware of.

Cooper grabbed the butt of his pistol with two fingers and tossed it at the man's feet. He put the cuffs on and lay on his stomach. The man came and patted him down, finding his spare pistol and knife.

"Up you go. Walk down the hill toward that tower you see in the distance." Cooper pushed himself up and started walking.

"Didn't I see you yesterday?" Cooper asked.

"Uh-huh. Keep going." The man started whistling. Was that a sea shanty?

"Really?"

The man ignored him.

"Can I at least get your name?"

"Nope."

"Then what am I supposed to call you?"

"Not supposed to call me anything. Won't matter once we reach the wall." He started whistling again.

They continued on.

"Crazy weather, huh?"

"Uh-huh."

He'd have to try a different tactic. Unlike Talia, this one didn't fall for his "get 'em talkin'" strategy.

"You're pretty smart sneaking up on me like that. Not many can."

The man just whistled louder. So, ego-stroking wouldn't work either. Damn-it.

The tower loomed in front of them. It stood over twenty feet tall, enclosed at the base in high-grade steel or something equally as difficult to penetrate. The perch at the top had a 360-degree view. He squinted his eyes and craned his neck. *Was that a rail gun?* No, there were two. How the hell had they transported them here? And gotten them to the top of the wall?

A piece of black fabric fluttered down from the top of the tower and landed on the ground. His captor pushed him against the wall and leaned down to pick it up—a shroud.

"Time for lights out."

"I'm not putting that on."

"It's either this lights out." He held up the shroud. "Or this lights out." He held up the butt of his pistol. "Your choice."

Cooper had been in far worse situations. Hell, he'd created

far worse situations. Sweat dripped into eyes, and his heart raced. The shroud hung there, a simple piece of fabric. Innocuous, really. Most likely hemp.

His left eye started to twitch.

A smell like burning chlorine drifted in the air and he leaned over so he wouldn't vomit. *Get a grip. This isn't Oklahoma.* The self-talk didn't help.

He closed his eyes as black dots floated across his vision. They didn't disappear. *Damn it.*

Cooper opened his eyes as his captor moved toward him. He had said something, but Cooper missed it.

"What did you say?" The words echoed in his head, hollow. The black dots persisted.

The man raised the butt of the pistol, and Cooper's world went black.

Dim light lit the metal box of a room where Cooper sat. Only two other things adorned the cell: a single toilet in one corner and a hatch in the door. He rubbed the side of his head where blood had dried in flaky patches. His brain ached and he worried about Kiva and Jorge.

Cooper stretched his legs in front of him and straightened his back to align with the wall, stretching every kinked muscle. A row of letters and numbers next to his hand caught his attention. *The Lord is close to the brokenhearted and saves those who are crushed in spirit, Psalm 34:18.*

Cooper wasn't a religious man, but many of the settlements he'd come across still held to their faith and prayer in whatever form that took. He had felt abandoned by his faith a long time ago. Finding a Christian bible verse in a cell of the Basin Territory shouldn't have surprised him; prayer in prison made a certain kind of sense. It surprised him nobody had washed it away.

Somebody moved outside the door, clinking keys against the metal. He rose to his feet and braced against the wall. It opened, and bright light glared across the threshold. Two guards he didn't recognize came through the door. One threw a pair of handcuffs at him. He calculated distances and analyzed the two men. They both stayed just out of reach, one outside the door and one to the left of the jam. Neither of them had the green rookie feel of Talia. The duo reeked of trained killers.

Time to see what they wanted.

He ratcheted the cuffs into place. "Lead the way."

The guards remained silent, their expressions neutral. One strode in front, and the other followed him, effectively sandwiching him down a narrow hallway. Doors to what he assumed were other cells lined the passage. They each had the same hatch in the doorway, probably for food trays. The hallway looked like something from a pre-Collapse mental institution he'd seen in a movie once.

The interrogation room resembled an old legal drama with a two-way mirror on one wall and a large steel mechanic's table, a loop for his handcuffs welded on the top, bolted to the floor in the middle. Two metal chairs sat on opposite sides of the table.

Cooper grabbed a chair and scraped it across the tile floor with a *screech*. He plopped down and held his hands out arrogantly towards one of the guards. "You gonna hook me in?"

"Is that necessary?" The guard who captured him walked through the door and sat in the chair across from him.

"I could probably clear this room but then where would I go?" Cooper stretched out in the chair and crossed his ankles, lacing the cuffed hands on his stomach.

"You might have a more difficult time getting through me than you think." The man mimicked Cooper's casual pose.

Cooper grinned. "So, what brings us here today? Can't a man go on a stroll through the hills anymore?"

"We both know you weren't just taking a stroll. Where's the

kid?" The man cocked his head to the side and looked like he actually expected Cooper to answer.

"I don't know who you're talking about." He countered.

"I'm not playing word games with you. We don't need another northerner dead. Now, which direction did he go?"

"I'm not too great with cardinal directions. Always get them mixed up out here in the desert. Sorry, I can't help you."

The man glanced at the two-way mirror and Cooper smirked. Somebody watched them from behind the glass. Cooper could work with this.

"How's your boss? Jorge hit him pretty hard. He's getting a little slow in his old age."

A muscle twitched in the big man's jaw. Most people would have missed it. Cooper's smile widened.

"Mr. Cooper, you're still alive due to the fact we need Jorge in one piece and you saw him last. Don't make us rethink that." His interrogator leaned forward and placed his hands flat on the table. "Now, where did he go?"

"You should work on your interrogation skills. You just told me that I'll be expendable if you find Jorge." Cooper clucked his tongue and shook his head. "I actually thought you were better trained than that."

The larger man slammed his hands down on the metal table making the chains rattle. Cooper raised an eyebrow. Now he was getting somewhere. You agitate the enemy enough and you have a better chance of gaining the upper hand. At some point. With some enemies.

The door opened and in walked Daniel. "It's okay, Tobias."

Tobias. One of Daniel's personal guards. Now he remembered. Cooper had never worked with him directly. Shield had treated him well.

His interrogator stood and allowed Daniel to sit.

Huh, that didn't take very long at all. Cooper let out a disappointed puff of breath.

"Well, if it isn't the fearless leader himself. How's the head?" Cooper cocked an eyebrow.

"Killian, I don't have time for your crap. Where's the kid?"

Cooper looked behind his shoulder. He turned back and touched his cuffed hands to his chest. "Oh, you're talking to me?"

Daniel stalked to Cooper and grabbed him by the throat. "This may not kill you, but it will sure hurt like hell."

Cooper coughed at the increasing pressure of Daniel's hand. "Grghls—"

"What did you say?" Daniel's grip lessened.

"Go to hell." Cooper ground out, his throat raw.

Daniel upended Cooper and his chair to the floor and kneeled on his throat to keep him there. If his reaction time had slowed, his strength sure hadn't.

A thin smile tipped the edges of Daniel's lips. "You remember Trevor Kreskin?"

Icy fingers tripped their way down Cooper's spine. "The Commander of the Montana regiment."

"Think about what I did to him after what he did to all those people and reconsider your position. We won't hurt the kid. We're just sending him back home. Use that brain of yours, Killian."

A tangled knot of blood and frost punched through Cooper's memories. So many militiamen and cannibals had died, not standing a chance against Daniel's soldiers and the effects of Shield. Daniel's world operated in a cold, hard, black-and-white logic. Some of Kreskin's regiment had surrendered. Daniel didn't believe in surrender. Not with the kinds of horrors the people at Butte had inflicted. Without prisons, the quick, unyielding corporal punishments of the Wild West had regained their momentum in the years after the Collapse—for better or worse.

"Why the extreme reaction? Makes me wonder what you're hiding." Cooper relaxed his muscles and let his body go limp.

"I owe you no explanation. Where's Jorge?" He slammed Cooper's head against the concrete floor.

Stars obscured Cooper's vision. He blinked them away.

Another, younger guard came to stand by Tobias. The two men side-eyed each other. Not enough for Daniel to see but Cooper spotted the uneasy glance.

"Well, see, I wouldn't know that since your thug over there captured me before I could determine Jorge's route. Though, I wouldn't tell you, even if I did know."

"You expect me to believe that? I taught you better. Always have an escape route, always have a viable exit. If one doesn't exist, make one. Now, where is the kid."

"Daniel, let's just call a spade a spade. This isn't about the kid. This is about our history. You already have scouts out looking for Jorge. You don't need me to tell you a thing. What's it going to be? A headshot? Those can rattle the brain, even for the Shielded." Cooper taunted him. Daniel leaned into the knee on his neck.

"Tell me why you're really here, Killian."

Cooper cleared his throat, the pain subsiding, and he stared up at the untextured ceiling from his place on the floor. "The fabulous accommodations. Why else would I venture into hostile territory?"

"I don't know. Who are you working for these days?"

"Isn't that question getting old? I mean, think of another way to ask it."

"It sure will be satisfying not to feed or water you for a week. We'll see if that loosens your tongue."

"Still torturing people to get the answers you want, eh? Still a slave to the Serum? Damn, Daniel, I thought *you* were better than that."

Daniel flinched the slightest bit. Not enough for the others in the room to notice but Cooper's enhanced eyesight could pick up the slightest flare of an eyelid, or twitch of a jaw muscle. Cooper had been there in Butte. He had seen what the early version of Daniel and Eva's Serum could do to its users if left untreated—some never recovered. How Cooper had avoided that fate still eluded him.

Daniel changed his focus to Chet across the table. "If you can't get Jorge's location, lock Killian in his cell. Nothing for a week."

"Am I your pet now, Daniel?"

"You're the one who deserted, Killian. I am well within my rights." Daniel turned on his heel and walked out the door. It slammed behind him.

Tobias came and righted Cooper's chair. The blood on his face flowed again, and he almost ended up back on the floor from the head rush.

"You heard him." Tobias sat and laced fingers on the table.

"You guys are like a broken record." Cooper had no intention of letting them lock him up for a week. Time for an exit strategy.

A knock at the door, and the other guard opened it.

Mia strolled in. She ignored him and looked at Tobias. "Father needs to talk to you. Wanted you to catch up with him before he heads to the Council House."

The man nodded. "Copy that."

He strode through the door and disappeared.

Mia closed it behind her. "Hey, Adam. Mind leaving me with the prisoner for a second? It won't take long. Daniel thinks he might talk to me."

The guy shifted from foot to foot. "I was told not to let him out of my sight."

Mia nodded her head like she agreed with him. "I really am sorry about this."

She shoved a syringe into Adam's neck. The guy never stood a chance. He gave her a startled gurgle and collapsed to the floor. Mia grabbed him by the legs and dragged him out of the way, then opened the door. Somebody else, a young woman, peeked in. Mia's arm snaked out with another needle and dosed her. She dragged the other woman into the room and laid her next to the guard.

"Well, hello," Cooper told the woman in front of him. She looked haggard. Dark circles rimmed her eyes, and tension crackled and snapped along her entire body. Her perfect bun had fallen from grace, and strands streamed around her face. Stormy hazel eyes met his.

"Cooper, you better be useful."

Cooper held up his cuffed hands. "We will certainly find out, won't we?"

CHAPTER 12

COOPER

Friday, September 9, 2072
10:43 A.M.

ia unlocked one of Cooper's cuffs and dangled the key in front of him. He snatched it from her hand before she could touch his bare skin, and uncuffed the other wrist.

"Took you long enough." The words cut through the stillness from the unconscious guards and the cold fluorescent lights. Mia raised an eyebrow at him and turned back to check the halls. The disabled cameras dangled on frayed wires. She threw him his pack, gun, and knife. He grabbed them out of the air with cat-like reflexes, too quick for any normal human. Mia didn't react to him showing off.

"I didn't know you were expecting me." She moved out the door and took a left. "Come here."

Cooper hesitated—not an action he had much familiarity with.

"Why?"

Mia's lips thinned in annoyance. "Cooper or Killian or whatever the hell your name is, nobody knows I just took out these two. They're going to regain consciousness soon. The fastest way out of here is through the main part of the Dam and down to the steam tunnels. Between us and them is about twenty guards and who knows how many other personnel. I'm escorting you."

"It's just Cooper." He sidestepped out the door, shoving the pistol into his jeans at the small of his back. Covering the weapon with his shirt, he crossed his arms and stood in front of her. "If that would require me to put those cuffs back on, that is not happening."

She glared at him and took out a shroud from her pack.

"This is how we're getting you out of here."

Panic tugged at his insides, and he took a step back from the piece of fabric. Not again. "And that is definitely not happening."

"It's just a shroud. Your hands will be free, we won't close the cuffs all the way, and you can take it off if we run into trouble." She took a step forward.

Cooper took another stumbling step backward. This time, an evil glint entered Mia's eyes.

"Is Just Cooper afraid of a little shroud?" She waggled the fabric in front of him. He yanked it out of her hands.

"We don't have time for this." Irritation infused his voice. The PTSD hadn't kicked his ass this hard for a very long time. It was a little disconcerting, to say the least.

"No, we don't. Now put the damn things on, and let's get out of here." She moved to the door, glancing in either direction.

Come on, Coop, there has to be a better option. He tilted his head back and contemplated the ceiling. It had been patched, and drywall tape outlined an uneven, dirty white square.

"I didn't take you for the praying type."

"Huh?" Cooper blinked and focused his attention back on Mia.

She pointed to the ceiling.

He shook his head. "No. I was just searching for inspiration."

"You can always take your chances by yourself, but I don't

think you want to do that. When my father gets back and finds you gone, he's going to mobilize. Choices, Just Cooper, choices." She nodded at the cuffs and shroud. "Best options to get through this with minimal conflict. I may want your help, but it doesn't mean I want to hurt my people unnecessarily."

Cooper hung his head, and the familiar tug of panic riffled through his innards. Damn it. He could clear what, ten, maybe twelve guards before being incapacitated? Maybe more on a good day, which this most definitely was not. Serum or no serum, his body could still be damaged. Maybe not permanently, but enough to be recaptured.

"Fine. Do it." He handed both items back to Mia and donned his gloves. The panic welled, and he closed his eyes, clasping his hands behind him. Mia closed the handcuffs on his wrists, but they didn't click. He opened his eyes, and their eyes locked. That fission of awareness zinged between them. She narrowed her eyes, not giving him an inch.

"I'm at your mercy." Cooper tried to control the dizzying feeling of suffocating in dry air. So much for the tough guy act. God, he hadn't had a panic attack in years, and now two in one day? At this point, he'd be a pile of sludge by midnight.

Her lips twitched, and he took a deep breath. Down came the shroud, and his world went dark. Little pinholes of light peeked their way through like some claustrophobic night sky. He breathed. Or tried to. Pointed darts of memory crept around the edges of his mind and jabbed at his control.

"Don't speak. Don't struggle. Once we get to the tracks, we'll find a cart."

Cooper couldn't find his voice. His breath drew the fabric into his mouth when he breathed.

In and out, in and out.

"Stop that or you're going to hyperventilate." She took him by the elbow and marched him down the hall.

A door squealed open and their clicking footsteps echoed against the walls of a much bigger room.

"Hey, Mia, where you taking him?" A male voice asked from somewhere in the room.

"My father wants him out at the MUC." Mia's smooth, commanding voice must have appeased the man because they weren't detained.

They picked up the pace, clipping along across another echoing room. A low, insistent hum from somewhere nearby vibrated through the air. Nobody else stopped them, though he heard shuffling steps and clinking glass. A cafeteria? Probably not. No food smells. Maybe a lab? Mia paused, and they strode through yet another door.

"Stairs," Mia murmured. The stagnant air had warmed. "First one. We're heading down."

"I figured when you said the words 'tunnels.'" Cooper tried for glib but fell short. The damn shroud needed to come off.

Her hand on his arm tightened to just shy of painful and he grunted.

"Shh."

Round and round, they descended. Sweat popped out on his forehead and dripped down his face. Some of it soaked into the shroud, and it stuck to parts of his face. Miserable damn thing.

Two more flights of stairs, and they stopped. A swish of a panel moving, a couple of beeps, and the click of a lock opening signaled another door. The humidity inside the shroud became damn near unbearable. He and Mia stopped, and somebody nearby scuffed against the ground. The smell of heavy sweat, cooked meat, and mildew wafted through the porous material covering his head.

"Whatcha doing with the prisoner, Mia?"

Tobias.

"My dad wants him out at the MUC." No hesitation. No nerves. An ember of respect sparked deep inside Cooper, where he stashed such things.

"That's a bald-faced lie."

"Everybody lies. Isn't that what you told me, once? Now, move." Mia didn't give a thing away in her voice.

A tense silence fell. Cooper would have given his other backup weapon to see the look on Mia's face at that moment.

"Can't let you do that, Mia."

Mia let go of his arm, and he unlaced his fingers, working at loosening his hands from the cuffs. He kept the movement minimal and worked one hand free. He waited for her signal.

When was the last time you waited for anybody's *signal, Coop?* Cooper kept his inner monologue in check and flexed his fingers. The need to take control had him twitching out of his skin.

"And why is that?" Her words were mild with a thread of steel.

Cooper widened his stance.

"You should have taken him out the front door. It would have been more believable, kid. Your father would never permit a prisoner in the tunnels. Even with you as an escort." Tobias's voice came closer.

"And why would you say that? Dear ol' Dad has been doing a lot of strange things lately."

"So have you."

"I've just been investigating. That's all. It's for my mom. Wouldn't you do anything you could for your family?" Her voice had moved. She was giving herself space.

"And you trust this man over your people? Hell, I thought I was family. Do you even know *who* this is? Don't be a fool, child!"

"Who said I trust anyone? I do have a better handle on his motives than whoever used a preCollapse bioweapon to kill an old man within the Inner Territory. Or nailed a skunk and dead rabbits to the sides of the Council House and tunnel walls. *Or,* took potshots at me and Jack." Emotion had seeped into the cracks of her controlled voice. The woman was furious.

"Leave it alone, Mia. You need to let others better prepared handle all this." A hard note entered Tobias's voice.

"And what is 'this,' Toby?" No doubt about it, Mia had crossed the barrier between control and wrath.

"Give me Killian. Now."

A shuffling step and then a crash. Cooper yanked the shroud off to find Mia standing over the unconscious man.

"What did you do?"

She shrugged. "Throat kick, knee sweep. He taught me that particular move. You'd think he'd be better prepared to handle it."

"Remind me never to piss you off."

"He'll be fine. We need to get out of here, though. Where he is, my father is usually not too far behind."

They stood on a concrete platform at the outer edge of an immense tunnel. A multitude of pipes lined the walls and ceilings. Dim utility lights descended from the ceiling in even intervals, and two sets of train tracks ran down the center. Access walkways followed the tracks on either side, and Mia took off along one to a waiting mining cart, complete with welded benches and a control panel. Cooper wiped the sweat from his dripping face with the bottom of his t-shirt and followed.

"Fun." He climbed in and sat next to the controller.

"Up." She swatted at him to move.

He glowered at her. "You, on the other hand, are no fun."

"You don't even know where we're going."

"Obviously straight. Unless you have some superpowers I don't know about?" Cooper pointed down the tracks.

Mia shot him a withering glare. "You want me to put the shroud back on your head?"

He sighed and heaved himself to the other side of the cart. He'd get a better look around, anyway, if he wasn't fiddling with the controls.

"So not just straight. Where else does it go?" He crossed his arms and legs.

"I'm not telling you that. I've already broken more rules than I can count today."

"Why are you doing this? Releasing me? It can't just be to find Jerome's killer. I know your dad. He doesn't take disobedience lightly."

Mia got the cart moving, and the warm breeze stirred the stagnant air of the tunnel. "About that. How do you know him?"

She didn't recognize him. "Well, the man did just interrogate me."

She quirked an eyebrow. "Uh-huh. You're full of crap. Spill it, Killian Cooper. I remember your name but not much else at the moment."

Cooper narrowed his eyes, all joking banter dissipating with the full use of his name.

"My name is Cooper. Only Cooper and nothing else."

"My mother used to call you by your full name. I read it in one of her journals. I'm assuming you're the person she was talking about. There can't be too many people still around with that name."

Shock rattled through him. Eva had written about him in her journals? "What else did it say?"

"That she considered you a friend. She was sad that you left, though my father called you a deserter. Which one are you? Friend or traitor?"

Cooper digested her words, the cart rumbling on the tracks and the overhead lights flashing by.

Mia laced her fingers together and leaned forward, an amused edge to her voice. "I have a feeling you're not struck speechless very often."

Cooper cleared his throat. Mia had rescued him. He owed her something. Owed Eva. "They saved me, you know. They killed my parents but saved me. My family was a part of Project Shield, one of the initial test subjects before the bombs fell."

"You were five, almost six, when your parents signed you up." Her voice was soft.

"You knew? Did Eva write about that, too?" Bitterness coated the words. "Have you gotten to the part about Montana yet, and why I left?"

"No, Cooper, I haven't." She looked at him steadily, no pity in her eyes, just patience.

"It should be a hell of a read if she told it right. Talk to me afterward; we'll compare notes." If he was even here that long. Cooper looked at the bottom of the mining cart. The dented metal floor bubbled up in the middle. He stretched out in his seat, and the floor creaked. He had to change the subject, fast. "So, where are we headed?"

Mia slowed and turned the cart along a branch tunnel. "We're heading to Track Three."

Cooper jerked at the name of the tunnel. "Well, this should be interesting."

CHAPTER 13

MIA

Friday, September 9, 2072
12:01 P.M.

The emergency lights flickered in this part of the tunnel. Mia's black-leather booted toes touched the seam between new and old concrete. An imaginary border between the past and present. Her pack hung heavy on her back.

Only three people had access to Track Three through its titanium-plated door—Daniel, Eva, and Jack. Why not herself or even Rani? Mia didn't know.

"What's that symbol?" Cooper pointed to the circular symbol above the number 3, along with a series of letters naming the branch, endpoint, and midpoint.

Mia didn't even have to shine the light on it. "Ouroboros, the old symbol for the Western Coalition. It's their tunnel. It starts clear on the East Coast, and branches of it go as far south as Mexico. The Western Coalition and the US government built multiple subterranean railway lines across the old United States At least according to my mom's journals."

"You're mom's sure chatty in her journals." Cooper hopped out of the cart, anger in every stride.

She grimaced. Yesterday, the man had been calm and collected. Intense and observant.

Today, he was twitchy and unsettled.

What in the world had compelled her to break him out of prison?

"You good?"

"Just peachy." Cooper examined the keypad, running a hand along the handleless door jam. "Daniel was serious in keeping this place off-limits."

Built to withstand about anything, the wall the door was encased in had used the last of their titanium supply; the rest went to the door at the tunnel entrance to the MUC itself. It plated both sides in thick layers over concrete and rebar. Damn hard to penetrate. Which was of course the point.

"He does take security seriously."

The string of numbers in her mother's journal had been her birthday combined with Eva's. Had her father really been that sentimental? She tapped them into the keypad. The door clicked open.

Well, damn. Sentimentality for the win.

Right past the wall, two sections of track had been removed. A single caged light shone from a dangling wire. The concrete brick curvature of the newer tunnels transformed into something resembling the pictures of old subway tunnels in New York City but instead of the white subway tiles, these were dark blue surrounded by brick and concrete. Ductwork ran along the top portion of the wall for air, yet there were no irrigation pipes, only conduit for electricity.

She clicked on the flashlight.

"You think that's wise?" Cooper asked.

"There's nobody down here. My father's topside. So is Jack."

"Open your ears, Mia. Don't you hear it?"

Mia clicked off the light. Shield heightened her senses, but too much input overwhelmed her. She'd learned at a young age to tune out all the stimuli of the world if she wanted to stay sane.

It had been a long time since she'd dropped her guard all the way.

Cooper's brow furrowed, a line of dark brown barely seen in the ambient light cast by the single bulb behind them.

She closed her eyes and relaxed. Air whispered through the tunnel, the low hum of TMRWS underlaid by a rattle of pipes behind the titanium wall in the mainline. The most minute sound within half a mile filtered through her ears. Topside, she could hear farther if she tried. The mustiness of dust and mouse droppings assaulted her nose, and she held back a sneeze.

And then she heard what Cooper had. A low metallic thumping sound. Tinny, and far down the track. Her eyes flew open.

Daniel was on the surface, probably out at the MUC piecing together how somebody could have gotten ahold of an old bioagent. At least he would be until Tobias woke up, then he'd be hunting for her and Cooper. As far as she knew, Jack and the guards she'd sent out to help him were still waiting for Sector Nine to show up at his old place. So, who was down here? Her mother?

Or somebody else?

Ambient light cast Cooper in shadow, but she felt his regard.

"I remember you, you know, as a girl. Before I got shipped off to the military camp out at the dam," his voice was but a whisper, unlike the teasing tone he usually employed.

"You were one of dad's Shielded militia. Of course you would recognize me." It wasn't a question.

"Yeah. We never got to come into the Sectors too often after that. He didn't want us to lose focus on the objective, but I remember you when you were about five or six. I was twelve or so and had to come to pick something up for Daniel. You were helping pick green beans with Rani in the raised beds. You wore your hair in a braided bun around the top of your head. I wondered what would happen if I yanked it down. It looked too much like a crown. Yanking the braid of Daniel's daughter—I was very impulsive back then."

"Oh?" No other words would form on her lips. His eyes drifted behind her, lost in thought or memory. Or both.

"A couple years later, we were sent out to find Daniel and Eva's lost daughter. It was right before I left for Montana. I found you reading a book by yourself near the wall. Dark hair in a braid this time, no crown in sight. You looked so young and alone. I sat and talked to you. Apparently, some girl named Gabby had stolen your strawberries and you had punched her. You were afraid to face the music, so you ran away. With just a book and the rest of the strawberries. It took me almost an hour to talk you into returning to Eva."

Mia blinked. A faint memory of him as a blond teenager, perturbed yet kind, worked its way to the front of her mind. "I remember that. That was you?"

"Yeah. And later, right before I left—"

She finished the thought, the memories flooding back in a rush now. "I found you, sitting by yourself in the adit to West-bound-2. I was supposed to be going to special training and hated being singled out. I started walking and ended up there. You called me a pipsqueak and told me to go home, and I called you an asshole. And then you asked me if I had any strawber-ries. I didn't, but I ended up reading you the book I brought, *A Wrinkle in Time*. You told me not to stop, and I think I read to you for a good hour."

"'Nothing is hopeless; we must hope for everything.' Great quote. It was the part of the story you read from that book that finalized my decision to leave." Cooper took a step closer. "You're very different now."

"I should hope so. I'm all grown up." Her heartbeat tripped over itself. So did Cooper's. She could hear it. He hadn't laid a finger on her, and yet, she felt a tug, a pull like a magnet yanking scraps of metal from the air.

"I can see that. Happen to have any strawberries?" Cooper took off a glove and extended a hand toward her as if to shake.

Mia reached out her own hand. "Not at the moment."

When their fingertips met, a spark, like static electricity, zipped through the air between them, arcing bright and blue in the dim light.

She startled and jumped back. "What the hell was that?"

Cooper backed against the wall to the walkway, his hand clenched to his chest. She could no longer see his face. "We need to go."

Mia heaved gulps of air to calm her racing pulse. "You know, don't you, what that was?"

His shadowy form hopped onto the walkway. "Not now. We need to find the source of that noise."

Mia growled in frustration. She knew he was right. Whatever had just passed between them could wait. The distant clang of sound could not if it meant somebody else was down here.

Not saying another word, she yanked her pistol out of its holster and stalked down the track, leaving Cooper to do whatever Cooper did.

He disappeared along the walkway. Her head ached, and she could now sense his presence, strong and magnetic, a little way ahead and to her left. It felt like a tracking beacon on a handheld device, the light blinking to show location. Shield had done this.

Not now. Don't think about it now. Later. Like a mantra, she repeated the words over and over in her head. She tried to raise her guard again, but Cooper's light was too bright.

Dammit all to hell. What had he done?

She strode forward.

Daniel maintained a lab or office of some kind in the depths of the tunnel in one of the maintenance rooms. The only reason she knew this was because she'd overheard him telling Jack one day.

An unfamiliar musty smell filled the air, something between mold and cat piss. Mia wrinkled her nose. Similar to yesterday by the dead animals. Whoever had spiked those animals to the wall had disappeared back here somehow.

The clanking became clearer, like metal hammering metal, and the tunnel brightened as they neared its origin. A dozen shallow mechanic's bays that could house a single engine or train car, lined the tracks on either side, and a sidetrack branched off to her left. It reminded her of the children's books with *Thomas the Train*.

Track Three continued on straight in front of her, a makeshift wall on the right hiding something large behind it. A light shone around the edges. Several locked doors appeared before the wall, but Mia didn't bother. They weren't what she needed.

She sensed Cooper on the opposite side of the track coming around the other side. Mia shivered. Could he sense her like this, too?

The smell of cat piss and mold intensified.

A faint song reached her ears: Bob Seger singing about running against the wind. Whoever it was didn't seem to be worried about visitors.

She waited until Cooper paused almost directly across from her on the other side.

The song changed to Credence and their bad moon rising.

Somebody really liked the classics. Definitely not Daniel.

The clanking stopped, replaced by the sound of a welding torch.

Mia side-stepped around the corner of the makeshift wall, the gun held in a three-point stance, and her jaw hit the floor.

A massive black train engine, bullet-shaped like a miniature submarine on rails glared back at her. God, she wanted to examine it closer, but Cooper was already moving toward the source of the noise.

She sped around the end of the long engine. Cooper had engaged a person in overalls and a welding helmet. They wrestled before he got the upper hand and whipped them over his hip, throwing the person to the ground. The figure whacked their helmeted head against the cement and slumped to the floor.

Behind them, a metal access door opened, a caged emergency light shining on the area like a spotlight. A small generator purred, one of the pre-Collapse reduced noise models that operated on refined corn diesel.

The train engine was pulled into a mechanic's bay. Well-lit, it extended the entire length of the limited track. Behind it was a mechanic's room. Rows of thin drawered tool cabinets, a desk, and at the back of the room, a large, clear case the size of a microwave, gloves reaching inward. She focused on that. It reminded her of the case that used to hold the Tau-159 sample down in the MUC.

Cooper raised his eyebrows in question, pistol pointed down at the person in a crumpled pile at his feet, helmet askew from the blow, half-concealing their face.

A numb kind of certainty gripped Mia.

Not her mother. But damn close.

She knelt and shoved the welding helmet all the way to the side.

Rani.

CHAPTER 14

COOPER

Friday, September 9, 2072
2:32 P.M.

Before Mia, Cooper hadn't touched a Shielded in years.

He flexed his gloved fingers at the remembered spark. It most definitely had never done that.

Rani groaned, slumped in the chair where he'd planted her. Unbound and regaining consciousness. Cooper remembered her as easy but pragmatic. He pushed her boundaries every chance he got before Daniel took him to train at Camp Havoc near the Dam.

Her eyes startled open and she gasped. Cooper examined the gloves box where a jet stone the size of a basketball, a metallic sheen glinting from its surface, laid on a piece of memory foam.

Mia leaned against a toolbox, arms crossed. After scrutinizing the stone, she'd stayed as far away from him as possible in the small room and hadn't uttered a single word since the tunnel. But then again, neither had Cooper.

He sensed her every movement, like water gliding through a glass tube.

Nothing unusual stood out in the mechanic's room—at least not to him. Everything except for the stone.

"Mia?" The woman's voice wavered. She was Shielded, so the wound on her temple was already closing up.

"What is this place, Rani?"

"No, not with him here." She glared at Cooper, eyes puffy and red. He didn't really blame her. He'd walloped her good.

"Cooper? Rani and I need to talk." Mia didn't take her gaze off the older woman.

He raised his hands by his head and defaulted to a lazy grin. "I know when I'm not wanted. I'll just wait outside."

It would give him a chance to survey the engine anyway. Mia either didn't care or didn't think it was important that he was left alone with it because she simply nodded, her entire focus on Rani.

He walked out and closed the door behind him, leaving it cracked in case she needed help.

A single light shone above his head. Mia had shut the Bluetooth speaker off and only distant sounds from outside the tunnel reached his ears. He looked up at the windows of the engine and froze.

Eva stood framed in a window inside the engine.

She didn't run, she just nodded at him and gestured for him to come up into the interior.

Come into my parlor, said the spider to the fly. Cooper kept her in his sights, walking to the set of narrow stairs at the front.

Sloppy work, Coop. He hadn't cleared the interior of the train after taking Rani out. God, where had his mind gone on this trip? Ever since he'd crossed the boundary into the Territory, it was like an emotional switch had flipped in his brain, and all his training had flown out the door. All the memories from that time long ago, previously bottled up, started fizzing out in stops and spurts. He couldn't afford memory lane. Claire couldn't afford it.

Hardening his heart, he faced the woman who'd shaped him more than any other.

###

The interior of the engine was not what he expected. On one side, a few large black chairs remained, like the kind that used to be in airplanes. The other side had stubby metal posts where chairs used to reside, the weld marks straight and clean. A wall with a narrow door opened behind Eva, and the opening to his right led to a conductor's chair and controls.

He stopped at the top of the steps.

Time hadn't touched Eva at all. Her long black hair was braided tight against her head, wispy strands sticking out in puffs, a testament to the heat. She wore cargo pants and a t-shirt, its sleeves cut off revealing muscular arms. A rifle strap hung off one shoulder and a toolbox laid open at her feet next to an open hatch.

"Coop." The word was wary, and her hand tightened on the strap of her rifle.

"Ma'am."

Her chest rose and fell in a deep sigh, but her eyes remained steady on his. "I heard you were back."

"Yeah, from who? I only arrived yesterday and nobody but Daniel recognized me." No use in keeping it to himself. Daniel and Eva had always been thick as thieves, even after their split.

Her lips pressed together. "Are you sure?"

"Yep. Nice train." This had to be the same one he saw her on in Virginia so many months ago. How many of the things could be out there? Track Three must be one hell of a long tunnel.

"What are you doing here, Coop?"

"Like, here in the tunnel," he pointed at the ground, "or here in the Territory?"

"You know what I mean." A line of irritation creased her forehead.

"Well, let me see. I had some vacation time coming and thought I'd visit my old stomping grounds. Catch up with old friends, visit the ol' homestead—"

"Stop it, Cooper," Eva interrupted. "I know you're working for Sarah, I recognized you in Virginia, and I don't want any more of your bullcrap."

He narrowed his eyes. "Then why did you ask?"

"To give you a chance to explain. I'm not Daniel. I will listen to what you have to say."

"No, you're not him." A hard edge of exhaustion knifed through him. He'd been fighting for survival for so long he didn't know what peace looked like. Cooper had made the choice to leave after the mission to Montana fifteen years ago, and he hadn't looked back since. Through all the death, killings, and manipulations, he'd kept the core of himself that still hoped for a different future locked away deep inside.

Eva blinked away tears.

A manipulation or the truth? He couldn't tell anymore.

"I'm so sorry, Cooper. I'm sorry we let you down." It came out as little more than a whisper. She didn't try to cover the moisture in her eyes.

Something shifted deep inside him. He felt her sincerity. Not enough to tell her the entire truth, he wasn't that far gone with the useless emotions now roiling inside of him, but he believed her enough to tell her part of the truth. "I have a foster daughter, Claire. Your sister will have her killed if I don't bring back intel. It's how the twisted remnants of the Western Coalition operate. She brings them intel, and they leave her alone for the most part. WC handlers dose loved ones of the people they're trying to control with *Oblivion's Curse,* or as your science types like to call it, *necrotizing putreflorum.* Then, they hand out the daily dose of dampening agent each day if we're doing as we're told. It's very effective."

Eva's body stiffened at the name of the old bioagent the Eastern Bloc had created before the Collapse. The Western Coalition had replicated it early on and still had doses deep in the bowels of their facility beneath the mountains of western Virginia. He'd tried to gain access to those sublevels without luck. They had them locked down tighter than a fallout shelter after a nuclear attack.

"Oh, Cooper," she breathed. She took a step toward him.

Cooper stepped back, his back coming up hard against the half-wall of the engineer's cab. "I neither want nor require your pity, Eva. Now, why were you on this train?"

Her features hardened. "So you can bring the information back to Sarah? Not going to happen, even to save your daughter."

He kept his eyes steady on the woman in front of him. "As far as I see it, you have a golden opportunity here. She said to bring back intel on the train and the power source. What you give me on either of those two things is totally up to you. True or false, I'm not going to know the difference."

She blinked. "Double agent?"

"I wouldn't go that far. I just need to get as far away from this place as possible. It's doing weird things to my system. But, I can't leave without intel," and Shield, but he had to keep that to himself, find a way to get it without anyone the wiser. Claire's life was too precious to gamble with. "Give me something. Anything, and I'll be gone."

"And not finish out your agreement with me?" Mia said on the staircase below him.

Cooper had felt her leave the mechanic's room and knew she'd hear his words. All of them. He still had Plan B or, rather, Plan C at this point. But it was a doozy, last resort kind of option.

She brushed past him, the nerve-endings tingling up and down his body at the close contact. A shiver hunched her shoulders, and she didn't meet his eyes. She had felt it too.

"A promise is a promise." He crossed his arms over his chest.

"Good. Hello, mother. I hope you can tell me what the hell is going on. Rani won't say a word."

"As well, she shouldn't." Eva's lips thinned, and her eyes flicked back and forth between him and Mia. Her brows drew together. "Sarah will know if you're lying, Cooper. It's one of her superpowers."

"She won't. I've gotten away with it before."

"Are you sure?"

A trickle of unease seeped into the cracks of his confidence. "I am."

"Hmm. Or she could have allowed you that belief. It's too risky." She shook her head and walked toward them as if to exit the engine.

Mia sidestepped in front of her. She directed her next question at Cooper without taking her eyes off Eva. "What do you need to know about the power source, Cooper?"

Eva's eyes narrowed. "Don't you dare."

This was interesting. "How much output it has, where it's located, and how guarded the facility is."

"Thirty mega-watt hours, though it can produce a lot more, it's located at Lower Monumental Dam, and its energy is piped underground. It's protected by an old Nike air missile defense system and many guards. Some of that is a lie. I'm not telling you what. Will that help get your daughter back?"

Cooper blinked and straightened from his perch by the cab. Shock penetrated his hardened defenses. Had she just defied her mother? In front of her? *Both parents in the span of two days.*

He really liked this woman.

"It'll definitely help."

"That was stupid, daughter."

"No, stupid is not asking for help, mother. Now, what have you been up to?"

CHAPTER 15

MIA

Friday, September 9, 2072
4:43 P.M.

va cupped her elbows in a tight-knuckled grip. Dark circles gouged half-moons beneath her eyes, and her clothes were filthy. She looked like she hadn't slept in forever.

Rani hadn't elicited any useful information; she just kept directing Mia to talk to her mother. So here she was, attempting to speak to the woman she hadn't seen in over a year. Not the homecoming she thought it would be.

"Well?" Anger drove Mia forward and she stepped farther away from Cooper, his presence like an electrical field at her back.

The older woman looked past Mia. "Could you give us a moment, Cooper? I need to have a conversation with my daughter in private."

Cooper snorted. "Don't take too long. She and I have a murderer to find. I promised."

He clomped down the steps. Mia cocked her head to the side. The spot in her mind that indicated Cooper's whereabouts moved back toward Track Three and the tunnel system. When she deemed he was far enough away, she zeroed in on her mother.

"You can feel him. In your head." Her mother set the rifle down, slumping into a seat on the right-hand side of the train. She gestured to another seat across from her, angled like it had just been moved. The metal stumps of legs on the left indicated it probably had.

Mia backed up to where Cooper had been standing and crossed her arms. Her mother's eyes followed the motion, a look of resignation in their depths.

"Excuse me?" Tightness gripped Mia's chest. This was the conversation her mother wanted? After all this time?

"With Cooper, it's like the enzymes in his system can sense the other enzymes outside his body. An unanticipated side effect I studied once it was discovered. Part of the leftover Super-soldier modifications. I never observed the same in you. I deduced it was because everybody responded to the stable version of Shield in slightly different ways."

"This is what you want to talk about? Not the fact I haven't heard from you in months. Sector Nine has been wreaking havoc and there's been all kinds of crazy crap going on. I think some-body wants the settlements, well, unsettled." Mia couldn't keep the bitterness from her voice.

Her mother winced. "Sometimes it's easier to focus on what you know. If you can reciprocate the extra-sensory benefits now, that's fascinating."

The fanatical spark of a scientist on the scent of new research flickered across her mother's face.

"So none of what I just told you just registered? Got it. Good talk." Mia stepped down to the stair, ready to gather Cooper and leave.

Eva leaped to her feet. "I'm sorry. Wait, please."

Mia turned. "You're not studying me. Or him. We have bigger issues. Like, for starters, why were you hiding?"

Eva only hesitated a beat, her brow furrowed. "Because we have a traitor. Maybe more than one."

Before she could fully process her mother's words, Rani appeared on the stairs by the engine cab, holding a small, unfamiliar style of radio in her hand.

"Daniel and Jack need help. They're pinned down back at Jack's old place."

Adrenaline shot through her veins, and Mia rose. "I'll get Cooper."

CHAPTER 16

COOPER

Friday, September 9, 2072
5:05 P.M.

Mia's presence pulsed in a maddening wave of sensation throughout Cooper's skull. In all seriousness, he wanted to plunge a sharp object into his brain, wiggle it around a little, and scoop the nuisance out. That would fix the problem.

Lacking the proper implements, he paced instead. Back and forth, across the track in front of the first, empty maintenance bay.

Rani stepped out of the shadows of the walkway above him. "Penny for your thoughts?"

"Do you have a quarter?" Another pass over the tracks.

She didn't even blink an eye at the old joke. "You were always a serious child. A smart ass, sure, but a serious one."

Rani scooted to the edge of the walkway and sat down, her legs dangling.

"So, you're helping Eva?" He didn't even try his usual bag of tricks. Rani wouldn't have succumbed to his charms, anyway.

She waved a hand toward the surface. "And the other two.

The Council likes to think they have control, but between you and me; Jack, Eva and Daniel will always have the final say on anything that matters around here."

"Ha. That's giving Jack and Eva a lot of credit." Political small talk it was.

"They can sway him when others can't." Rani crossed her arms like she was protecting something deep inside. "You've been missed, young man."

That stopped him in his tracks. It almost sounded…sincere. "Rani, what are you doing out here?"

"You banged me over the head before I could say hello. Sorry for my reaction when I came to. I almost didn't recognize you." She motioned at her own chin like she had a beard. The bruise on her hairline had almost faded.

"Ahh, I understand. You drew the short straw. Baby-sitting duty doesn't suit you."

"Dammit, Killian. I just wanted to talk." Rani jumped down. Her head reached about mid-chest. She peered up at him, a concerned expression wrinkling her forehead.

"I doubt that, Rani. I doubt that very much."

Her lips tipped down in a frown, and her shoulders hunched forward as she crossed her arms. Very unlike the old Rani he knew.

"You were like my child, Cooper. I helped raise you, and you never even said good-bye before you left."

"I had to leave. After Montana…" The words were barely above a whisper.

"I know, kid, I know. Next time, say good-bye."

His chest tightened and he enveloped the petite woman in a bear hug. She squeaked and he let her go.

Before he could respond, a sharp whistle pierced the darkness.

Mia appeared. "My dad and Jack need help. You're coming with me."

"You didn't say please."

"I don't need to, jailbird. Now move your ass, mom has a shortcut." She threw the words over her shoulder as she walked back toward the maintenance room.

His lips twitched.

"You like her." Rani eyed him.

"Now, wouldn't that beat all? It's been fun Ranimayi."

And he sauntered after Mia.

###

Mia and Cooper wove through the corn stalks without a rustle or a word. The woman moved like a cat, light and smooth on her feet, and she held the pistol like an extension of her arm. Eva had accompanied Rani back to the MUC to make sure the place was secure. With Sector Nine on the move, they couldn't be too careful. Too many secrets to protect, he guessed. It had to be exhausting.

Mia had called Talia, and more support was on its way, but for now it was them, Jack, and Daniel taking on whoever from Sector Nine had come for the two young men in Jack's bait hole. The two guards Mia had sent earlier had been taken out en route and couldn't be found.

Another gorgeous sunset lit the sky, the thick haze ablaze with a deep vermilion, as if the sky were on fire.

They needed to wrap this up quick; his intuition told him he was running out of time to find a vial of the Shield Serum and get the hell out of this place.

The two of them reached the edge of the field. A plume of dust off in the distance wound its way toward the house. Eight minutes away by ATV, maybe ten? It could be Talia and the guards, or backup for the Sector Nine goons retrieving their lost kids.

God, what the hell was he still doing here? *Claire, that's why.*

Jack's house and barn was situated next to the top of a broad canyon on the backside, an old train track visible at its base.

Corn surrounded the rest of the outbuildings, hiding them from sight except for the roofs.

All in all, lots of places to hide. Goodie.

"Another one at your eleven o'clock," he murmured to Mia.

She squinted her eyes. "Did you see the one behind the left-hand poplar tree and well house?"

"Yep. I count eight total."

"Me too."

"Isn't your father going to be pissed? You know, with you breaking me out of his super-secret holding cell and all and now dragging me out for some good, old-fashioned fun."

"He already knows you're coming. Mom told him on the radio. Just don't antagonize him." She stood and ghosted through the cornstalks toward the back of the barn to get a clean shot of the four along the tree line. As soon as backup arrived, they'd surround them and incapacitate

"You apparently don't know your father," he grumbled to her departing backside.

She disappeared from sight but he could still track her through the green stalks.

Minutes ticked by.

He could leave right now and not look back. Initiate Plan C.

Mia was in position. Cooper drew in a breath. *Just a little longer, Coop. You can't leave a lady in distress.* He snorted at the thought of Mia being in distress.

The soft swishing of stalks alerted him to somebody coming toward him. The young guard, Talia.

Mia signaled her to stay where she was, and she nodded, indicating with her hands the positions of the other guards.

Cooper padded around the edge of the field, making sure some of the goons saw him. Distractions for the enemy were always good. A shot rang out. He returned fire.

Another shot. Mia made it to the back of the machinist's shed attached to the barn and banged on it three times, paused and banged two more to let Daniel and Jack know they were ready.

The massive barn doors opened, and an engine roared, the harsh chemical smell of petroleum gasoline drifting in the air.

The distraction of the noise from the barn was their cue.

Cooper dropped to a knee and fired at the goon behind the well-house. He tagged a leg, and the person howled, dropping from cover. The following bullet shut him up.

Four of the Territory guards filtered out of the corn and found cover on the porch and around the side of the house. The others were to spread out in the field.

One of the goons ran for the fields.

Talia clipped the woman in the shoulder and spun her around.

The shooting started in earnest after that, like a Wild West shootout he saw once in an old movie.

Shards of wood splintered off the barn and house, holes like Swiss cheese peppering the siding.

Another shot. He ducked for cover back in the corn.

Daniel squatted behind an upended steel machinist's table and aimed for the shooters behind the poplar trees. A round whistled inches from Cooper's head.

He shot up and cleared the space between the field and the backside of the barn.

A spear of pain knifed through his brain, and stars needled his vision. He dropped to his knees and gripped his head, pistol and all.

No blood. He wasn't shot.

Mia.

Another knife of agony lanced through him, and he collapsed to the ground. All nerve endings raw, like electricity shooting down a high-voltage wire. Death would be a blessing at this point.

The blackness of unconsciousness dragged him over the edge.

CHAPTER 17

MIA

Friday, September 9, 2072
7:00 P.M.

Mia awoke to almost complete darkness, crammed in the back of a side-by-side and knees up to her chest. Pain sliced through her synapses.

The vehicle jostled and jolted her against the hard metal sides and back of the seat. Tight plastic zip-ties fastened her arms to an eye-hook in the bottom of the vehicle.

Chet's old ATV. Somebody had stolen it.

Mia stilled. The seat against her back rose high enough the driver couldn't see her entire body. They didn't give any indication anyway, and she re-settled.

Think, Mia.

The spark that indicated Cooper's presence was thready and weak, more a gray patch than a bright presence. She couldn't tell if it was from distance or from her being knocked out. It moved somewhere to her right, but the internal map had dissipated in a haze of brain fog.

The last thing she remembered was turning toward a noise

and twin electrodes from a taser hitting her in the chest. Rage simmered hot inside of her.

With effort, she lifted her head. Wherever she was, it was underground.

The glow from the ATV's light bar bounced off the dirt walls and wooden support beams, creating havoc with the shadows. Rustic and narrow, the path they drove on was bumpy and uneven, the sandy soil loose with stones. Mia had explored all the tunnels throughout the Territory at some point in her life—with the exception of Track Three. She didn't recognize this one. Just how long had people been working down here without the Council's knowledge? Months? Years?

Mia's head fell back to the cradle of her shoulder. The Territory hadn't built a new tunnel since the last had been completed five years ago.

The ATV descended farther underground.

More tunnels. The side-by-side took three more turns. Left, left, right, each turn imprinted onto her mind.

How far do these tunnels go?

She estimated fifteen minutes had passed before they stopped for good in a large cavern. Water dripped in even intervals and a wet mossy smell infused the air.

Were they even still within the Inner Territory's borders?

Mia closed her eyes, feigning unconsciousness.

"I know you're awake." An unfamiliar male voice intoned, a flash of brightness from a headlamp blinding her for a split second.

Rough hands wrapped around her bound wrists, releasing them from the eye hook. His face was covered.

It was an odd angle but she whipped her head forward, connecting with the man's face.

"Son-of-a-bitch!" The man stumbled back, cradling his face. Mia leaped out of the vehicle. Tingles shot down her legs from being scrunched in a fetal position for too long. Ignoring the sensation, she ran back the way they had come as fast as her weakened legs could carry her. If she could disappear into the darkness before her kidnapper could recover, maybe she'd stand a chance.

Strong arms tackled her from behind. She fell hard to the ground and struck out with a kick. It connected with something soft. More cursing.

She rolled to standing, only seeing the shadow of the person she'd hit. Mia balled her bound hands together and punched toward the vague outline of his mask-covered head.

The man grunted but regained his footing.

Heart beating out of her chest, she regrouped her sore body for another attack.

It never came.

A zing through the air and twin pinpricks of electricity sizzled across her arm. *What the hell?* She slapped her hands over the metallic filaments now attached to her. She didn't have time to pull them out before agonizing electricity fired off every nerve-ending.

She collapsed to the ground.

Paralyzed but conscious this time, the man threw her frozen body over his shoulder. Mia throbbed from head to toe.

A door in her peripheral bobbed nearer. The metal rectangle looked like something from the MUC, a locking mechanism crisscrossing the surface with hydraulic bars with a keypad where a doorknob should be.

Agony soaked into every pore, but if Mia didn't get free now, she might not have another shot. She willed her limbs to move through the torturous needles coursing along every inch of her body, Mia jerked off the man's shoulder.

And landed on the hard ground, a poof of dust encompassing her. She rolled but couldn't find the energy to stand. The man grabbed her legs.

"If you won't stay put, I'll just drag you like an animal." Dark eyes glared at her through the eye slits of the balaclava, thin lips pursed. He yanked her towards the door. A single LED bulb hung on a wire above the entrance, its light limited.

"Screw you," she said through numb lips. Every muscle was jelly.

He punched in a code, and the locking mechanism clanked open.

The man dragged her to the center of the dim room and closed the door as he exited, lock clanking into place.

Mia lurched to sitting. A threadbare cot, barely fit for an animal, sat positioned in one corner. A plastic bucket, red streaking the sides, huddled against the wall. A simple wooden chair, a single missing spindle from the back, was stationed to one side of the door. Another light dangled from an ancient orange extension cord from the ceiling, the cinder block walls dull under its yellow glow.

Where were they getting power?

Crawling on wobbly hands and knees, she collapsed onto the cot.

The door clanked open, and a tall woman walked in. Her long, dark hair was greased into a braid, her features sharp and watchful. A scar puckered her temple. Alarm skittered down Mia's back. The pictures didn't do her Aunt Sarah justice.

Mia allowed the wall to prop her up. She didn't flinch. "You're my Aunt Sarah."

The other woman widened her stance, hands folded in front of her. Prepared. Ready for a fight. "You look like my grandmother. You have your father's eyes, but the Zapada genes bred strong."

It was a clinical assessment, nothing of normal emotion accompanied the statement. The woman was like a robot, flat and hard.

"So, I've been told. What are you doing here?" A cold calm entered Mia's voice, despite the turmoil roiling beneath the surface.

"Plan B." She banged on the door. Another man with a balaclava mask—they must have scavenged an outdoor store—entered carrying a box the size of a first aid kit. He waited by the door. "We won't drain you, but we will be taking your blood. I would've rather hoped to just take you, but I'm not ready to face my sister yet. Some of your stupid people went off the rails earlier than anticipated. Work with idiots, get idiot results."

Pins and needles coursed through Mia's limbs as sensation returned.

But not fast enough.

Sarah laid across her, pinning her to the bed. The man in the mask came over and brought out a blood collection needle and an IV bag.

"You're not getting my blood." Mia jerked and bucked to no avail. She was still too weak to dislodge Sarah.

"Move again and I will put you down. Shielded or not, your system will not enjoy three tases in under an hour."

The needle pricked her vein, and blood flowed through the tubing down to the bag. Her skin healed around the needle, again and again. Like nails boring into her veins. The man didn't seem concerned. Just jerked it out and reapplied.

"You won't get away with this." Mia croaked, her throat dry and raw from yelling.

"Don't you realize? Your blood is power. It absorbs the tellurium enzymes, stops them from overreplicating. And Daniel has been hoarding you like a damn dragon. You know how much relief you could offer? I will retrieve the rest of Shield stored in the MUC for myself, screw the Western Coalition. If I have your blood, there's not a damn thing they can do. Poison and antidote. Isn't that how true control works? That old man from Colville certainly must have hoped for an antidote in the end." Sarah narrowed her gaze, a glint in her eye. "I should have taken you long ago, *sobrina*. Too late now."

Mia's eyes widened. The woman was mad. "Are you behind the poisoning? The attacks?"

"It's easy to manipulate people when they want something." Sarah placed the vials in a padded case.

Silver flashes floated in Mia's eyes, and a sharp pain bit into her head. The still, gray patch representing Cooper's presence brightened to a spark. But something was wrong…really wrong. He felt off somehow.

Focus.

"My mother is a great woman. She's helped save a lot of people. A lot more than what you've done. I've read about you in her journals."

Sarah quirked a brow. "Are you sure they're accurate? Those accounts?"

"Screw you. You're a liar."

"It runs in the family, dear. Time for me to go. I'd bring you with me, but your parents planted a tracking device in you at birth, and I don't have time to go exploring to dig it out. You ever want the truth, you know where to find me." With that, Sarah closed the door with a click of bolts, leaving Mia trapped inside to stew on her final comments.

CHAPTER 18

COOPER

Friday, September 9, 2072
7:08 P.M.

pikes of pain ping-ponged around Cooper's brain, the bumpy farm road exacerbating the sensation. The Seeking with Mia had receded but only a little. He'd never had one so strong that it had knocked him out. Obtaining Shield and getting the hell out of dodge was still his number one goal. He couldn't let complicated relationships and homecomings get in the way of that—or unusual side effects of the Seeking. A little girl depended on him.

At least somebody did.

The side-by-side sped along the dirt road, dust billowing behind it like an angry cloud. Cooper's hands clasped his head, eyes squinting ahead. Daniel drove the compact vehicle like a demon on crack, Jack by his side. Always.

"Can't this thing go any faster?" Jack leaned forward, peering out the front window at the cloud of dust a couple of miles ahead of them. "Are you sure this is the right way, Coop?"

Mia's presence pulsed in his head."Yeah, she's up there somewhere."

Daniel gripped the steering wheel hard and a calm anger had settled over his features. Dust, sweat, and blood speckled his neck and arms. He'd said fewer than three words to Cooper since they'd left Talia and the other guards to clean up the mess at Jack's house.

Cooper cleared his throat. "What are we dealing with?"

"What the hell does it look like we're dealing with?" Jack didn't look back at him, "You were supposed to be covering her. At least that's what she told us on the radio despite our warnings you couldn't be trusted."

Daniel's focus didn't waver, and he remained silent.

Cooper shifted in the tight space. "I did. She indicated she was going towards the back door of the barn to signal you. I provided a distraction and covered the front. Then zap, I was down, and she was gone."

"Zap? What does that mean?" Jack craned his neck around.

Shit. Lie or tell the truth? He liked Mia. In any other circumstance, he would explore the growing connection; spurred on by childhood memories and Shield. But he couldn't afford it, not with Claire's life on the line. If the two men in front of him found out how strong the Seeking was between him and Mia, Daniel would bind his hands again and use it until the last ping. That couldn't happen. Not if he wanted to escape at the first possible opportunity. Initiate his Plan C.

"I don't know. I think I must have gotten shot or something. The Seeking's already starting to fade. We need to hurry before I lose it." Cooper lied.

Jack cursed.

Daniel's eyes flickered briefly to the other man. "We'll get her."

"We better, or we're all dead. What the hell was Sector Nine thinking?" Jack snapped the glove compartment open and pulled out full clips, the metal of a 9mm round peeking out of the top of one of them. He handed one to Cooper over his left shoulder and shoved the other in his back pocket.

Cooper hid his shock with effort.

Daniel rammed the wheel left, then right to avoid something in the road.

A shovel.

Another object laying in the road almost took out the right wheel and Daniel cursed. He tapped the 4-wheel drive button and swerved into the potato field to avoid another obstacle. Large pine and poplar trees lined one side of the road. The other side housed eight-foot tall rows of corn. They *thwapped* the wheel wells as the vehicle mowed them over.

"They'll run out of crap soon." Cooper braced against the back and held on, head pounding, body aching. Shield wasn't catching up quick enough for him to feel like his old self. *Another anomaly.*

A grumbled reply was all he got in return.

His prediction came true, and the ATV bounced back onto the gravel road. Mia's bright presence in his brain zipped farther away.

"We'll all die, huh?" Cooper aimed his question at Jack but kept his eyes trained on Daniel, whose jaw muscle clenched and unclenched.

Cooper heaved a sigh of resignation. Neither man had the capacity to let go of their secrets.

This time Daniel surprised him.

"Mia's blood can be used to make an anti-serum against the Shielded." No further explanation, and yet it was more than Cooper had expected.

"And you didn't lock her up?" Incredulity laced every one of Cooper's words. What the hell had the mad scientist done this time?

"I don't owe you an explanation." Daniel deflected in an even monotone.

"Then why don't you just drop me off at the wall, and I'll be on my way."

"You're not going anywhere." Jack this time.

"Then give me something. If I get her blood on me, am I done? Or is it more complicated than that?"

Another side-eye from the two men in front of him and Jack answered. "It's more complicated than that."

Cooper noted they didn't say how much, but he could live with that. "And who knows about this superpower?"

"Who are still alive?" Jack turned.

Cooper raised an eyebrow. "Yeah, let's go with that."

"Four, including you. At least four that we know of. Her kidnapping probably has nothing to do with it, it's probably just an internal conflict, but neither of us want to take that chance."

"Why let me in on this?"

"Who said you're going to be allowed to leave with it?" Daniel's voice held firm. He'd been silent during his and Jack's interplay and met Cooper's eyes from the rearview mirror.

"And how're you going to keep me here? Lock me up at the dam? I won't work for you or anybody else." Cooper shook his head, wishing it was true.

"You would, if it's in your own best self-interest. You want something or you wouldn't still be here." Daniel refocused on the road. The plume of dust had turned a corner up ahead, and now followed a cornfield. If they weren't careful, they would lose sight of it altogether.

"You two sure haven't changed much."

Daniel took the corner to the side road at full speed, and the side-by-side swayed on its shocks, the back tires skidding in the loose powder. Cooper locked his arms around the right side roll-bar where it slanted to the frame.

No houses loomed in the distance this far to the northwest of the inner Territory. The large sprinkler irrigation systems stretched out their long silvery arms into the fields, their booms moving on wheels at a snail's pace, the wall of metallic junk hunkering in the distance.

Jack and Daniel swore. What now?

A large log lay across the road in front of them.

Daniel slammed on the brakes and Cooper almost careened into the front seat. The dust in the distance dissipated.

Cooper snorted and jumped out of the vehicle, leaving the other two men to deal with the log. Mia's presence had stopped about a mile ahead and was moving at a slower pace. He could probably reach the spot sooner by running at this point.

And anyway, what were Jack and Daniel going to do? Shoot him in the back?

He paced along the side of the road. The stalks stood tall and green, loaded with cobs almost ready to harvest. The musky scent of plants growing filled the air and Cooper took in a deep breath. It smelled of life.

Tracks from various vehicles and animals wove together along the road, going both directions. Jack jogged to his side. "Get back in."

"I'm good."

Mia started moving again, taking a hard right and then coming back toward him. But *below*.

What the heck? "Is there a tunnel underneath this road?"

Jack eyed him. "No, why?"

The side-by-side pulled up beside him and Cooper and Jack hopped back in. "Drive ahead and stop when I tell you."

Daniel narrowed his eyes.

"Why else did you assign me as tracker back in the day, Daniel?"

"It definitely wasn't because you followed orders well," Daniel put the ATV in gear and rolled forward.

Cooper ignored him. "I do believe at one point you called me the best tracker in your militia. And that," he pointed to two faint partial tire tracks veering off the road between two circles of corn, "is something to investigate."

"Huh." Jack tilted his head and examined them closer.

Cooper hopped out and the other two men followed.

They all unholstered their pistols. Tension They walked in

silence for a few minutes, the tension an undercurrent Cooper tried to shake.

Only a broken leaf or occasional divot marked the other side-by-side's progress until the tracks just stopped.

They all turned in circles.

Nothing else stood out.

"Stop for a second," Daniel ordered and his eyelids closed and he tilted his head as if listening for something making noise far away. "There's a clicking. Can you hear it?"

Jack and Cooper mimicked Daniel's pose. A faint metallic clicking, like gears falling into place, emanated beneath them. Underground. *Always.*

Cooper dropped to his knees and started scooping the fertile soil away from the ground. The other men followed suit.

"Here." A metallic hatch. The three men dug harder and faster, unearthing the dirt until they found the edges of a metallic electrical box with two directional buttons on a long cord.

"You want to do the honors?" He extended it to Daniel.

Rage sparked behind the other man's eyes. "Let's see what we have."

And he pushed the top button.

\#

The three men descended into darkness. It wouldn't be the first time Cooper had done so with these two. The rungs of the stairs ran parallel to the mechanized lift shaft next to them. Chains and pulleys extended within arm's reach. If the lift were to ascend, it would be a tight squeeze.

There were no emergency lights and Daniel held the only flashlight, but none of them needed much more than that.

Daniel's light stopped bobbing and spotlighted him in its orangey glow. Daniel had reached the bottom.

"Get a move on." Daniel's clipped tone was reminiscent of past missions.

Cooper slowed down.

Jack snorted, the sound echoing down the shaft.

"Fine. When whoever's behind this gets Mia's blood, we can just tell them to wait before using it because you have lead in your ass. Now hurry up."

He and Jack landed at the bottom. Dust motes danced in the beam from the flashlight. The pulley lift sat on the ground beside them, large enough to hold an ATV. Daniel played the beam around. They were in a long tunnel that extended either direction.

Cooper crouched by the lift and inspected the tire tracks coming off of it, confirming the fading sensation of Mia's presence. "That way."

He pointed to the right of their present position.

They trudged along the tunnel in silence.

At one time, all three of them had worked as an efficient unit. Cooper didn't know if it was because of their shared training or because of the bonds of war and struggle. Maybe it was both. Montana had changed that. The men beside him had turned from mentors—family—to something else entirely. Had it ever been real? Those bonds?

"Cooper." Jack's impatient voice startled him from his thoughts.

He blinked and focused on the other man who had turned to walk backwards to get his attention.

"What now, Jack." His words were rough and hard.

"Why are you here? What do you want out of all of this?" Jack swept his arm in front of him like he was encompassing the Territory.

"Well, Jack, there's a lot of things I want."

"Spill it, Cooper. We know you're working for somebody, though, after Montana, I can't see you working for Cordova and what's left of the Eastern Bloc, or Hensley in the Midwest. And the remnants of the Western Coalition on the East Coast are only moderately better than those two. So which one is it?"

"That's rich. Nobody is on the side of angels these days, Jack, even this Territory."

Daniel remained silent but Cooper had the distinct impression he was listening. Carefully.

"We're feeding five different settlements besides our own." Irritation tinged Jack's voice. "I'd say that was a lot closer than most."

So, he didn't like being compared to warlords?

"You give them the illusion of control while they live constantly on the brink of starvation. Isn't that almost worse? About thirty years after the Collapse and everybody is still only out for themselves." God, Cooper had enough of this BS. He needed to find help for Claire and vacate. If he had the Shield Serum, she could fight the poison and they could disappear into the world somewhere for awhile, everybody else be damned.

"Enough." Daniel's icy tone chilled the air.

"Truth hurt, Daniel?"

"No, Cooper, because you have it all wrong." Daniel pointed the light to an upcoming intersection. "Which direction?"

"Another left."

Daniel raised an eyebrow at Jack. Jack nodded back. "After you two."

Cooper hesitated a split second but proceeded Daniel down the tunnel.

They turned left at the next intersection. This tunnel held strings of small white lights spread out in even intervals. Somebody had attached them with small nails to the rough-hewn wooden beams that supported the passage.

Daniel clicked the light off.

"We're getting close," said Cooper.

The next tunnel to the right yielded nothing. Cooper swore he could still see the signs of an ATV passing not long ago, but they'd been in these passages for almost an hour. Jack felt like they were spinning in circles.

At the next intersection, Cooper's face wrinkled in confusion.

Mia's spark was all over the place, and he couldn't pin it down. Was she on the surface or nearby? "There was a struggle here. See? Blood droplets there, there, and here on the wall."

He ran his hand over the compact dirt of the wall and motioned with his hand for Daniel to give him the flashlight. Each smear of blood pinged inside his skull when he touched it.

Cooper clenched his hand into a fist and dropped it to his side. His head buzzed.

The area brightened. Chunks of rock and clay lay on the floor and deep grooves slashed the wall at chest level. Cooper combed over every inch of the wall and did the same on the other side of the tunnel and tried to shake the blood's calling.

"What are you seeing?" Jack walked closer to peruse the area Cooper had examined.

Daniel stood in mute silence, observing Cooper with an impassive expression on his face.

"I don't know, yet." He soft-stepped along the passage and came back, confusion overlaying all else. He pointed the light to the ceiling, down the intersecting tunnel and back to where they stood.

"Tracks have disappeared, and I can't get a fix on her." Cooper gave the tunnel a once over, again.

"That's impossible." Daniel stated. He snatched the flashlight from Cooper's hand.

Cooper put his hands up like he was surrendering. "Go for it, Danny-boy. I'm telling you. They're gone. We can split up and investigate each tunnel, but the signs point to the side-by-side stopping here. She fought back, and now, no more tracks."

Daniel took a step toward Cooper, and Jack placed himself between them.

"Damn, you're stupid sometimes, Coop." Jack huffed out an exasperated breath.

"Yeah, but at least I don't let people die unnecessarily."

Daniel lunged and it took everything Jack had to restrain him.

"You deserted after Butte. You took it upon yourself to disobey direct orders and would have got all of us captured or killed. For what? You're morals?" Daniel stilled but tension emanated from every muscle.

"Yes, my morals. Isn't that all we have left? When non-combatants were involved, and you were going to blow the place to hell and back. I had to try to get the rest out, you cold-hearted son-of-a-bitch. Somebody in the group had to have some common decency." Cooper strained against Jack, each word spitting out of his mouth in anger.

"Common decency? The only logical course of action was to do what we did. We needed that equipment to save thousands of lives, not just dozens."

"Screw you and your logic." Cooper threw the flashlight on the ground at Daniel and Jack's feet and strode off through the side tunnel.

"Follow him," Daniel told Jack as he walked away.

Cooper's flashlight bobbed in the murk, the scent of must and mildew thick in this part of the tunnel.

"Cooper, wait." Jack loped to catch up to him.

"Daniel's even more of an ass now than he was fifteen years ago." Cooper didn't slow down.

"What did you expect? Damn it, stop. You can't keep running."

Cooper turned around to walk backward. The dim tunnel was getting dimmer and there were no side passages. "I didn't run. You all left me there and I had to track you down on the road back. You were my family, and *you* deserted *me*. I didn't follow his damn orders to kill innocent people, and he was going to leave me there to rot. I didn't desert, I chose a different path and he can't stand being defied."

Cooper flipped back around, picking up his pace. Distance. He needed distance from Jack, Daniel, and all the memories that had haunted him since he'd stepped foot on his family's old farm.

The tunnel dead-ended. Such a metaphor for his life thus far —except for Claire. She represented life, a chance at family that had always been taken away from him, time and time again. He looked all around and there it was, on the ceiling. Purpose settled in his bones.

"There's a hatch," Cooper called back to Jack.

"I'll be damned." He halted next to Cooper. A circular hatch above their heads was just out of reach.

Cooper looked him up and down. "I better lift you up, old man."

"Screw you," Jack huffed.

A familiar grin lit Cooper's face and he laced his fingers in a cradle. Jack sighed and placed his foot in it. Cooper lifted.

The handle squealed and he pushed it up until it slammed to the ground on the other side. Jack pulled himself up to sit on the edge. Bright daylight streamed into the passage. It must have been at a gradual ascent for them to be this close to the surface now.

"We're outside the wall." Jack hollered down to Cooper.

"Help me up."

Enough of this playing prodigal-son-come-home. He needed to get Shield for Claire and split. Mia or not, he had to stay on mission. There was one option left. An option he'd left as the last recourse because it could be deadly—even to him.

Jack braced himself and reached for Cooper's outstretched arm. He jumped, and Jack hauled him to the surface.

"Sorry about this, Jack." And Cooper shoved him back down the hole.

To be continued in All Things Hidden…Check out the Sneak Peak at the end…

ALSO BY D.L. BUNCH

All Things Hidden

All Things Found-*Pre-Order Now!*

Visit www.dlbunch.com for more information on prizes and deals! You may find a survivalist tip or three as well!

ABOUT THE AUTHOR

About the Author: D.L. Bunch

D.L. Bunch is an author based in Southeastern Washington, where her passion for storytelling intertwines with her love for the great outdoors. With a heart for adventure, D.L. draws inspiration from camping trips and family escapades, weaving these experiences into her gripping narratives. Her debut work, *The Territory Series*, is a thrilling post-apocalyptic saga that explores survival, sacrifice, and the enduring power of hope in a fractured world. When she's not crafting tales of resilience, D.L. shares her expertise through survival tips and exclusive deals on her website, inviting readers to embrace their own adventures. Join her on this journey through the wilds of fiction and the wilderness alike at www.dlbunch.com.

SNEAK PEAK:

ALL THINGS HIDDEN: PROLOGUE

The Dig
May, 2055

If Chloe ever made it back to the Basin Territory, she'd never steal again.

Compared to her current surroundings, her home in the Pacific Northwest was heaven. Here, enormous mountains of debris lined the double-tracked railway tunnel for as far as she could see, a product of clearing the massive cave-in. Two miles at least.

It felt more like a hundred.

Chloe sighed and picked up a heavy rock with gloved hands, the dusty, earthen smell tickling her nose. She threw it onto the growing pile next to her. Yep, stupid decisions never paid off.

Pickaxes clanged all around. Curved walls, cracked and broken, towered above while roots and globs of dirt hung between the concrete slabs still holding the tunnel together. Rebar poked out like shadowy, skeletal fingers, the girders like a giant's ribcage. Kansas City's dead and buried carcass. Chloe shuddered. Her mother had always told her she had too much of an imagination.

Pools of light dotted the already cleared tracks here and there, highlighting the other workers in their worn jeans and cracked leather boots. Their supervisor and guard, Neil, leaned against the tunnel wall by one of the emergency lights, flipping through an old paperback he'd picked up topside along the way. A rifle hung on his back to stop them from escaping, and Chloe snorted. As if any of the workers wanted to leave this hellhole for the hellscape above.

Kansas City had fared worse than others in the Collapse.

Except for those first few days her crew spent clearing the underground tunnel from just east of Basin Territory to somewhere beneath Nebraska, they hadn't had any run-ins with scavvies.

The nickname suited the almost feral humans that Neil and the other guards called *hostiles*. Even better, *local hostiles* like they were in some freaking old war movie. The long days spent here in Kansas City hadn't produced a soul from topside. Thank God. She hated huddling in the makeshift mining carts with the other workers while bullets whizzed overhead.

Kerchunk. The pile next to her grew.

One more hunk of the dense concrete and she could take a break.

The crash of rock against rock, followed by a sharp curse shook her out of her pity party.

"Aaah! Help!"

Torrance.

One of her few friends in this shithole.

Clambering over the rubble, Chloe's feet hit the exposed ground running. She rushed over the double tracks, a median, and past mountainous piles of excavated debris. Others in the general vicinity did the same and they all converged on a slim man, bloody rivulets trickling from a head wound.

She and Neil reached him at the same time.

A huge black hole yawned above them all, the giant sections of concrete Torrance had dislodged lying atop one of his legs.

That wouldn't have been too bad except for the slender shaft of rebar pinning his other leg to the ground. Blood seeped out around the metal sticking out of his torn jeans. Teeth clenched and face set in a pained grimace, he panted out breaths of pure agony.

"Grab the other side." Neil directed, picking his way around the gravelly earth beneath where Torrance lay. Chloe gingerly placed her foot next to the downed man and found the edge of the table-sized hunk of concrete. Two more sets of hands grabbed the rough edge next to her, and they hoisted it together. Groaning and swearing, somebody moved Torrance from under the rubble, lifting him from the rebar in a swift jerk.

He howled and then fell silent in unconsciousness.

Please don't die.

Chloe's group lowered the slab, careful to miss gloved fingers and leather-covered toes.

"Anybody see what happened?" Neil tore the jeans further, revealing that the rebar had just missed the femoral artery. She closed her eyes for a beat, relieved, and then moved to help. Neil batted her away.

A murmur of 'no's' circulated through their group.

"Looks like he moved an unstable piece," A thin, scraggly-haired woman named Colleen said.

Neil quirked one bushy eyebrow. "This entire blockage is unstable. This is why we have a spotter, people."

Feet shuffled and everybody avoided eye contact. Nobody wanted to spot. A spotter would have to watch every move, every piece of debris for movement, and yeah it made things more safe, but it also made the day drag by at a snail's pace. Some had volunteered or been ordered as guards for this mission, and others, like her, were here as punishment.

She would have much rather got wall-building duty back home.

"Don't touch that. Ally, go get Saul and the med kit. Dan, bring the cart down here so we can load Torrance up. Colleen and Chloe, check the wall and that hole. If we've finally found the end of this blockage, we need to shore up the opening so we can send a crew to check the other side. The rest of you, back to work," Neil ordered.

Torrance moaned, his hands reaching for the source of all his pain. Neil gripped the other man's hands to keep him from touching his leg.

Nobody moved.

"Now!"

The crew jumped as if electrocuted by a cattle prod and moved to their various locations. Colleen and Chloe eyed each other.

Colleen wrinkled her nose and turned toward the gaping maw above their heads. "You're young. Climb up there and see if you can make out anything on the other side. I'll spot ya."

"Seriously, Colleen? You're not that old."

"But I have more experience spottin'. Now, get your skinny ass up there. I'll let you know if anything shifts."

Chloe glared at the other woman but turned on her booted foot and mounted the chunk of concrete they'd pulled off of Torrance. Pieces of subway tile clung to it like a reminder of a more structured world. It wobbled a little but didn't tip. The rubble, like an alluvial fan, spread out below her as she climbed higher. Nothing shifted. *Thank God.*

"You're doing good," Colleen called behind her. She resisted the urge to flip the other woman the bird.

Slipping a bit on some of the loose gravel at the top, Chloe caught herself.

Something clattered on the other side of the blockage. She froze.

"I think there's something over there."

"What did you say?"

Chloe gripped the edges of a table-sized hunk of concrete, rebar shooting out of it like mutated porcupine needles. "Hello?" she called through a narrow opening.

Stupid. Chloe chastised herself.

Seriously? Was she really announcing herself to some unknown presence on the other side of a barrier dividing them from what was most definitely hostile territory?

"Local hostiles," she murmured to herself and ducked down for a moment, heart pounding.

"Who you talking to? Get up there and scout it out." Colleen shouted.

Chloe pulled herself to the top of the ledge and peered over to the other side. Stale air met her nose, musty and stagnant. Darkness punctuated by more darkness. She squinted her eyes. Was that a flash of light? Couldn't be. There. Again. Farther away this time.

She tried to climb higher, head craning forward over the edge of the rubble. One more time. In the distance down the tunnel. Twin sparks of—of something. Like the small narrow luminescence in the eyes of some small animal.

Her foot slipped.

Arms and legs spun to grasp at the nothing of thin air, her ass and then head crashing against the rough slab. The tumble to the base of the pile of debris wasn't as dramatic as Torrance's, but it was close. Breath wheezed out in painful gasps and stars danced in her eyes, every muscle screaming.

"Ow." She rubbed at the back of her head.

Colleen smirked down at her. "Serves you right for not paying attention. You know better than to climb through those holes before we stabilize them."

"You told me to look! And I wasn't trying to climb through. I thought I saw something."

"I said peek, not climb. Your imagination is getting away from you. There's nothing over there but years of dust and whatever the old government was hiding. You were probably just seeing reflections from the emergency lights." Colleen extended one muscular arm.

Chloe looked at the hand and then back up at the older

woman. Grimacing a bit at the motion, she grasped it and wobbled to her feet. "I know what I saw."

"Uh-huh. Best keep your fantasies to yourself. Now come on, Neil's probably going to have us working overtime now that we've almost got this section cleared."

Chloe held her pounding head with one hand. "I hope not."

She glanced one more time up at the gaping hole. What had those lights been?

————

Eva Zapada
May, 2055

Condensation streaked the windows of the observation room to the TMRWS device. Eva swiped her finger through the rivulets, breaking the flow and catching droplets on her fingers. She rubbed her forefinger and thumb together. She'd have to have a crew check the seals on the output shafts carrying water from the TMRWS to the surface. Too much humidity indicated a possible leak and a risk of total system shutdown. With planting season upon them, the Basin Territory couldn't afford the chance of losing power—or water.

Eva checked the sensor units on the console for the hermetically sealed room that held the machine. Green lights glowed on the panel above the door. Her ever-present guard was just visible through the narrow rectangular window looking bored. Too bad.

The observation deck was positioned toward the top of the TMRWS, the enormous cylindrical device resembling a turbine once used in the old dams. A panel of inch-thick glass ran the length of the small room, steel frames holding it in place and separating it from the abyss below.

The scientific gloves-box container with the smaller sample of the tellurium meteorite—Tau-159—sat on a table, a dark reminder of the much larger sample they hid in a cavern only a mile away, its presence thrumming in her consciousness dark and deep. *Ignore it.*

The constant pull exhausted her.

For some reason, the smaller sample didn't have the same effect. Because of the mass? Or something far simpler?

Eva placed her entire hand in the cool droplets, the body heat fogging up the window each finger outlined in stark relief.

The sleek titanium surface rotated in a smooth motion, never touching the sides of the cavernous shaft surrounding it, the magnetic field intact and stable. The hum of white noise it emitted calmed her, the break from her, Rani, and Amrit's work necessary for sanity's sake.

Their work to uncover the mysteries of Tau-159, the enzymes within, and the effects it had on everything from the TMRWS to the Shield Serum weighed on them all.

Eva slapped her fingers against the glass, splattering droplets like tears to the ground. *Wasted water.*

Her and Daniel Burgess's predecessors in military research had kept it all hidden. The TMRWS in plain sight at the dam, the meteorite in the black site in that godforsaken cavern, and the Shield Serum buried beneath the ground in the MUC. All tied together. All falling apart. Just like society had done during the Collapse. So many hidden depths, so many hidden deaths. And for what? She'd done it for life, for good. To save people. The old government…well, she wasn't so sure.

Nobody should have the power to control the weather. And that's exactly what the TMRWS did. Nobody should have been allowed to do human experimentation, but they did that too.

With your and Daniel's help.

A cold presence shifted inside her, foreign and demanding. She locked it down with a force of will. It slithered there, beating against her mental defenses. Seeking…something. *Home.* The single word grasped her and squeezed. Eva massaged her temples, breaths coming in and out in gasps. Sweat pooled beneath her arms, soaking her shirt.

She jumped when the door opened, the console above turning a bright red.

"Sorry, didn't mean to startle you." Daniel closed the metal door with a clang, and the light panel returned to green. He stopped by the glass and peered into the turbine room, his slender fingers catching a droplet of water. Daniel frowned, his reflection on the glass hazy in the dim lighting. He didn't come closer.

The pain vanished in his presence, receding like the tide at dawn. Could she blame him for his distance? Somehow, he'd avoided the cold presence of the enzyme's influence. Due to more injections of Shield—the small amount of enzyme in the human strengthening serum acting like a vaccine—or for another reason was what she and the others had been studying. As the leader of the community, if he became controlled by this unpredictably violent force, they were all sunk. How had she become infected? Why hadn't others? Was it even like a disease or something far more sinister?

Eva crossed her arms, hunching her shoulders.

Daniel's hair brushed his shoulders in dark waves, his beard trimmed neat in contrast. Today, he wore jeans and a sweatshirt with work boots. Her breath hitched.

"What are you doing down here? Don't you have people to micromanage and a mine shaft to finish drilling?" Eva leaned against the glass.

He'd been working on drilling out the shaft where the tellurium meteorite, Tau-159, had been buried. A wave of guilt hit her. The explosion she had caused played on repeat in her head. *Not your fault. It made you.*

That foreign presence wormed around her mind, and her right eye twitched.

Daniel cocked an eyebrow and regarded her. "I don't micromanage."

"If you say so."

He turned back toward his contemplation of what lay beyond

the window. "We broke another drill bit. It'll take a while to replace. I wanted to catch you before you left for the day."

"Oh. Not Amrit or Rani?" Most communication went through her so-called lab assistants these days. Mother-hens more like.

"Just you. It's about Track Three and the black site."

Eva shook her head, heading him off before he could even ask. "No, I'm not going back down there. I come out here to the dam, and that is close enough."

The main shaft hid there in her nightmares. When she slept. When she was awake. She breathed through her pinging headache and focused on the side of Daniel's face. It eased.

"Just hear me out, please, before jumping to conclusions. The outside world isn't going to leave us alone forever. The cannibal stories are getting worse…I've seen it firsthand. The guards have already caught several scouts sniffing around our borders. Can't tell who they're from. Probably Sarah. If they get a whiff of what we have down here, they'll come to take it from us. And it'll make that dust-up with her crew a while back look like child's play. Without adequate power for the wall…" He clenched a fist and tapped it against the sill of the observation window. "We have to be ready."

"Ready for what, exactly? War?" Eva resisted the urge to reach out and touch his shoulder. Seven years ago, her crazy sister Sarah brought a crew into the Territory. A fight where many had been injured and some had died. Eva had questioned why. Killing one person in the hidden tunnels beneath the territory wouldn't be enough to start a war. There weren't too many people left. Eva had deduced it had been some kind of distraction, like they were looking for something.

"Maybe. That and with Sector Nine constantly preaching that we're not sharing our technology enough, and claiming the MUC scientists are just using the Basin settlers for slave labor." He gestured toward the TMRWS, "That won't stay secret for much longer, either. I don't know how they keep building followers. People either have to be stupid or desperate to believe their lies. At this rate, we'll have a civil war before much longer."

Eva regarded Daniel's tense back. "People need to feel connected to their leaders, Daniel. I'm not saying I agree with their ideologies, but Sector Nine does offer that—connection."

She regretted the words almost as soon as they passed her lips. Instead of lashing out, though, Daniel surprised her.

He ran a hand through his hair, brows drawn together. "Relationships have never been my strong suit. This territory doesn't need me to be kind. It needs me to be strong and decisive. Jack's there to be the go-between. The people person."

Eva took a hesitant step towards him and laid a hand on his arm. His muscles tensed under her touch, but he didn't move. "It needs both."

Daniel continued looking straight ahead. "We stirred up a hornet's nest in Montana when we retrieved the mining equipment. Eventually, they'll come for us again. And it'll be worse. Sarah's hell-bent on destroying the MUC. The only thing I regret about Montana is…Killian leaving. I don't regret much, but I regret that. He wasn't wrong; he just didn't see the bigger picture."

Her heart clenched. Killian Cooper was one of their own, one of their survivors, only a kid when they burrowed out of the MUC a year after the Collapse. "He'll come back. Just give him time. Not a lot can kill him."

"He's a walking top-secret project, Eva."

"He's still a young man, Daniel. And there are no more top-secret projects because there is no more government. I doubt Killian will announce his abilities to what is left of the world."

He regarded her finally, his hazel eyes a darker steel in the dim lighting. "I still don't like it."

Eva shrugged. "We have bigger things to worry about. Like Sarah and Tau-159. Are you sure her only motivation is to destroy the MUC?"

"What else could a cannibal traitor want?"

Gah, he could be so myopic. "A lot of things. Hopefully, you're wrong, and we're not heading toward war. There's been enough of those to last the next hundred years. And Killian Cooper made his own decision. He'll see what a horrific mess is left out there and be back within six months. Trust me. The outside world can't be that wonderful."

Daniel snorted and took a step closer until their bodies almost touched. Like the last few months had faded away. Like he wasn't afraid she was infected with some mysterious disease that could spread through a touch or a simple kiss. "Assholes, death, and tyrants. That's what's out there."

"Only out there, huh?" Eva deadpanned, arching one eyebrow.

"I'll only admit to the asshole part." His lips hovered over hers.

Eva closed her eyes, savoring the moment.

At the last minute, he pulled away, his eyes dark storms. "I need to show you something."

The abruptness startled her, but she recovered. Her voice came out rough, "Now?"

"Yes."

Eva cupped her elbows. She had followed him to the ends of the earth, cared for him, fought with him, fought for him, and probably would for the rest of her life. Could she really say no now? *If that's not codependent, I don't know what is.* "Fine. Lead the way."

He turned on his heel, the door buzzing on his way through.

They descended into a control center, expanded last year to accommodate a small lab and a second office for her research into the tellurium meteorite.

Another, newer door opened to a metal ramp staircase down to the hub connecting the Mainline between the MUC and Lower Monumental Dam, and the small branch that took off toward Track Three—the old government tunnel system that marched underground clear across the defunct United States.

Dread slithered in her gut.

A mining cart waited to take them the few miles to the intersection. Tamara had modified it for seating and to run on old car batteries, and had done the same with many others to make travel easier on the old tracks. There were so many of the carts now, they'd even sent out the track clearing crew with them.

She went past this intersection on a daily basis. Newer tunnels branched off the mainline, toward the interior of the Territory—even below her own house. But this hub, this turnoff to Track Three always felt…ominous and foreboding. *Ye Olde Evil Mineshaft*, she'd nicknamed it in her head. But, was it evil or just so completely alien she couldn't come up with a different name?

A tug, like a magnet attracting a chunk of metal, pulled at her. Eva ignored it again, but for how much longer?

She and Daniel curved around the branch as it connected with the main Track Three, emergency lighting shining in pools of light, each one an oasis in the shadows. And then she saw it—an enormous black engine sitting in the middle of the track.

"What the hell, Daniel?"

"We found it on our last expedition down the track. Intact, just this side of a cave-in somewhere under Wyoming."

"What is it running on?"

"It runs on that new fuel Bio-Nova that came out before the Collapse. We found an enormous cache of it in Idaho. We're going to take it to the end of the line, Eva. Find the rest of the TMRWS before they suck all the water from the atmosphere, and any other sources of Tau-159 before it destroys everyone." Daniel's face hardened into a stony, determined mask.

"A working train?"

"Yeah, but we need to finish clearing the tracks…and find the other map with the rest of the locations of any other TMRWS. If we can't fix them and contain the remnants of Tau-159, it won't matter if there's another war. We'll *all* be dead. " His next words surprised her. "I want you to join the search team."

"Is that smart? We don't know..." The foreign cold slithered along her veins. Was that anticipation? What would happen if the presence took control again?

"One of the workmen on the mining rig tried to blow the operation up yesterday. He looked like a zombie. It's spreading. Slowly, but it's here in the Territory now."

Eva backed away from him, hugging herself. "I'm surprised it hasn't happened more often. What do you want me to do with the train?"

He bowed his head for a moment, then straightened. "I want you to do what we talked about now that the track is almost cleared through Kansas City. Lead the teams to track down the other TMRWS. You...you might be able to sense if there is more meteorite nearby."

Eva's brows furrowed. Should she tell him? Tell him that she sometimes almost lost control of herself and her senses? That she held on by a thread most days?

No, I need to find answers before this thing turns me into my sister. He won't let me go if he knows.

Instead she said, "What about Mia?"

Their daughter was her lifeline. Her hope for the future. Her blood and Killian's were their greatest accomplishment.

"She starts her advanced training soon. As soon as the blockage in Kansas City is clear, you'll head out. Plus, we need to find another cache of Bio-nova or adapt another energy source. It'll take a lot of fuel if we're going to make it clear across the country. I'll get Rani and Tamara on it."

Eva stared at him. "You have it all figured out, don't you?"

He blinked. "Well, yes, or I wouldn't have told you about the train."

To continue reading, please visit: All Things Hidden FREE with Kindle Unlimited!